Also by Beth Rinyu

The Exception to the Rule

An Unplanned Lesson

Beth Rinyu

An Unplanned Lesson Beth Rinyu
Copyright © 2013 by Beth Rinyu
First Printing, 2013

Cover Design by LLPIX Photography
Editing and Formatting by BZHercules.com

ISBN-13: 978-0615779485
ISBN-10: 0615779484

Acknowledgements

A great big thank you to . . .

My mom, my Aunt Rita, and my cousin Sharon for being my guinea pigs once again and encouraging me to keep writing this story. A double thank you to my aunt who muddled through those somewhat risqué scenes, even though I made her blush. Remember, Aunt Rita, this is purely fiction!

Marcie and Joanne for being the first round of editors before I sent it off to the editor!

My husband for always being so supportive.

Stephan and Aidan: no more late nights on your Xbox because your mom was too busy writing away to realize it! So you guys better hurry up and help me come up with an idea for my next book!

An Unplanned Lesson

Table of Contents

Chapter 1

I stepped into the hot muggy air, immediately wishing that I had opted to wear my sleeveless summer dress instead of the blazer and pants that I was wearing. I battled in my head whether I should run back in and change, but I quickly chased that thought from my mind, knowing that I had just enough time to make it to my job interview and that was *if* I didn't hit any traffic or red lights.

My car had been acting up and I was hoping that it would be on its best behavior this morning, just long enough to get me to my destination, which was Pineview Elementary School. I was interviewing for a second grade teaching position, most likely along with twenty other people. It was early August, which meant that the summer crowds were out in full force in my tiny New Jersey bayside town that I called home year round.

The humming of my car's engine as it turned over at the first turn of my key was music to my ears. Much to my surprise, I pulled into the school parking lot with five minutes to spare. I pulled down my rearview mirror and gave myself one last glance. My thick, raven-colored hair, which I had meticulously blown out and flat ironed just a few short hours ago, had expanded from the humidity. I grabbed the ponytail holder wrapped around the gearshift in my car and pulled my hair into the best possible bun that I could manage. I applied another quick coat of mascara to the lashes of my hazel eyes and a thin coat of lip-gloss to my lips. *Well, this is going to have to do. It's not like I'm going to get the job anyway. But at least the interview will be a good experience.* This had become my mantra for the past year while pursuing a teaching job. I was working at a local preschool, but my degree was in elementary education. Even though this was my second interview round, I wasn't getting my hopes up. There were plenty of times that I had been called back for a second interview and I didn't end up getting the job.

I stepped out of the car, instantly breaking out in a sweat as I put my blazer back on. My first interview had been at the Board of Education office. This was the first time I had actually been inside the elementary school. My jaw dropped as I walked into the enormous, state-of-the-art building. It was full of windows, allowing for an abundance of natural light. There was a grand staircase leading to the second floor that was open to the downstairs. *Wow, I guess this is what astronomical taxes buy you,* I thought. I reminded myself that I wasn't in my modest little town anymore, but instead the next town over - which happened to be very affluent.

I walked into the main office and waited for the secretary to end her phone conversation. I took a deep breath as she placed the phone down. "Hello, I'm Nicole Morgan; I have a two o'clock interview with Dr. Joyner and Mrs. Kane," I said to the heavy-set woman sitting behind the desk.

She looked down at the paper on her desk. "Okay, have a seat. They'll be right with you."

I sat down and waited while I read the signs hanging on the walls over and over, trying my best to calm my nerves. I heard the door of the principal's office squeaking open and the faint sound of voices. I gave a smile to the woman who was exiting, clearly knowing that she was here for the same reason as I was. She looked to be about 40 years old, which meant she had fifteen years experience on me. Her poker-straight hair was cut in an asymmetrical bob; obviously, the humidity outside wasn't an issue for her. She was wearing a long printed summer dress and I was half-tempted to ask her where she had bought her adorable red peek-a-boo toe sandals.

"Cute shoes," I said as she made her way past me.

"Hey thanks." She smiled as her blue eyes glistened.

I rested my head against the wall. *Yes, she was what they were looking for; someone who had it all together. Probably had a few kids of her own, a great husband, and a big house. Not someone like me, a twenty-five-year-old girl who tried on twenty different outfits before coming to this interview, all of which were either lying on her bed or on her bedroom floor at this particular moment. Someone who would misplace her car keys as soon as she put them down or couldn't maintain a relationship to save her life because she was too busy*

10

harboring the guilt of her past. Oh well, Nicole, another one you're not going to get.

"Miss Morgan, they're ready for you now," the secretary said before she led me back to the principal's office.

Dr. Joyner, the school superintendent, and Mrs. Kane, the principal, were sitting around the conference room table with a copy of my resume laid out before them.

They both stood up and shook my hand. Mrs. Kane reminded me of your typical soccer mom. I could tell almost immediately during my first interview that she was a very warm and caring person.

Dr. Joyner, on the other hand – well, he was just the opposite. He was a tall African-American man with a very deep, intimidating voice. He made me feel like I was being interrogated as a murder suspect in my first interview. I thought for sure that I had blown it, never in a million years expecting a call back.

"Well, Nicole, you must have really impressed us to have made it down to the final three out of fifty applicants," Dr. Joyner said with a smile.

Wow, what a boost of confidence, three out of fifty! And, Dr. Joyner actually smiled at me, I thought to myself. I smiled back, trying my best to contain my excitement.

"We just have a few more questions for you and then we will be making our final decision by the week's end," Mrs. Kane chimed in.

"Okay Nicole, what makes you think that second grade would be the right fit for you?" Dr. Joyner asked.

"Well, I love children of all ages, but to me there's something about the primary grades that allows you to make such a lasting impression in their lives. The preschoolers that I'm teaching now are great, but they are much too young to be inspired by a teacher's enthusiasm. Once you get to the older grades, they seem to think they know it all and will reject anything that you have to offer. I think that second grade is the perfect grade to motivate a child through the rest of their school years." I took a deep breath and waited for their reaction.

Mrs. Kane quickly smiled as if she were happy with my answer. They continued on, going over the salary and benefits *if* I were to get the job.

"Okay, do you have any other questions for us?" Mrs. Kane asked.

"No, I think you pretty much covered everything," I said.

"Okay, like I said, we will be letting you know one way or the other by the end of the week, then of course the final approval must come at the next Board of Ed meeting," Mrs. Kane said as she extended her hand to me.

"Okay, that sounds great," I said, shaking her hand and Dr. Joyner's before exiting the office.

I walked out of the school and back into the heat with a newfound confidence. I was really happy with how the interview went, but I still wasn't going to get my hopes up. I pulled my phone from my purse to find two text messages. One was from my best friend, Donna, asking me how the interview went and to call her as soon as I got done. The other was from Drew, my ex-boyfriend. I hadn't spoken to him in months and was anxious to see what it said. My hands were shaking as I hit the button to read it: *Was hanging with a few mutual friends last night and they told me about your interview, good luck, I know you will do great.* My heart sank just reading his words. I missed him so much and wished that things could have been different between us. We had been together for two years. I was the happiest that I had ever been until he began to talk about marriage and children. I was still battling the guilt from my past and shuddered at the mere thought of those two things. The more he tried to get me to break down that wall the further I pushed him away, eventually leading to a very painful breakup. He was a great guy and I hated myself for not being able to open up to him, but it hurt too much to reveal my secret to anyone, so I kept it buried deep within my heart. I cried for days when I heard he was dating someone new. But through my tears, I knew that he deserved to be happy with someone who was willing to give him all that he wanted in life. As for me, I was done with the relationship scene. I was just going to focus on getting my life together and putting my past behind me for good. Yes, it would be a long road, but as

I got into my car and looked up at the beautiful bright blue sky, something was telling me...you can do this!

Chapter 2

The week dragged on at a snail's pace and each time my phone would ring, my stomach dropped. When I hadn't heard anything by Friday afternoon, I just assumed I would be receiving the usual form letter that always started off with, *"although you were highly qualified..."* Oh well, just another one to add to my collection. I was heading out to lunch with my best friend, Donna, and her boyfriend, Michael. I was hoping that they would help take my mind off my impending rejection.

We were meeting at our favorite casual bay front restaurant. It was a beautiful day and I opted to ride my bike instead of driving. I placed my bike in the bicycle rack and walked into the outside dining area where Donna and Michael were already waiting for me.

"Look at you, riding your bike," Michael joked.

"Leave her alone, Michael; that's why she's so skinny. I should be doing more of that and maybe I wouldn't look the way that I do," Donna said, looking down at herself.

"Donna, just stop, you're beautiful," I said. And she was, both inside and out. Donna had been my very best friend since middle school. There wasn't anything we didn't share. She was always there for me and vice versa. She had been there for me through my worst and I was so grateful for that. Her long blond hair blew in the breeze and her dark sunglasses hid her beautiful blue eyes. She was always so down on herself, particularly about her weight. She was always on some crazy diet or joining one gym after another to which she never went. She was by no means fat. She had curves, which looked perfect on her.

"Oh, Nicole, you are too sweet. But you know I would kill to have your body." She smiled.

"We ordered you a Corona," Michael said, pointing to the bottle that was on the table as he took a sip of his.

"My favorite," I said.

"Well, have you heard anything about the job?" Donna asked.

"Nope," I said, disappointed.

"Well, the day's not over," Donna said enthusiastically.

"Yeah, I guess." I took a sip of my beer. "So what's going on with my favorite couple?"

Donna beamed. "Only this!" She dangled her left ring finger in front of my face as the sparkle from the perfectly cut pear-shaped diamond reflected off the sun. I had just taken a sip of my beer and choked at the sight of an engagement ring on her finger.

Michael had never mentioned anything to me, but then again he was wise if he was trying to keep it a secret. He knew the relationship I had with Donna. But still, I think I would have been able to have kept something like this from her.

"Oh my goodness, it's beautiful!" I said as I held her finger across my hand. I got up from the table to give both her and Michael a hug and kiss. I held back the tears that were stinging in my eyes. I knew part of it was over my happiness for the two of them. The other part was over sadness for me; this could have been me and Drew, if only I weren't so screwed up.

"We haven't exactly set a date, but we're thinking next summer and of course you are going to be my maid of honor," Donna said.

"Of course!" I said as if it were a no-brainer.

The waitress came over to take our order; I didn't even have time to look at the menu. I was too busy ogling Donna's ring. So I decided to go with my usual BLT.

Donna told me how Michael had proposed to her early that morning during a romantic sunrise stroll along the beach. I sighed, wishing that I could have someone in my life like Michael, and then I painfully reminded myself that I once did and I screwed it up. The food arrived as we continued to talk about the wedding plans. Donna already knew her venue, the color of her bridesmaids' dresses, the type of flowers that she wanted, and what their wedding song was going to be. She had it so together and I wondered how she could have been best friends with someone like me, who was her exact opposite.

Donna was an ER nurse and Michael was a police officer who just happened to break his ankle two years ago in a foot chase.

Luckily for Donna, it just happened to be on the same shift that she was working. They had the type of relationship that most people would die for. Michael was so carefree and Donna so regimented; it was the perfect balance that worked well for them. I looked at Michael, who seemed to be beaming just as much as Donna was. He had such a cute boyish way to him that made you like him instantly. He had short-cropped brown hair and dark brown eyes. He was only a little bit taller than Donna, about five feet, eight inches, but the two of them looked like they were made for each other.

We finished our lunch and were still engrossed in wedding conversation. I could tell that Michael was getting bored from hearing about different types of flowers and styles of wedding dresses.

"Are we ready?" I asked finally.

Michael nodded as if I had said the magic words. I went to get the check, but he grabbed it from my hands. "Michael, let me get this; you guys have a wedding to pay for!" It was of no use; he was already fumbling for his credit card.

I looked over at the entryway and hoped that my eyes were fooling me. It couldn't be Drew and his new girlfriend - but it was. I wasn't even ready to face Drew yet, let alone his new girlfriend. Donna placed her hand on my arm in support. I took a deep breath as they moved closer. *You can do this; you can do this*, I kept repeating over and over in my head.

The girl was grasping Drew's hand tightly. I wondered if he had told her who I was when they were making their way to our table.

"Oh boy," Michael whispered as he finally looked up from filling out the credit card information on the check.

I was so grateful that there was no humidity today and my hair was in perfect form; honestly, the things I thought at a time like this amazed me. They stopped right at the edge of our table as I secretly examined his new girlfriend from head to toe. She had very blond hair; with a little help from her hair stylist, I was sure. I could see her darker roots peeking out of the top of her head. She definitely had a much bigger chest than my average-sized one and she was a lot taller than my five-foot, five-inch height. She looked to be almost as tall as Drew, who was about five feet, ten inches. She was dressed in a teal green T-shirt and short khaki skirt that accented her long thin legs. After I was done with my assessment of her, my eyes moved to Drew. He was so handsome, wearing tan shorts and a blue T-shirt that showed off his rock-hard chest. His beautiful thick brown tousled hair blew in the light bay breeze and his warm brown eyes still made me melt. I had looked into those eyes so many times, never able to convey all that needed to be said.

I forced my best smile. "Hey," I said, realizing I sounded a little too fake.

Drew knew me better than almost anyone. He realized my false sense of excitement right away and secretly raised his eyebrow at me. Drew shook Michael's hand and Donna got up to give him a hug. I remained seated. Somehow, I didn't feel that giving your ex-boyfriend a hug in front of his new girlfriend was appropriate, especially when you still had strong feelings for him.

"Heather, this is Michael, Donna, and Nicole," Drew said. I noticed that it almost pained him to say my name.

"Oh," she said, looking a little surprised as her blue eyes began to focus directly on me. She wrapped her arm around Drew's waist, pulling him closer. I stood up immediately to shake her hand, even though it was killing me inside to see Drew with another woman clinging to him so tightly. She extended her free hand to me, never loosening her grip on Drew.

"Very nice to meet you, Heather," I said, this time trying to sound a little more genuine even though I could feel my lunch churning in my stomach. I sat back down and looked away as Donna and Michael followed suit and shook her hand.

"Babe, my brother and his girlfriend are at the bar waiting for us," Heather said in an effort to break up the uncomfortable reunion.

"Babe?" Did she really just call him "babe" in front of me? "Okay, you go ahead; I'll be right there," Drew said. She looked reluctant to leave him alone, but finally loosened her grip.

"Okay, but don't be long," she said, planting a kiss on his cheek, clearly for my benefit.

After she walked away and things were a *little* more comfortable, Donna held out her finger to Drew. That beautiful smile that I adored appeared on his face. "That's awesome! Congratulations, guys!"

I had to look away; I knew all too well that's what Drew wanted more than anything - to get married and start a family. That's what had ultimately led to the demise of our relationship.

"Well, I better get going," Drew said.

"Yeah, we were just heading out," Michael said as he got up quickly. Donna and I both stood up as well. Michael pulled his ringing cell phone from his pocket and looked at the caller ID. "It's my aunt calling to congratulate us, no doubt; you know she's going to want to talk to you too, Donna." He quickly shook Drew's hand once again before answering his phone and exiting the restaurant.

"We'll meet you outside, Nicole," Donna said as she went trailing after Michael, leaving me alone, standing face to face with Drew.

For the first time ever alone in his company, I didn't know what to say. "Did you hear anything about the job?" he asked, trying to make small talk.

"No, I'm sure my rejection letter is in the mail as we speak," I said, trying to act as if I didn't care.

"Don't be so negative; you never know," he said optimistically.

I shrugged. "She seems really nice," I said, trying to sound sincere as I looked over at the bar where Heather was chatting away with her brother and his girlfriend as she peered over at Drew every now and then.

"Yeah, she is," he said, almost as if he didn't want to admit it.

"Are you happy?"

"Yeah, I really am." His brown eyes looked so emotional.

"Good," I said genuinely. He was a great guy and he deserved nothing but happiness. I was just sorry I wasn't the one who could provide it to him.

"It was really good seeing you, Nicole," he said as he touched my arm lightly.

"You too," I said as I forced a smile and walked away, just waiting for the dam that was holding back the tears to burst.

Chapter 3

I arrived home to my one-bedroom apartment and flopped down on my bed. I stared at my lavender-colored walls as I tried to get the image of Drew and his girlfriend out of my mind, but I couldn't. It all seemed too real for me now. Drew and I were really over. I closed my eyes and thought back to that warm May night. It had been the anniversary of that dreaded day, the day that I would always shut myself away from the rest of the world and just feel sorry for myself because it brought back too many sad memories for me. Memories that I wasn't ready to share with Drew, so I tried to act as if everything were as normal as possible, even though on the inside I was an emotional train wreck.

We were cooking dinner at Drew's house. I decided to take a break since my inability to focus was leading me to screw up our Chicken Marsala. Drew continued slicing the mushrooms. "I'm sorry, I'm just so out of it today," I said, knowing exactly the reason why.

"That's okay, I'll finish up," Drew said. I smiled at him, loving the way he always took over when he knew things were too much for me to handle. Drew continued slicing and sautéing until his masterpiece was done. I poured us each a glass of wine as we sat down to eat.

"This is great," I said, taking a bite.

"Thanks," he said.

I began to banter about my day and the latest escapades of my four-year-old pre-school class. Drew always got such enjoyment from these stories. He listened closely and then smiled at me. I could feel him staring at me as I took another bite of my chicken.

"What?" I asked, wanting to know why he was looking at me.

"You are going to make such a great mom someday, Nicole."

I choked on the sip of wine I had just taken. "These potatoes are really great too. Did you cook them differently than usual?" I ignored his comment and tried to change the subject.

"Why do you do that?"

"Do what?"

21

"*Every time I bring up the subject of marriage or children, you turn white and change the topic. I don't get it, Nicole — is that not what you want?*"

"*No, yes, I mean - I don't know.*"

"*You don't know? What do you mean you don't know? I thought we loved one another.*"

"*I do love you, Drew; very much.*" *I wished we could just get off the subject.*

"*Well then, why does the thought of being with me for the rest of your life and having my children make you look like you're going to pass out?*" *he asked with sadness in his eyes.*

"*I don't know, Drew, but please don't ever doubt my feelings for you.*"

"*Nicole, I need to know if marriage and a family aren't what you want. Because I know that's what I want. Believe me, there is no one that I want them with more than you. But if I'm wasting my time here, let me know.*"

"*Drew, can we please just talk about this later?*" *I pleaded.*

"*No, I'm tired of sweeping this under the carpet. I'm twenty-eight years old and I want to get started with my life and if you're not willing to–*"

"*If I'm not willing to, you'll what, Drew? Fall in love with someone else and have children with her?*" *I got up from the table and grabbed my purse. I knew I had no right to be angry with him; he was just being honest.*

He got up and walked over to me. "*Nicole, what the hell is wrong with you; why can't you break down this wall that you've built up around you and tell me why - why are you so afraid of being happy?*"

"*Because I can't; I wish that I could, but I just can't. You deserve so much better than me. You deserve a girl who is willing to give you all the things that you want from life and I'm not that girl.*" *I knew that I had to get out of there before the tears began to flow.*

"*Nicole!*" *Drew shouted as he followed me to the door.*

"*Don't ever second-guess my feelings for you, Drew. I always loved you and I probably always will. Because of that, I have to let you go.*" *I softly caressed his face and kissed him gently on the cheek.* "*Just be happy,*" *I whispered in his ear before walking out his door for the very last time.*

The sound of my phone ringing broke me from my daydreaming. I grabbed a tissue from my nightstand and wiped my eyes before answering. I looked down at the caller ID on my cell phone and did not recognize the number.

"Hello," I answered, trying to hide the fact that I had been crying.

"Nicole Morgan, please."

"This is she."

"Hi, Nicole, it's Valerie Kane from Pineview Elementary."

"Oh, hello, Mrs. Kane," I said, trying to hide my excitement.

"Nicole, we want to offer you the second grade teaching position at the salary and with the benefits that we discussed in the interview. I understand that you may need time to think about this, but if you could let us know by Monday at the latest, that would be great. We would like to get a resolution, making it official at the next school board meeting, which is Tuesday night."

I didn't want to sound too anxious, but I also knew that I wanted the job and there was nothing for me to think about. "I accept the position, Mrs. Kane; I've had all week to think about my decision if I was offered the opportunity and I know I want it."

"Okay, great then!" She seemed impressed with my ability to make a decision quickly. Little did she know this was the only time in my entire life that I had made such a swift decision. "Well, like I said, it won't be official until the resolution is passed, but there should be no problem with that; it's just a formality. I'm having a meeting with all staff members on August fourteenth at ten a.m. at the elementary school. You will be getting your class assignment and can start setting up your classroom as well," Mrs. Kane explained.

"That sounds great; thank you so much, Mrs. Kane." I was unable to wipe the smile from my face.

"Please call me Valerie, and welcome aboard, Nicole."

I hung up and threw my phone on my bed. I began to jump up and down with excitement. *I did it; I got the job!!* I quickly texted Donna, informing her of the news.

I was so excited that I didn't know what to do next. I picked up the phone and began to dial the number that I so often avoided - my parents. As excited as I was, I was hoping that I would get the machine. I knew that talking to either of them would bring me down from my happiness and I wanted to relish in it for as long as I could. My relationship with my family was somewhat strained. It had all changed with them seven years ago, the same time my life had changed so drastically. My mother and father never came out and said how disappointed they were in me, but they didn't have to; their actions spoke much louder than words. They had moved from our hometown three years ago and were now living two hours away, to be closer to my older sister, Renee, and her family. Renee was the perfect daughter. She was five years older than I was, had a great husband, a huge house, and two adorable little boys. My parents reminded me every time I spoke to them just how perfect Renee was. If they weren't gushing about Renee or her kids, they were going on and on about my little brother, Justin. Justin was twenty-two years old and a Marine. My father, who was a retired Marine, couldn't have been prouder. I was also very proud of Justin; out of everyone in my family, he was the one with whom I was closest. He never judged me and was always there when I needed a shoulder to cry on. In return, I did the same for him. I was happy that he got the same vibe from my parents as I did that Renee was the chosen one. We would commiserate a lot over that fact. But I knew that even though Justin sometimes felt that way, it was I who was the black sheep of the family. I was the one who had humiliated my strict Catholic parents so much that they could barely even look at me for years and were still having a hard time dealing with my past.

"Hello," my mother answered in her usual hurried tone.

"Hi, Mom," I said cheerfully.

"Nicole, where have you been? You know it would be nice if you called once in a while to let us know you're alive."

The phone does work both ways, you know, I thought to myself. "Yes, I know. I'm sorry. I've just been really busy. But I called to let you and Dad know that I got a job teaching second grade."

24

"Hold on one second, Nicole." My mother took the phone away from her ear and began to yell. "Christopher and Joey, please stop fighting—I'm trying to talk to your Aunt Nicole." She placed the phone back up to her ear. "These kids are driving me crazy; you know Renee started volunteering at the hospital, which is really a great thing, but all these kids do is fight..." She continued telling me all about my nephews and what a great opportunity my sister had going for her at the hospital, not even hearing the reason that I had called her. "So what's new with you, sweetheart?" She finally came up for air after talking non-stop for five minutes.

"Nothing, Mom," I said, feeling disheartened. Donna's name beeping in on my caller ID was a welcoming distraction. I had heard enough about my sister, her kids, my mom's back acting up, and every other topic she had just spewed about during the phone call, none of which had anything to do with me. I couldn't wait to gush with my news to someone who genuinely cared. "Mom I have to take this call coming through; I'll talk to you soon. Give Daddy my love, please."

I clicked over to Donna. "Congratulations! I knew you would get it!" she said as I answered the phone. I smiled on the inside and out. This was the kind of reaction that I had wanted from my mom. Instead, she was so busy talking about herself and my sister that she was totally unaware that I had even gotten a new job. I was quite sure that I would be scolded later for not telling her once she found out about it, even though I had just tried to tell her.

"Thanks, Donna," I said, trying my best to sound upbeat.

"You don't sound very happy about it," Donna said with concern.

"No, I am; I just got off the phone with my mom and, well, you know how that goes." Donna didn't need an explanation. She knew all about my relationship with my parents.

"Oh, Nicole, I'm sorry, but don't let that ruin your happiness. You should be proud of this."

I felt my excitement from earlier rushing back. "I am," I said with a huge smile.

"I'm working the night shift for the next three nights, and then I'm off for four days. We have to plan a night out; we have a lot to celebrate!" Donna said cheerfully.

"We sure do," I said.

"I have to run; I'll call you tomorrow!! Love you, girl!"

"I love you too." I hung up the phone feeling much better than I had just a few minutes earlier.

Donna was right; I should be proud. I looked in the mirror and smiled. My hazel eyes were glowing back at me. "Good morning, class; I'm Miss Morgan," I said to my reflection. I giggled at my silliness as I made my way out into the kitchen to pour a glass of wine and start the celebration a little early.

Chapter 4

I spent two whole days preparing my classroom. I planned out all my bulletin boards and worked tirelessly on them until they were absolutely perfect. I made up place cards with my students' names on each of them, so they would know exactly where their desks were on the first day of school. By the time I was finished, I was quite pleased with the outcome of Room 114.

The first day of school had come and gone and it was hard to believe that I was already wrapping up my second week. The school was great and the staff even better. Everyone was so warm and welcoming. The second grade team consisted of five teachers and I was the youngest. I was afraid that the others might look down on me for being so young and inexperienced but they didn't; instead, they welcomed me with open arms and appreciated having someone younger with fresh ideas. I instantly bonded with Sarah Webb. Her class was right next door to mine. She had been teaching at the school for the past twenty years and was a wealth of information. I found myself running to her quite a few times within the first two weeks.

The parents, on the other hand, weren't as sweet. Pineview Elementary was located in a very wealthy community. Many parents traveled into Philadelphia and some even into New York City for work. It was more common to have a nanny than it was *not* to have one. I could tell just from the few e-mails I had already received from some of the parents that they felt a sense of entitlement. *Make sure my child doesn't sit next to this one,* or, *I specifically asked that my child not be placed in a classroom with that one.* It was going to be a very long year, but I was up for the challenge.

I was sitting at my desk, grading spelling tests. All of the words were a review of what the students had learned in first grade, so I was expecting everyone to get as close to a hundred percent as possible. I looked down at the spelling test in front of me and began to mark my red pen over every word. I quickly looked up to see whose paper I was grading and wasn't very surprised by the name: Ryan O'Maley. Over the past week, Ryan and I had gotten to know each other quite well. I had to talk to him about lifting up the girls' skirts when standing behind them in the recess line. Then there was the talk about appropriate and inappropriate language. The final straw was when Ryan overflowed the toilet in the boys' room by flushing a whole roll of paper towels, forcing me to have to sit through a fifteen-minute lecture from the custodian, as if it were my fault.

Sarah had filled me in on Ryan's home life; his parents had died in a tragic car accident at the end of the previous school year. Now he was being shuffled between his aunt and uncle. I tried to take this into consideration, reminding myself that this poor little boy had gone through far too much heartache in his short life. But still there were moments when Ryan could wear the patience of a saint.

I decided to call it a day as I put the final grade for the spelling tests in my grade book. I was heading out for drinks with Donna and Kara, another friend of ours, and was anxious to get the weekend started. I glanced over my e-mails one last time before turning off my computer. There were four new messages, all of which were from parents and all were basically asking the same thing – what was I going to do about Ryan O'Maley? I leaned my head back in my chair and sighed. These were second-graders; of course, they went home and told their parents every aspect of the day. For the past two weeks, Ryan had become a major aspect with the constant disruptions. I tactfully answered each parent in the same manner, stating that the students were all still adjusting to the second grade and I would be working with Ryan to improve his classroom behavior. I was hoping that this would be enough to keep them happy for now. With that, I knew it was finally time to address the situation with Ryan's uncle, with whom he was living. I pulled out Ryan's contact information card from my file and typed in his uncle's e-mail address.

Dear Mr. O'Maley,

I would like to see if we could set up a time to meet and discuss Ryan's recent behavior and grades in school. I understand that it's only the second week of school, but I would like to address this matter as soon as possible so that we can work on a solution before it gets out of hand. I am available to meet any day before or after school. If you would just let me know what works best for you, I would be happy to accommodate your schedule.

Thank you so much for your support and I look forward to working together in making this a successful school year for Ryan.

Sincerely,

Nicole Morgan

I hit the "send" button, hoping that I could get this all resolved easily and have a great school year.

"Hey, you're still here?" Sarah poked her head in.

"Yeah, just finishing up. I'm meeting my girlfriends for happy hour," I said.

"Oh, happy hour, those were the days," Sarah said.

"Would you like to join us?" I asked.

"Oh, no thanks, sweetie, I have to get up early; we're going to college open houses for my daughter tomorrow. But have a drink for me!"

"I will," I said with a smile.

"Have a great weekend," she said as she headed down the hallway.

I was just about to turn my computer off when I heard the dinging of an incoming e-mail. Another Ryan O'Maley complaint, no doubt. But when I looked at the e-mail, it was a response from Ryan's uncle instead.

Dear Ms. Morgan:

I believe, as a teacher, you are responsible for Ryan's behavior from the hours of 9:00 to 3:00. That is what you get paid for. If Ryan is not excelling academically, I believe that falls under your realm of duties as well. With that being said, I really don't understand what benefit meeting with me would have. I am a lawyer, not a teacher. That is what you have your degree in and if you are any good at your job, you should be able to do that without any assistance from me.

If you still wish to meet, I will be out of town for a good part of next week so unless you are willing to travel to Boston to accommodate my schedule, I won't be available until next Thursday afternoon at 4 pm.
    Yours truly,
Dailan O'Maley

My jaw dropped upon reading his e-mail. *What a jerk!* I immediately became more sympathetic toward Ryan, having to deal with an uncle like him. He was no doubt some stuffy old lawyer who thought he knew it all.

I quickly responded so I wouldn't have to deal with Mr. O'Maley any more until Thursday.

Dear Mr. O'Maley,
    Thank you for your quick reply. Thursday afternoon at 4 p.m. works for me. I look forward to meeting you.
    Sincerely,
Nicole Morgan

I finally logged off my computer and called it a day. After that e-mail from Ryan's uncle, I was in desperate need of a drink. I quickly ran home to freshen up. I changed into my favorite boot-cut jeans, a white tank, and a pair of black flip-flops. I reapplied my make-up and ran some styling cream through my loose waves. Donna and Kara were meeting me at my house, which was right up the street from the bar to which we were heading. I was just finishing up when I heard them coming through the front door.

"Leave it to Nicole to make just a plain old pair of blue jeans and a tank top look totally glamorous," Kara said upon seeing me.

"Yeah, well, the fact that she's toothpick thin helps a lot too," Donna said as she went into the fridge to grab a bottle of water.

"Are we ready?" I asked as I grabbed my black blazer off the chair.

"Yup," they said in unison.

We decided to walk, just in case any of us had too much to drink. I filled them both in along the way about the nasty e-mail that I had gotten from Ryan's uncle. They both formed the same opinion of him as I had – he was a jerk!

We entered PJ's Bar and we were immediately greeted by '80s dance music that was being played by the DJ. We sat down at a table and ordered a round of margaritas. Two hours and many margaritas later, we were all feeling our problems wash away. We would giggle hysterically over something the other had said, make fun of the drunken women out on the dance floor who were making fools of themselves, and check out every handsome guy that walked through the door. Donna would remind us constantly that it was okay for her to look as long as she didn't sample the merchandise, causing us once again to giggle like cackling fools.

We decided we were done with the drinks and we were just going to finish up our chips and salsa and then leave, when the waitress came over with another round of margaritas.

"Oh, we didn't order those," Donna said.

"Those two gentlemen over there did," the waitress said as she pointed to two men standing at the bar. From what I could see in the dim lights, one of them had sandy blond hair and was wearing khaki pants and a black polo shirt. The other, who was much taller, was wearing blue jeans and a white button-up Oxford shirt.

The shorter blond made his way over to our table and asked Kara if she wanted to dance. She smiled and looked at me and Donna. We both raised our eyebrows and took a sip of the margaritas that were placed in front of us. We watched as Kara became one of those drunken women out on the dance floor that we had just been making fun of. I was shoveling in the chips and salsa in an effort to sober up, when I dripped some salsa on my jeans.

"Damn," I shouted over the music.

"Club soda," Donna screamed.

"Oh yeah, good thinking!" I said as I got up to walk over to the bar, spotting Michael, Donna's fiancé, walking toward us.

"Oh boy, looks like I'm going to be driving the drunks home tonight," he said, laughing and giving Donna a kiss on the cheek.

I tried to make my way in at the bar to order my club soda. I found an opening between two businessmen and the taller brown-haired man who had bought us the margaritas.

"Hey, thanks for the drink," I screamed, hoping that he would hear me over the blaring music.

"What?" He looked at me, confused.

"You and your friend bought me and my friends a round of margaritas," I said.

Once I got up closer, I realized just how handsome he was. He looked as if he were in his late twenties or early thirties. He had blue eyes and light brown wavy hair. His nose looked like it may have been broken at one time, but that only added to his character. He towered over me; I guessed him to be somewhere around six-foot two.

His smile made my stomach flip. "Oh, that was my mate there, trying to pick up your friend," he said in a very Irish accent, making my stomach now do a double flip. "But if I was half paying attention and had seen how cute you were, I would have bought you a drink myself."

I smiled at his compliment. "Well, aren't you sweet?"

He ordered himself a beer and another margarita for me. "Oh no, I can't have any —"

"I'll be insulted if you drank the margarita that Tommy bought you and not mine," he said, flashing that sexy smile again.

"Okay, if you insist," I said as I looked over at Donna and Michael sitting at the table. Donna smiled and gave me the thumbs-up.

I sipped my margarita, totally forgetting about the club soda. "Do you want to dance?" he asked.

"Sure," I said, taking one last swig of my margarita, licking the salt from the rim off my lips. "He's so hot!" I mouthed to Donna as he walked in front of me to the dance floor.

He was just as good at dancing as he was handsome. I was having so much fun. I was usually never this forward or loosened up. I knew it was part alcohol, part hot Irish guy. The pace of the music changed into a slow dance. I was a little surprised when he pulled me closer and wrapped his arms around me. I didn't resist. I rested my head against his rock-hard chest and *accidently* pushed my stomach into his arousal, which was leading me to believe that he was just as turned on by me as I was by him. I breathed in the delightful scent of his cologne, a blend of cedar and musk – delicious. I wasn't a one-night-stand type of girl but tonight, being here in the arms of this gorgeous guy, I was considering bending the rules.

"Wow, this is a great ending to a horrible day," I said as we swayed back and forth.

"Why's that?" he asked.

"Just a horrible day at work."

"What do you do?" he asked.

"I teach second grade and my day ended with an obnoxious e-mail from a pompous ass who's the uncle of one of my students."

He stopped moving as he placed his hand on my shoulders and gazed down at me with a smile. *Yes, I think I would definitely bend the rules tonight.*

I moved my head back to his chest and closed my eyes as we continued to dance. I was beginning to feel a little dizzy from the alcohol. "Do you have a name, hot Irish guy?"

"Dailan – Dailan O'Maley. It's a pleasure to meet you, Miss Morgan."

Chapter 5

I quickly removed my head from his chest. His arms were still wrapped around my waist as I looked up at him. He had a wry smile on his face. I felt my insides trembling. I wanted to run but my legs felt frozen.

"Oh my God, I'm sor-" My legs finally thawed as I pulled away from his embrace, running past Donna and Michael and out the door, trying to escape my humiliation. I made it out into the parking lot just in time as all the alcohol and what little food I had in my stomach came rushing to the surface.

Donna and Michael came running out behind me. Donna held my hair back until there was nothing left to come out. I turned to both of them, rubbing my temples.

"Are you okay--what happened in there?" Donna asked with concern.

"Did that guy try something with you?" Michael asked as he went into police officer mode.

"No, not at all!" I wanted to make that clear to Michael before he went back in and made a scene. I looked at Donna. "He's the uncle of the student that I had told you about earlier."

Donna's grin was a mile wide. "Oh my God! Well, he may be obnoxious, but he's certainly easy on the eyes."

"I'm standing right here, you know," Michael joked.

"I'm sorry, sweetie; you know I only have eyes for you," Donna said playfully as she batted her eyelashes at him.

"I was rambling on in a drunken stupor and told him about my horrible day. When he asked me what I did for a living, I told him, and then stupid me continued by telling him about the e-mail I received from the pompous ass uncle of one of my students."

"Yikes!" Donna exclaimed. "Well, relax; maybe he didn't put the pieces together and realize you were talking about him," she said with fading optimism.

"Oh no, he knew. Right before I ran out, he made a point of saying, 'It's a pleasure to meet you, Miss Morgan.' What am I going to do?" I sat on the curb, running my hand through my hair.

"Well, there's not much you can do; what's done is done."

I looked up at Donna. She clearly knew that wasn't the answer I wanted to hear.

"What if this gets out to the other parents? I mean, really, I wasn't exactly model teacher material tonight. I swear if I hadn't just realized who he was, he probably would have been in my bed tonight."

Donna looked at me as if she were a little shocked by my out-of-character statement. "How's it going to get out to the other parents? Somehow, I don't think he's the PTA type and besides, he looked to be just as into you as you were into him. Just let it blow over; I'm sure in a couple of weeks, he'll have forgotten all about it."

"Donna, I'm supposed to meet with him Thursday after school," I said painfully.

"Oh," Donna said through clenched teeth. "Well, just try not to think about it. Go home and go to bed; you'll be able to think more clearly in the morning. Michael will give you a ride. I've gotta go find Kara before she does something foolish too. I'll call ya in the morning and help you think of what to say." She headed back into the bar to find Kara.

Michael grabbed my arm as I stood up from the curb.

"How do I get myself into these messes, Michael?"

"I don't know, Nic, but you sure do keep us all amused," he joked.

"Oh gee, thanks," I said sarcastically as I got into the car.

* * *

Much to my dismay, the week was flying by at a rapid pace. I didn't receive any more e-mails from Dailan O'Maley. I tried my best to deal with Ryan's constant disruptions in class on my own, not wanting to draw any further attention from his uncle. I had spent every single planning period with him, going over the math unit with which he was struggling. I didn't care if it meant spending extra time after school or at home preparing lesson plans. It was all worth it when I actually saw Ryan solve a math problem at the blackboard with complete ease one afternoon.

The day I had been dreading all week long was finally here – Thursday. I still hadn't thought of what to say to redeem myself with Ryan's uncle. I was hoping that he was really that nice guy that I met in the bar and not the obnoxious jerk in the e-mails.

All the kids were gone for the day and I was savoring the golden sound of silence. I glanced up at the clock on my desk as I was grading papers. It was 4:30 - *Looks like Mr. O'Maley is a no-show – thank God!* My head was pounding from stressing out all day over this meeting. I just wanted to get home and park myself in front of the TV for the rest of the night. I was hoping that I wouldn't have to deal with him for a while – as in never. Ryan had actually gotten a 75 on his math quiz, which was a big improvement from his usual 40s and 50s. I only had to talk to him twice today and the librarian told me he was excellent during library time. Maybe Ryan was finally starting to adjust to second grade.

I got up from my desk and decided to call it a night. "Damn," I said as I wrestled with the stack of papers, trying to get them to fit in my bag.

"Now that's not very nice language for a teacher to be using." I looked up quickly to find the handsome man whose arms I was in just the other night standing in my doorway. He was even more handsome than I had remembered as I got an even better look at him in the bright light. He looked as if he hadn't shaved in a few days and the stubble on his face made him even sexier. I swallowed hard at his captivating smile and I could tell that underneath his perfectly tailored suit was a perfectly sculpted body.

"I would introduce myself, but I believe we've already met," he said.

"Look, I'm really sorry about the other night. I had a little too much to drink. I don't usually act that way."

"No need to apologize; don't you know that being called a pompous ass when you're a lawyer is a compliment?" he said and began to move closer.

I backed up and leaned against my desk. I didn't know if it was his good looks, his sexy smile, or his thick Irish accent that was making my heart feel like it was going to leap out of my chest.

"Please, have a seat," I said, directing him to the chair on the other side of my desk.

I sat at my desk and fumbled through my papers, trying to locate Ryan's progress report that I had made up specifically for this meeting. I looked up quickly from my pile and noticed him gazing at me. I realized that I had taken my cardigan off when the kids left and I was only wearing the camisole that I had on underneath. I quickly grabbed my cardigan off the back of my chair and buttoned up the middle button to cover what little cleavage I had.

"I liked it better off," he said with a crooked smile.

I shifted my head up from the papers and shot him a look of disgust.

"I'm sorry; just being honest," he said playfully.

I quickly put my head down and continued fumbling through the stack. I could feel my face starting to flush. I silently scolded myself for being so unorganized. *Why was he making me so nervous?* I finally located Ryan's progress report and placed it in front of him.

"Like I said in my e-mail, I don't know how I'm going to be of any help in this situation," he said, barely looking at the paper that was just placed before him.

"Mr. O'Maley, I have been working with Ryan and will continue to work with him at school. But it will do no good if these things are not followed up on at home as well."

"Okay, and what are these *things* that you're referring to?"

"Well, I had to talk to Ryan several times in the past few weeks about his behavior. In particular, lifting up the girls' skirts during recess or when they are standing in line."

He began to laugh loudly. "There's nothing wrong with that; I'd be more worried if you told me he was chasing after the boys."

"Mr. O'Maley, clearly it is a problem when I'm being inundated with e-mails from the parents of these little girls asking me what I plan to do about this."

"Tell them to fuck off," he said nonchalantly.

"That's the other thing; the language that he's using in school is totally inappropriate."

He looked at me smugly. "Oh, so now you're worried about what's appropriate. You sure weren't the other night when you were pressing yourself up against me, were you, darlin'?"

I felt my face begin to burn and I knew that I was turning red. I pushed my hair behind my ear and tried my best to compose myself and ignore his last statement.

"Look, I'm willing to work with Ryan during school and I can even schedule some time after school to get him up to par with his academics. I'm just asking that you work with me a little?"

"Oh, I'd like to work with you a lot." His smile broadened.

I stared at him blankly, trying to get him to take me seriously. It was as if I were talking to one of my students. "I could schedule Wednesdays after school for tutoring. There's a late bus that Ryan can take home as well."

"Oh no, he doesn't have to take the bus; I'll come and pick him up."

"Well, I just thought the bus would be a better option. I know you said you're kind of busy with work."

"I can adjust my schedule for my nephew, especially if it means I get to see his pretty teacher once a week," he said as he got up from the chair. "It was a pleasure to meet again, Miss Morgan." He extended his hand to me and raised his eyebrow.

I placed my hand in his and quickly released it. "Thanks for your support with this, Mr. O'Maley."

"Oh, sweetheart, the pleasure is all mine," he said as he turned around and exited the room.

I took a sip from the bottle of water that was sitting on my desk. Part of me was melting inside; the other part was loathing this man. He clearly had no interest in Ryan's education. He was using it as a tool to get me in bed, which would happen over my dead body. I cringed when I thought about how close I had come to having a one-night fling with him. My new mantra - *I will never drink again.*

Chapter 6

I was anxiously waiting for my little brother Justin to arrive. He was home on leave for a few days and we were spending the day together before he went to meet up with his best friend tonight. I had just hung up the phone with Donna when I heard the knock on my door. I ran to answer it and was unable to wipe the smile from my face at the sight of Justin standing in the doorway. I hadn't seen him in over a year. He looked exactly the same as he had the last time I saw him, but so different from that little boy I always had in my mind whenever I thought about him. He was about six feet tall. The dark brown stubble of what was left of his shaved hair covered his head and his muscles rippled through the black T-shirt he was wearing. The only thing that remained the same about the bratty little boy from so long ago was his big brown eyes.

He effortlessly scooped me up into his arms as I went to embrace him. "How's my little Pooh?" I asked as I gave him a kiss on the cheek. Justin was only three years younger than I was, but I always had a protective instinct over him as if I were so much older than he was. Growing up, I always did my best to cover for him to keep him out of trouble with my parents. I thoroughly inspected all the girls he dated and would become furious if they broke his heart. But I always made sure I was there to help him pick up the pieces if they did.

"I think you're the little one now, Nicole," he said, placing his hand on my head as he towered over me.

"Justin, no matter how tall you are, you will always be little to me."

We sat down on the couch and began to catch up. Justin had been staying with my parents for a few days and couldn't take it anymore. He decided to pack up and spend his last day with me before heading off to see his best friend, Johnny. He told me that he wasn't sure where he would be sent to next, as his orders were top secret. My stomach clenched, knowing that it was probably someplace dangerous. Even though I knew that Justin was living out his dream of being a Marine, the selfish part of me wished that he had chosen a different career; one that was a lot less risky. We spent the entire morning talking. It felt so good to catch up with him, even if it was just to listen to him complain about my parents and my sister. He knew I could relate to them all too well.

I had been dying to try the new Italian restaurant that everyone had been raving about near my school. I knew that Italian was Justin's favorite so we quickly agreed on our venue for lunch. After we placed our orders, I began to tell Justin about my job. He listened closely when I stopped mid-sentence upon seeing Dailan O'Maley and a very tall, super-skinny redhead walking through the door.

"What's the matter?" Justin asked.

I took a sip of water, hoping that he wouldn't see me, but it was too late as our eyes locked.

"Just play along with me, Justin," I whispered as Mr. O'Maley and the leggy redhead moved closer to our table.

"What are you talking about?" Justin had a look of pure confusion on his face as he turned around to see who I was staring at so intently.

"Miss Morgan, how are you?" Mr. O'Maley asked in that thick accent that made my heart leap out of my chest.

"I'm well, thank you," I said in a very matter-of-fact tone. "Oh, this is my boyfriend, Justin." I suddenly realized that I was a little too quick to offer up the information and hoped that I was believable.

I could see Justin giving me a strange look out of the corner of his eye. I kicked him under the table to play along. Justin stood up to shake Mr. O'Maley's hand. He was still much taller than my brother.

"Nice to meet you; you're a lucky guy."

"Yeah, I guess," Justin said with an uneasy look on his face as he shrugged.

"Well, enjoy your lunch," I said, trying to dismiss him as quickly as possible before Justin blew his cover. I took a deep breath as he walked away from the table and I realized he hadn't introduced us to the girl he was with. *So rude but so typical of him,* I thought.

"What the hell was that about?" Justin asked.

"Nothing." I tried to play it off as the waitress brought out our food.

"Um, nothing? You just made me pretend that I was your boyfriend; you better spill your guts, girl."

I filled Justin in on my botched introduction to Mr. O'Maley and the way I had made a complete fool out of myself. I just wanted him to think that I had a boyfriend so he would realize that I had no interest in him whatsoever and that my forward attitude that night was a result of the alcohol – which it was. I was also hoping that it would curtail him from making his uncomfortable remarks, which he considered compliments.

"Nicole, you are too much, you know that?" Justin laughed.

I smiled at him. "I know, now eat your chicken parm before I give you a big boyfriend kiss," I joked.

We finished our lunch and headed back to my place. Justin had to go to Johnny's house even though I wished that he could have stayed longer. We were standing outside of my apartment as Justin prepared to enter his car.

"Why don't you meet up with us later?" he asked.

"I would love to, but I have a ton of papers to grade and I have to be up at the crack of dawn to go look at bridesmaid dresses with Donna. Besides, you're going to be trying to pick up the girls; you wouldn't want your *girlfriend* there tagging along," I said as we both began to laugh.

"I want you to take care of yourself and if anything happens, you just haul ass and get yourself out of the situation and don't worry about anyone else," I said, feeling my emotions starting to stir.

"You know you just told me the exact opposite of what we are trained for." He laughed.

"Well, I don't care; you listen to me, because I can be a lot meaner and a bigger pain in the ass than your drill sergeant will ever be."

"True," he said as he pulled me closer and hugged me tightly. "I love you, Nicole."

"I love you too, Pooh; just please be safe," I said.

"Of course I will; I have a beautiful girlfriend to get back to." He laughed as I lightly smacked him on the arm before he got into the car. I stood at the end of the driveway, watching him drive away until his car was out of sight. Then I let the tears begin to flow as all my fears for my brother began to surface.

I walked up the stairs to my apartment and realized that I had left my cell phone sitting on the kitchen table the whole time we were at lunch. Three missed calls, all from my mother. She had only left one voicemail. I reluctantly dialed the number so I could listen to:

"Nicole, is Justin with you? I told him to call me when he got to your house to let me know he made it there okay and he's not answering his phone and you're not answering yours. You kids drive me crazy – call me back."

I rolled my eyes, knowing that I had to call her back or else she would just keep calling, and then I would really have to hear about it. I dialed her number and waited in angst for her to answer. I was surprised when instead it was my dad's voice on the other end.

"Hey, Dad, how are you?"

"Nicole?" he asked.

Okay, what other female would be calling him "Dad" besides my sister, who I knew was at their house at the present time as I clearly heard her yelling at her kids in the background.

"Yeah, it's me. I was just calling Mom to let her know Justin was here and he's on his way to Johnny's."

"Oh, okay. You know your mother; your brother can go and fight in a war but God forbid he takes a two-hour drive alone," he said, trying his best attempt at humor. Not that he wasn't a funny guy - he just wasn't funny with me.

"Yeah." I laughed. "Well, if you could just let her know," I said.

"I sure will," he said.

"Okay thanks. Bye Dad, I love you."

"Bye, Nicole."

I hung up the phone, feeling the same low that I always had after talking to my father. There was nothing else to be said between us; he was so disappointed in me that he couldn't even say "I love you" back to his own daughter. He was the reason that I was so tough on the outside, never letting anyone see me cry, not even Donna, the one and only person I had ever let into my life. Through the years, I had mastered the art of holding in my sadness until I was all alone. My tears had become very personal and I was the only one allowed to see them, and right now, after hanging up the phone with my dad, they were all that I was seeing.

Chapter 7

"Okay, Ryan, spell the word 'great' for me," I said.

Ryan looked up at me inquisitively with his big hazel eyes. It was difficult to stay mad at him for long; he was absolutely adorable. His smile made me melt; he had two perfectly placed dimples on each cheek. It wasn't hard to see that good looks ran in that family. It had been a little over two months since I had my little talk with Ryan's uncle. Ryan was making leaps and bounds academically. His behavior was still somewhat of an issue, but it was improving, which led me to believe that maybe his uncle was working with him at home as well. I had been staying with him every Wednesday after school and his uncle would pick him up every Wednesday as promised. I always did my best to avoid unnecessary conversation with him, making sure that Ryan was all packed up and ready to go when he arrived. I made up progress reports, which I gave him every two weeks to keep him abreast of Ryan's grades and behavior.

"G-R-E . . ." Ryan paused for a moment looking like he was deep in thought. ". . . A-T," he continued.

I smiled and gave him a thumbs-up. "Now use it in a sentence."

"That was some great sex," he blurted out of nowhere.

I felt my jaw drop. "Ryan, no. Where did you hear that?"

"My uncle was telling someone that on the phone one day."

"Okay, well, that goes on the list of inappropriate things to say."

"Well, if it's inappropriate, then why does my uncle say it?"

"I don't know, Ryan; sometimes adults say inappropriate things without realizing it," I tried my best to explain.

"Well, then, I bet my uncle says a lot of things that should be on the inappropriate list."

I rolled my eyes as he continued.

"What does bast--?"

I tried stopping him before he could get the entire word out. "Ryan, if you think it's inappropriate, then don't say it."

"Well, then maybe I need to tell my uncle to stop saying those things too; maybe he doesn't realize they're inappropriate either," he said very sweetly.

Oh, I'm sure he knows, I thought to myself. "Yes, Ryan, that would be a very good idea. Remind your uncle every time he says something inappropriate." Something told me that would be a full-time job. "Speaking of your uncle, where is he?" I asked as I looked up at the clock, realizing it was already 4:40 and I only had twenty minutes to get to the bank before it closed. I waited another five minutes before I started fumbling through my files for Ryan's uncle's contact information. I picked up my cell phone and dialed his cell. *Three rings; great, it's probably going to go to voicemail and I'm never going to make it to the bank.*

"O'Maley," he finally answered in a stern tone. His voice gave me butterflies and my hands were actually shaking. *Why the heck was I shaking over this fool?*

"Mr. O'Maley, it's Nicole Morgan."

"Ah, Miss Morgan." His tone suddenly became softer. "What did Ryan do now?"

"Nothing."

"Oh, so you just called to hear my voice, did ya?" he asked playfully.

"Uh, no. I called to tell you that you're forty-five minutes late picking up your nephew and I should have been out of here — like ten minutes ago!"

"Oh, fuck!" he shouted. "I totally forgot today is Wednesday; I'm in a meeting about an hour away."

My eyes shifted to Ryan, who looked like he was being abandoned. "Look, I have to get to the bank before they close. I can take Ryan home with me if you'd like and you can pick him up from there."

"You'd do that for me, darlin'?"

"I'm not doing it for *you*. I'm doing it for Ryan," I clarified.

"Thanks, I owe you," he said.

"That's okay," I said sarcastically. I quickly gave him my address before hanging up the phone.

I had Ryan quickly pack up his backpack and we headed out the door. I pulled into the drive-thru of my bank with three minutes to spare. I waited for the teller to finish with my transaction and looked in the rearview mirror. Ryan was sitting in the back seat, looking out the window like a little lost soul. Less than a year ago, his mom and dad were here loving and caring for him. Now he was totally dependent on a self-centered buffoon who was less mature than he was.

"Are you hungry, Ryan?"

"Kinda."

"Well, I make the best grilled cheese sandwiches!"

"Okay," he said with a smile.

I turned up the radio to drown out the silence and headed home. I turned down my tree-lined street and pulled in the driveway. Mrs. Tallone, my landlord, was walking her little Pomeranian, Elmo.

"Hi, Nicole, I got a package for you that came from UPS."

"Oh great, my new purse!" I said.

Mrs. Tallone was in her seventies and was the sweetest landlady anyone could ask for. I wasn't sure if she still believed it was 1950 or if she really didn't care that she was charging me half the rent that she should have been. I didn't argue. I loved my cozy little second floor apartment; it was perfect. I especially loved the fireplace and bay view from my living room.

I did a lot to make up for my bargain rent. I would always pick up extra groceries for her when I was at the food store, which she would always accept in protest. I would take her to her weekly hair appointments when needed and we'd have dinner together quite often. She had become somewhat of a grandmother to me.

Ryan's face lit up when he saw Elmo. "Do you want to pet him?" I asked.

He nodded. He walked over to Elmo and petted him gently on the head. Elmo responded by covering Ryan in kisses. "He likes you," Mrs. Tallone said.

"What's his name?" Ryan asked.

"Elmo," Mrs. Tallone responded as she smiled, watching the two of them.

"Oh, Mrs. Tallone, this is Ryan; he's one of my students."

"Well, it's really nice to meet you, Ryan," Mrs. Tallone said.

Ryan looked up and smiled, still unable to break free from Elmo. Mrs. Tallone went in to get my package and brought it out to me. Ryan finally pulled himself from Elmo and we made our way up the stairs to my apartment.

Ryan walked in and took everything in. "Is this where you live?" he asked.

"Uh-huh."

He picked up the picture of my brother and me that had been taken at his graduation from the Marine Corps. "Wow, is he a soldier?"

"Yup, that's my brother," I said proudly.

"Cool," he said.

He walked around examining more pictures that I had set out, inquiring who was in each picture, and I explained. I took the frying pan out and made us each a grilled cheese sandwich. Ryan was finally done exploring my apartment and sat down at the breakfast bar.

"Here you go," I said as I placed the grilled cheese and a glass of juice in front of him.

"Thanks," he said.

Ryan began to talk non-stop. He told me that he had a nanny who would get him off the bus and take care of him when his uncle had to travel for work. He spent one night a week and every other weekend with his mom's sister, Lisa. He didn't have any brothers or sisters and the last thing he said broke my heart – he missed his mother and father more than anything. The tears began to roll down his face when he spoke of them.

I grabbed a napkin and wiped the tears away. "Oh Ryan, your mommy and daddy will always be in your heart."

He looked at me inquisitively.

"When someone we love dies, they're always nearby; they live in your heart forever. And I'm quite certain that your mommy and daddy are really close by; they would never be too far from a great kid like you!"

"But why can't I see them anymore?" He began to sob uncontrollably.

I hugged him tightly until his cries subsided. I dampened a washcloth and wiped his face. My heart was aching for this poor little boy. "Ryan, have you ever talked to your uncle about how you're feeling?" I asked.

"Sometimes, but he gets really sad when I talk about my daddy because they were brothers."

I made a mental note to talk to the school guidance counselor tomorrow. Ryan needed to express his feelings and for tonight, I was happy to listen. I looked down at his half-eaten grilled cheese. He picked it up and took another bite. When we finished eating, Ryan took out his homework and began to work diligently on it. He asked me to check his math worksheet, which I gladly did and was pleased to see that he only got one answer wrong.

"Good job, Ryan!" I went into my bag and pulled the Thanksgiving-themed stickers out, placing one on his paper. His smile lit up the room; he looked so proud of himself and he had every reason to be.

We were just finishing up our ice cream when the doorbell rang. I got up to answer it, not surprised to find Dailan O'Maley on the other side. "That bloody overgrown rat of a dog just tried biting me in the arse," he said as he made his way in.

"Elmo?" I asked. Elmo didn't have a vicious bone in his body.

"I don't know; we didn't have a chance to be formally introduced," he said sarcastically.

Ryan and I both began to laugh at the same time. If what they say is true and animals can sense a person's true personality, then Elmo was dead on.

"What's so funny? You know, Ryan, he could have bit off my hand," Dailan joked.

"Oh my God, I don't think he would even break the skin, let alone bite off your hand. Besides, according to you, that wasn't the part of the anatomy he was after," I joked.

"Yeah, well, what could I say, all the girls are after that part of my body." He raised his eyebrow at me and smiled.

"Oh, yeah, too bad Elmo is a *boy*! And don't be too sure of yourself; not *all* girls."

"Oh really? You wanted it, until you found out who I was."

I looked over at Ryan, who was in the living room packing up his backpack, making sure he was out of earshot.

"No, that was after a little too much alcohol and, trust me, I haven't had anything else to drink after that night. I realized just how much drinking affects my judgment." I gave him a sarcastic smile.

"Oh darlin', you really need to stop pretending that you don't like me."

"Oh, I'm *not* pretending, Mr. O'Maley."

He gazed at me with a mischievous smile. I stared back at him as if to challenge him.

"Okay, Uncle Dailan, I'm ready," Ryan announced.

"He had dinner and his homework's all done," I said, putting on my sweet teacher voice again for Ryan's sake.

Dailan opened the door as Ryan went out ahead of him. "Goodbye, Miss Morgan," Ryan said.

"Bye, Ryan; see you in the morning."

I looked up from Ryan, waiting for Dailan to make his way out the door as well. "Good night, Miss Morgan, I'll be seeing you in your dreams tonight."

I shook my head and rolled my eyes at him. "Oh no, don't say that, I need to get a good night's sleep tonight and nightmares always keep me up." *Take that, you egotistical jerk.* He shook his head and laughed. "Good night, Mr. O'Maley," I said as I closed the door behind him.

He drove me crazy with his sarcastic comments; things would go so much smoother if he would just act normal and not like the arrogant ass that he was. After getting to know Ryan a little better tonight and seeing how affected he still was over his parents' deaths, I realized that it was more important than ever that he have someone stable to talk to in his life.

I walked back into the kitchen and I realized the ice cream dishes that Ryan and I had eaten from were still on the breakfast bar. I went to load them in the dishwasher and saw, lying on the counter, Ryan's thankful composition on which he had been working for our Thanksgiving bulletin board. I picked it up and began to read it. I could see the indentation of his letters on his paper from him pressing so hard with the pencil; something else we had been working on together.

I am thankful for my video games my skate board my bike. I also like my teacher Miss Morgan lots she helps me all the time and doesn't get mad when I get something wrong or I do some thing that is wrong. She cares about every one and she's really pretty and easy to talk to. My Uncle Dailan is cool too he is funny and he likes to play video games with me.

I smiled and grabbed another sticker from my bag, placing it on the top of the page. Ryan O'Maley was slowly making his way into my heart, while his uncle was quickly becoming a big pain in my....

Chapter 8

Van Morrison filled the air of Room 114 while I replaced the turkeys on my bulletin board with Christmas trees and menorahs. I turned around when I heard someone loudly clearing his throat, to find Dailan O'Maley standing in my classroom doorway. *Speaking of turkeys,* I laughed to myself.

I stepped down from the chair I was standing on and immediately adjusted my wool mini-skirt over my black tights. He made no attempt to conceal that he was checking me out from head to toe as I grabbed my phone and turned off the music.

"You don't have to turn it off on my account," he said with that same crooked smile that made me angry and melt at the same time.

"What's up, Mr. O'Maley?"

"You know, you have my permission to call me Dailan – Miss Morgan."

"Okay then, what's up, Dailan?"

"Ryan called me while I was on my way home from work. He's upset because he forgot his math homework. So I told him I would try and get it for him."

I smiled, realizing just how much Ryan had progressed in these past few months. Two months ago, he would not have cared less about doing homework; now he was actually getting upset over *not* doing it. "Sure, no problem," I said as I walked over to my desk to hand him the math sheet that was tonight's homework.

"Thank you," he said, almost sounding sincere as he silently gazed at me. Even though I didn't want to, I still checked him out, up and down. He was dressed in black dress pants, a crisp tailored gray dress shirt, and a gray-and-black tie, which was loosened around his neck. This all was underneath his open black trench coat. He once again had the sexy, overgrown razor stubble on his face. I was finding that I preferred him with that look, rather than the clean-cut one. *What the heck was I even thinking? This guy is a jerk. The last thing I should be thinking about is whether I liked him with or without facial hair.*

"You're welcome. Oh, can you give this to Ryan?" I handed him the *Thankful Essay* that I had just taken down off the bulletin board.

I watched his reaction as he read the essay. He smiled and then chuckled loudly. "Oh, so you get a whole paragraph and I get two lousy sentences?"

I shrugged and smiled.

"Well, then again, I'm not as pretty as you." He looked at me, waiting for my reaction.

I just stared at him blankly and shook my head.

"So, I was wonderin' if you wanted to go to dinner and to the tree lighting in town with Ryan and me Saturday night?" he asked.

"Um, no, I don't think that would be a very good idea."

"Why not?"

"Because I'm sure somewhere in the school handbook it says something about teachers dating parents not being acceptable."

"Well, I'm not a parent and it's not a date. Ryan would be coming along." He argued true to lawyer form.

"Still, you're Ryan's -"

"Okay, it's settled then; I'll pick you up at six." He grinned before walking out the door.

I stood there, speechless over his arrogance. How could he just assume that I wanted to go out with him? Plus, as far as he was concerned, I *had* a boyfriend. After I introduced him to Justin that day, I assumed he would have backed off with his flirtatious efforts, but that just seemed to make him more determined.

I walked back to my bulletin board and started taking my frustration over Mr. Dailan O'Maley out on my Christmas trees. I punched the stapler into them as hard as I could. One minute I was thinking that I just wouldn't be home when he came to pick me up. The next minute, I was planning what to wear.

* * *

Saturday arrived and I decided that I didn't want to disappoint Ryan, so I would be home when Dailan O'Maley showed up. I was trying my best to bake gingerbread men. I was planning to bring them in to school and have my class decorate them. I wasn't having much success. When I looked down at the cooling rack, it looked like the gingerbread men had come straight out of a horror movie. Some were decapitated while others were missing limbs. I looked up at the clock and realized that I had just enough time to change out of my sweats before Dailan and Ryan arrived. I put the rest of the cookie dough in the refrigerator and chalked them up as a loss. I didn't want my students lying on a couch, years from now, telling a shrink that they were scarred for life by their teacher serving them maimed gingerbread men. So, I would have to go to the store and buy ready-made ones that had all of their body parts.

I quickly changed into my favorite worn-out jeans and my black turtleneck. My hair looked a mess so I pulled it up into a quick bun. I applied some blush to brighten up my pale skin and dabbed on a quick coat of lip gloss just as the doorbell rang. When I opened the door, Ryan was grinning from ear to ear. I tried my best not to stare at his uncle, but I couldn't help myself. He was wearing jeans and a gray t-shirt that looked like they were both fitted perfectly for his body under a black wool pea coat.

"Miss Morgan, can I go to the bathroom?" Ryan asked as if we were in school.

"Sure, it's right around the corner," I said.

"I just have to grab my coat," I said to Dailan as I led him into the kitchen.

He looked down at my gingerbread men on the cooling rack and began to laugh. "What the heck are these supposed to be?"

"Oh, I tried to make gingerbread men."

"What in bloody hell happened to them?"

"They stuck to the cookie sheet when I tried removing them."

"That's because you didn't let them cool off long enough."

"What?" I asked, shocked that he would know anything about baking.

"Did you try taking them off the cookie sheet right away?" he asked.

"I don't remember." I knew full well that I had, but I wasn't going to admit that to him. I only had one cookie sheet and was in a rush to get the other batches in.

"It's just like anything. You need to have patience and perseverance; it makes the outcome so much better," he said as he moved closer to me. I suddenly got the feeling that he wasn't talking about the gingerbread men any more.

"I'm all done," Ryan announced as he came out of the bathroom, breaking up the awkwardness I was beginning to feel.

We headed out the door and down the steps to Dailan's black BMW that was parked in my driveway. Ryan quickly jumped in the back as Dailan held the door open for me, closing it when I got in. *Okay, maybe he could be a gentleman when he wanted to be.*

"Can we go to Buster's…please!" Ryan begged.

"It's up to Miss Morgan," Dailan said, looking over at me with a smug smile.

"That's fine with me," I said. Buster's was a casual restaurant located in my town. I was hoping that because of the location, it would help lessen the chances of seeing anyone from school.

My phone began to ring and I fumbled through my purse to grab it. I looked at the caller ID and saw that it was Donna. I sent the call to voicemail; I knew she was just calling to confirm that we were still on for dress shopping tomorrow. I hadn't told her about my date with Dailan; I figured I would deal with that tomorrow when I saw her.

"Boyfriend?" Dailan asked sarcastically.

"Oh no, we broke up; he wasn't my type." Even though I didn't care what Dailan O'Maley thought of me, it bothered *me* to think that I was going out with another man when I had a pretend boyfriend at home.

He took his eyes off the road for a brief second, giving me a sly look of triumph, making me immediately regret telling him that I no longer had a boyfriend.

"What *is* your type?" he asked smoothly.

"Certainly not you," I said with a grin.

"You don't even know what type I am."

"Oh, I think I know enough."

"I think you may have your doubts or else you wouldn't be here tonight," he said.

"Well it's not a date – remember?" I reminded him.

We pulled into the parking lot and I was feeling much like I was incognito as we walked into the restaurant making sure that I didn't see anyone who was associated with school in any way. The hostess took us to a booth and I made sure to take the extra seat next to Ryan and not Dailan.

The waitress came over to take our order and I couldn't help but notice Dailan checking her out when she walked away. "You know that's just wrong," I commented.

"What?" he asked, clearly aware to what I was referring.

"The way you look at women like they're sex objects."

He rolled his eyes at me. "You know, I like that girl that I met at the bar that night better than the uptight school teacher."

"Good, 'cause that girl that you met in the bar doesn't exist," I said.

"Oh I betcha if that girl had a few drinks she would come back out," he said with a smirk.

I looked over, forgetting that Ryan was even there. He was coloring the picture on the back of his placemat, not paying any mind to the bantering going on between me and his uncle. I picked up a crayon and began coloring with him in an effort not to make any more conversation with his uncle. I finally looked up when I could feel him staring at me.

"What?" I asked in annoyance.

He was laughing and trying to play innocent. I had to admit that he looked absolutely adorable at that particular moment with his cute boyish grin.

"Why are you staring at me?" I asked.

"Because I think you're hot," he said as he chewed on his straw and his smile became even wider. Ryan started to giggle, never taking his eyes from his coloring.

I pursed my lips and shook my head. "What, are you twelve?" His only response was the arrogant smirk that I had become so acquainted with over the past few months. "You know what – why did I even agree to come out with you tonight? Oh wait—that's right, I didn't agree, you just took it upon yourself to barge into my classroom and demand that I go," I said, not finding any humor in his immature behavior.

"Do you always take demands like that from a man, darlin'? If so, I think I need to get you in the bedroom," he said as he rubbed the scruff on his cheek.

I couldn't take his obnoxious behavior anymore. I shook my head and shot him a dirty look before giving him a swift kick in the knee.

"Ouch, that wasn't very nice," he said as he rubbed his knee under the table.

"Keep it up and I'll aim just a little higher."

"Then that would be your loss."

"Oh, I'm sure it wouldn't be," I snapped.

Ryan seemed unfazed by it all as he continued to color. I realized now exactly where Ryan got his colorful vocabulary - from the immature, arrogant male chauvinist sitting across from me. Did I mention incredibly sexy as well?

Chapter 9

The town square was adorned in lights. Every single lamppost was decked out in green garland and red bows. The upscale shops were all open and in full swing, while Christmas music filled the air. Soon, Santa would arrive and light the twenty-foot Christmas tree that was at the center of it all. It was my family's tradition as a child to attend the tree lighting every year. All of the memories came flashing to me as if it were yesterday; back to a time when I was still my daddy's little girl and not some stranger that he couldn't even look at. I felt heaviness in my chest; so much had changed from those happy Christmases so long ago.

We sat down on a bench while Ryan ran around with a little boy he had just met who seemed to be his age. I zipped my coat all the way up and wrapped my scarf tightly around my neck. I had forgotten my gloves and buried my hands deep within my coat pockets in an effort to keep them warm. Dailan pulled his gloves from his pocket and offered them to me.

"That's okay," I said.

"I don't have cooties, you know," he joked.

I reluctantly took them and put them on. They were much too big on me, but they served their purpose in keeping my hands warm. "So tell me about yourself, Mr. Dailan O'Maley."

"I thought you already knew everything you needed to know," he said with a smirk.

"Humor me," I said smirking back at him.

He began to open up and actually have a normal conversation. I finally felt like I was talking to a grown man and not one of my students. He was twenty-nine years old. His mother was from Ireland and his dad was Irish-American. He was born in the United States and moved back to Ireland with his mother when he was two years old, after his parents divorced. Growing up, he and his older brother Gerry would come back to the United States for a few weeks over the summer to visit his dad. He worked as a lawyer for a marketing firm that had offices in Dublin, London, Boston, Pennsylvania, and New Jersey. He attended college and law school in the United States and had passed the bar exam in three different states. He had also passed the barrister exam in Ireland. I was beginning to see that what he lacked in maturity, he made up for with intelligence. He was living and working in Dublin, until his brother passed away seven months ago. He was here temporarily to care for Ryan and he was working in the office based in New Jersey. He had planned on returning to Dublin with Ryan, once he had gotten the approvals from the courts to take him out of the country. His brother and his wife Connie had granted full custody to Dailan in their will. I couldn't help but wonder what the heck they were thinking when they did that and why they wouldn't have chosen Connie's sister, who was adamantly fighting Dailan on it. She didn't want him taking Ryan out of the country to live. I could see sadness in his eyes at the mention of his brother and I actually felt sorry for him.

"So you guys were pretty close?" I asked.

"Who?" he asked as if he were taken off guard.

"You and your brother."

"Yeah, we were." He looked away as if it pained him to talk about it.

"Well, I'm really sorry," I said sincerely.

He looked at me and nodded with sadness in his eyes. We sat in comfortable silence and watched Ryan, who was sitting by the Christmas tree, listening to a story being read by an older woman, who was supposed to be Mrs. Claus. Dailan began to chuckle as he watched Ryan take the hand of the little girl sitting next to him. *So much alike*, I thought to myself.

"You know, he's come so far in just a few months," I said.

"Yeah, most of it is thanks to you." He smiled.

Wow, was that a genuine compliment without any sarcastic edge from Dailan O'Maley?

The children began to cheer at the sight of Santa's arrival. They looked up at him in awe, making me miss those days when Christmas was still magical and Santa still existed. Within seconds, the enormous Christmas tree was shining brightly as Bing Crosby's *White Christmas* blared throughout town square.

Santa began to hand out goody bags to each of the children. I watched as Ryan waited patiently for his. Santa finally made his way to Ryan. He said something that made Ryan nod in response before handing him the goody bag. Ryan came running over with a bag filled with candy in his hand.

"Look what I got from Santa," he said proudly as he waved the bag in the air. "You want some Miss Morgan?" he asked sweetly.

"Oh, no thanks, sweetie, and I think it's a little late for you to be eating that too," I said, directing my comment to Dailan, who probably would have let him eat the whole bag before going to bed.

"Why don't you let me hold that," Dailan said as he took the bag and shoved it in his coat pocket.

"Can we get some hot chocolate?" Ryan asked excitedly.

"Well, that depends. Miss Morgan may have to get home before she turns into a pumpkin," Dailan said with a smile.

"I would love to have hot chocolate with you, Ryan." I said happily.

"Cool!" Ryan exclaimed as he looked up at me, placing his hand in mine, taking me a little off guard.

We drank our hot chocolate as we walked around the town. I never got sick of looking at the old beautiful houses that were so lovingly maintained decked out in Christmas lights. The clippity clop of horse hooves hitting the pavement and the sleigh bells ringing from the carriage full of people they were pulling made me feel like I was in a different place in time. I found it hard to believe, but I was actually enjoying myself with Ryan and Dailan.

"Uncle D, can we please go to the arcade at the end of the street?" Ryan begged.

"For what? So I can crush you in Death Race again?" Dailan asked as he placed his hand on Ryan's head, messing up his hair.

"That's because you cheated last time," Ryan said as looked up at Dailan with an adorable toothless grin.

"I cheated? You're just a sore loser," Dailan joked as he effortlessly picked Ryan up and flung him over his shoulder.

"Ahhh, help!" Ryan screamed, unable to control his laughter.

I smiled at the way the two of them were interacting. A very small part of me caught a glimpse into why Ryan's parents may have chosen Dailan in their will, after all.

The dinging of machines filled the air as we walked into the arcade. My brother and I would spend hours here when we younger. Ryan immediately jumped on the Death Race game and anxiously waited for Dailan to put the coins in to start it up. Dailan hovered over Ryan the whole time, teasing him every time he would make a mistake.

"Be quiet!" Ryan yelled, clearly growing agitated with the game and Dailan.

By the time the game ended, Ryan's frustration had doubled and Dailan's relentless teasing was only adding to it. "I don't like you," Ryan pouted as he punched Dailan in the arm.

"Oh, stop being such a baby," Dailan said.

"I'm not being a baby; you made me mess up!"

Dailan began to laugh. "How did I make you mess up?"

"I don't know. You just did!" Ryan looked like he was trying to hold back tears as he stood with his arms crossed, looking up in annoyance at his uncle.

"You know what, Ryan? Why don't you play this with me?" I said, turning around to the air hockey table that was right behind me. I smiled inside, remembering all of the times I had crushed my brother in this game.

Ryan's frown immediately disappeared as he whisked past Dailan. "Hmm…" Ryan said as he punched Dailan lightly on the arm again.

Dailan playfully got Ryan in a headlock, making a fist and rubbing his knuckles into Ryan's scalp. "Noogie!" he yelled.

"Stop." Ryan laughed.

"Not until you say 'my Uncle Dailan is the best and it's not his fault that I stink at Death Race.'"

"No," Ryan said as he tried his best to break free.

"Say it," Dailan demanded as he continued his assault on Ryan's head.

"My Uncle Dailan is the best." Ryan's words were almost inaudible, being masked by laughter.

"And?" Dailan was persistent.

"It's not his fault that I stink at Death Race," Ryan said reluctantly as Dailan finally released him from his grip. Ryan was out of breath and his dirty blond hair was sticking up all over the place.

"I didn't mean it," Ryan said once he had gotten far enough from Dailan.

Dailan took a step toward Ryan, acting as if he was going to grab him again.

"Ahh," Ryan yelled, exposing his adorable dimples. "I'm kidding," he said in defeat.

"How do you play this?" Ryan asked.

"It's easy," I said.

"I'll show you first, Ryan," Dailan said as he moved closer to Ryan.

"Okay, Ryan, prepare to watch your Uncle get beat!" I said.

Dailan rolled his eyes at me as if I had just said something ridiculous.

"Oh, please, I will kill you." I said.

"Okay, care to make a friendly wager?" Dailan asked.

I bit my lip to think about his proposition for a minute. "What are you proposing?" I asked.

"If I win, you have to come to my company Christmas party with me next weekend," Dailan said.

I rolled my eyes at the thought. "And if I win, you will stop with your off-color comments that you're constantly making and act like the adult that you are when you're in my company."

"Deal," he said as he held out his hand and we shook on it.

Chapter 10

"I'll pick you up at seven on Saturday," Dailan said with a mischievous grin as we pulled up to my apartment.

"Whatever," I said. I still couldn't believe I had lost. *I killed my brother so many times in air hockey; what the heck went wrong tonight?*

I got out of the car and looked in the back seat, "Good night, Ryan. See you Monday."

"Good night, Miss Morgan," he said sweetly.

I looked over at Dailan, who was still smiling in triumph and just shook my head. I couldn't help but give him a quick smile back as I shut the car door and headed up the stairs to my apartment.

I fumbled in the darkness for my keys, finally locating them in the bottom of my purse. I walked into my apartment, hearing the sound of Dailan's car pulling away once I was safely inside.

Another mess you've gotten yourself into, Nicole. I had to admit that I actually enjoyed myself tonight. But I was not looking forward to going out on a one-on-one date with Dailan O'Maley at all. I wondered if it would look too obvious if I suddenly came down with a rare twenty-four hour sickness on Saturday.

I took my phone from my purse to find three text messages from Donna. I wanted to change quickly into my pajamas before I answered her back. I took my phone into my room with me as it began to vibrate with another text. *Geez, give me a minute, Donna.* I looked down to see what she had to say and realized that it wasn't from her. I didn't recognize the number at all. I opened it up to read it.

You really should keep your front porch light turned on, especially when you're coming home late at night by yourself. Good night, Miss Morgan. P.S. I promise I will be the perfect gentleman next weekend.

I instantly thought back to the day I had called Dailan from my cell phone to let him know that he had forgotten to pick up Ryan. He must have saved my number in his phone. *Great, not only have you agreed to go on a date with him; now he has your cell phone number, stupid!*

I quickly changed and responded back to Donna's text message.

Sorry for just getting back to you. I agreed to go out with Ryan and his uncle tonight and although it pains me to admit – Dailan O'Maley is totally sexy. I could definitely see him in my bed, if only he weren't so obnoxious. I'll tell you all about it tomorrow; we're meeting up at 10, right?

I hit the send button and took my phone out in the living room with me waiting for Donna's reply. A few minutes into my *Sex and the City* re-run, my house phone began to ring. I answered it immediately upon seeing that it was Donna.

"Where the heck have you been?" she asked frantically. "I've been calling and texting you all night."

"I texted you back a few minutes ago," I said.

"I don't have any texts from you. That's why I called you on your home phone. I thought maybe something was wrong with your cell."

I looked down at my cell phone to see if the message I had sent her went through. My stomach dropped and I instantly broke out in a sweat when I saw that I had accidentally replied to Dailan O'Maley instead of Donna.

"Oh my God, oh my God," I shouted as I instantly turned off my cell phone in hopes that it would somehow erase the message I had just sent.

"Nicole, what's wrong?" Donna asked.

"I sent a person to the wrong message," I said in complete hysteria.

"Okay, slow down and breathe, that made no sense," Donna said.

"Donna, I sent a text that was meant for you to Dailan O'Maley." I went on to explain the content of the text to her.

After her laughter subsided, she finally responded. "Oh my God, Nicole, you kill me with some of the things you do. Did he respond back?"

"I don't know. I turned off my phone. I don't want to see."

"Well, you're going to have to turn it back on eventually and what is it with you and this smut talk. First, you want to have a one-night stand with him and then you're sexting me about him. What happened to the sweet innocent girl I used to know who never talked about sex?" she teased.

"What am I going to do, Donna? He's never going to let me live this down," I said, completely ignoring her last question.

"I don't know, crazy girl, but I have to run. Michael and I are heading out to a late movie. I just wanted to make sure you were still alive. I'll see you tomorrow at ten and I look forward to hearing his response," she said, laughing as she hung up the phone.

I tried my best to forget about what I had just done, but it was of no use. I finally got the nerve to power up my phone. I anxiously waited for it to boot up. I couldn't look as I placed it upside down. Even though I couldn't see if there was a text message there, I could still feel it as my phone began to vibrate in my hand. "Shit, shit, shit!" I turned it around and read it with trembling hands.

That could easily be arranged.

I covered my eyes and shook my head. I could almost see him reading the message with that sly grin of his on his face. I waited until my hands were done trembling before I replied.

Sorry, that was sent to the wrong person.

I hit the send button, displeased with that response, but it was the best one I could think of at that particular moment.

My phone began to vibrate once again.

Obviously, but I'm glad to see you didn't need alcohol in you this time to admit your true feelings.

I shook my head in disgust and threw my phone on the couch. I thought about how he had relentlessly teased Ryan tonight in the arcade. He surely wasn't going to let this go easily with me. I picked my phone back up and began to type away.

Actually, I'm taking cold medication that impairs my judgment far worse than alcohol. I probably won't even remember this conversation in the morning.

I knew that he wasn't going to fall for it, but I remained hopeful that it would put an end to this texting debacle.

I looked down at the vibrating cell phone gripped tightly in my hand.

Right…..Well, I'll just have to make sure I remind you the next time I see you. Sweet dreams, Miss Morgan.

"I'm sure you will," I said out loud. "Stupid, stupid girl!" I shouted as I threw my phone on the chair across from where I was sitting. I had just added more fuel to his obnoxious fire. How in the world did I keep getting myself into one mess after another when it came to him? I couldn't think anymore; my head was starting to pound. I took two Tylenols and headed off to bed, hoping that I would wake up to find that this was all just a bad dream!

Chapter 11

I felt like I had tried on every single bridesmaid dress in the store before Donna and I finally agreed upon the very last one. At this point, I was willing to wear a paper bag. We had been looking for the perfect dress for the past three months. We finally decided on a strapless chiffon cocktail dress with a soft sweetheart neckline in a light green color called "clover." I placed the order for the dress, glad finally to put my bridesmaid dress shopping days behind me.

We headed to lunch and were just digging into our salads when Donna bought the subject up, the one that I was trying to forget and thought I had avoided because we were both so absorbed in dress shopping all morning long.

"Well, what happened with the text?" she asked.

"Just what I thought; he made a wise-ass comment and will probably never let me live it down," I said as I took a sip of water. "Now I have to go to this stupid Christmas party next weekend, with him thinking I want to sleep with him the entire night."

"Wait a minute, what Christmas party?" Donna asked.

I filled Donna in on the events that transpired last night. She looked at me and shook her head.

"What?" I asked unable to read the expression on her face.

"I don't get you, Nicole; you obviously are attracted to him. So why are you fighting it?"

"Because he is the legal guardian of one of my students and is clearly a womanizer."

Donna shrugged her shoulders. "I don't know; he seems to only have one woman on his mind, the way he's pursuing you."

"Oh, I seriously doubt that. Besides, even if that were true, which it is not, the last thing I want right now is a relationship."

"Why not?" she asked.

"Do I need to remind you about the mess I made with Drew?" I asked, raising my eyebrows at her.

71

She looked at me sadly at the mention of Drew's name. "Well, then maybe you should just have fun with him. If you don't want a relationship and he doesn't, then what would it hurt?"

I couldn't believe the words that were coming from my hopeless-romantic best friend's mouth. She was actually telling me to sleep with someone – no strings attached.

"Can we please stop talking about this before I lose my appetite?" I asked.

Donna nodded as she took another mouthful of salad.

"Donna, one last thing, and then there will be no more Dailan O'Maley talk for the rest of this lunch."

Donna looked at me anxiously, waiting what I had to say.

"Would you mind helping me pick out a dress for this Christmas party?"

"Absolutely," she said with a mile wide grin.

We finished up our lunch and headed to the mall. We hit several different stores without any success and I decided that Macy's would be our last stop; if I didn't find anything there, I would just have to dig deep within my closet for something.

I was quickly losing my steam as I half-heartedly scanned the racks of dresses. I was just about to call it quits when Donna pulled out a little black velvet dress. It looked a little plain and not at all what I had in mind, but I decided to try it on anyway.

We went into the fitting room. I pulled the dress up over my body, and Donna zipped me up in the back. I looked in the full-length mirror at the bodice style dress with elbow length sleeves. It was a little shorter than I would have liked, but it was a perfect fit, looking like it was tailor made for me, molding perfectly to my body.

"Wow!" Donna exclaimed as she backed up to look at me.

I turned to try and get a glimpse of the back of it in the mirror and I couldn't help but notice how perfectly shaped my butt looked in it. I was feeling totally sexy. Then it dawned on me, there was no way in hell that I could wear this dress. That would be just asking for trouble with Dailan.

"Yeah, I don't like it," I said to Donna.

"Are you kidding me? That dress is perfect!" Donna said.

"Perfect if I was going out with someone I was actually trying to impress. Not with a grown man who has the maturity level and hormones of a teenager," I said.

"Nicole, you have to get this dress. I will not let you leave here without it," Donna protested.

"Did you not just hear a word I just said, Donna?"

"Yeah, I did and so what if it drives him crazy? Pay him back for his obnoxious behavior by letting him see you in this dress, knowing that he can't have what's under it," Donna said with a devious grin.

I quickly began to smile back, liking her way of thinking. I looked down at the price tag, knowing that I couldn't really afford it. I would just have to put it on my credit card. It would be worth it, if it meant beating Dailan O'Maley at his own game.

"Sold," I said with a huge smile as I lifted the dress over my head and hung it back up.

Our next stop was the lingerie store to find a bra to enhance my breasts, as Donna put it, or, in other words, to find a bra that would give the illusion that I *had* breasts. As we walked in, Donna began to fumble through the bras.

"Can I help you ladies?" A good-looking, well-dressed Spanish man asked. I looked at him, thinking that it was kind of odd to see a man working in a lady's lingerie store.

"My friend just bought this beautiful curve-hugging dress and needs a bra to make her little a little bigger," Donna explained.

"Do you have the dress with you, hon?" he asked.

I lifted the plastic that was covering the dress on the hanger.

"Gorgeous!" he said.

He led us over to another section of the store that looked like it had more of the risqué undergarments.

"What size are you?" he asked.

"32B," I responded.

I watched as he scoured the bras, finally finding my size. "Go try this on with the dress," he said.

I rolled my eyes at Donna. I had my fill of trying on clothes for one day. "Just do it," she scolded as she followed me into the fitting room to help zip me up.

I put the bra on, immediately feeling like I was carrying around two ten-pound weights. "What the heck?" I wasn't used to seeing my chest look so big. Donna helped me slip the dress on and then zipped it up for me. I looked at myself with my newfound boobs under the dress; there was no doubt in my mind now that I was asking for serious trouble.

"Let me see," the salesman shouted through the door.

"Seriously?" I whispered to Donna as she opened the door and pushed me out.

I watched as the salesman put his hand up to his cheek and his mouth opened a mile wide. "Ahh…girl, you are seriously rocking it in that dress. You are going to give your man a heart attack." Donna and I both began to laugh.

We went back into the dressing room to change. "Look out, Mr. O'Maley," Donna said, laughing as she unzipped my dress. Donna walked out of the fitting room while I finished changing. She was waiting for me at the counter. I gave the bra to the salesman, who began to ring me up as Donna handed him a sexy little pair of black lace underwear. I shook my head at her in protest.

"Yes, you can't look all smokin' hot and wear those granny panties that you wear underneath that dress," she said.

I watched as the salesman immediately shook his head. "Oh no, you definitely have to wear the sexy undies; no granny panties."

"I don't wear granny panties," I said in defense as Donna rolled her eyes at me.

"Fine," I said as I handed the salesman my credit card. This surely was an expensive lesson that I was going to be teaching Dailan O'Maley. My only hope was that it didn't backfire on me!

Chapter 12

I sat at my desk, waiting for my students to pile in. Monday morning at 8:58 am had to be the most dreaded time of the week for any teacher. I got up to greet the children as they started to arrive with the walkers/car riders first, then each individual busload. The silence that filled the air just a few short moments ago was now filled with laughter, gasps, singing, and every other sound in between.

I paid particular attention to Ryan, who came walking in with Kyle, another little boy in my class with whom Ryan was becoming close friends. It made me happy to see Ryan starting to form relationships with his classmates. He was looking absolutely adorable wearing a black ski jacket and a black winter hat. He was bogged down by his backpack and another bag that he was holding in his hand. He walked over to my desk, quickly taking the backpack off his back. I grabbed the other bag that he was holding to help him out.

"These are for you," he said, pointing to the bag.

I looked at him, puzzled, as I opened the bag to find two cookie tins. I slowly removed the lid from one of the tins to find layers of perfectly formed gingerbread men, with all their body parts intact.

"Did you make these, Ryan?" I asked with a smile.

He nodded, looking very proud of himself. "Well, me and my uncle did." He sighed as if he was displeased with something.

"What's wrong, Ryan?"

"Miss Morgan, my uncle said a lot of words on the inappropriate list yesterday when he was making those. I tried to remind him every time, but then he burnt his hand when he took them out of the oven and he started saying words that I never even heard before, but I think they were inappropriate. I told him to use the potholder, but he doesn't listen."

I smiled and shook my head just imagining the words that were spewing from his mouth.

"Miss Morgan, is that f-word still inappropriate when you say Mother before it?"

I looked at Ryan and nodded.

"Oh, then he really did say a lot of inappropriate things," Ryan said with disappointment.

"These are awesome gingerbread men, Ryan! Thank you so much for sharing them with the class," I said trying to shift the subject.

"You're welcome," he said as he ran off to put his stuff away.

Just when I was ready to get Dailan O'Maley back with the little black dress, he had to go and do something nice like this. I looked in the bag to find an envelope with my name on it. I tore it open, almost afraid of what it said.

"Dear Miss Morgan,
Not only am I incredibly sexy, but I can bake as well. If you'd like to thank me at a later date in your bed, I would be willing to let you. Hope you have a wonderful day.
Dailan"

I rolled my eyes and couldn't help but laugh. *Okay, Dailan O'Maley, the little black dress attack is back on!*

I finished up the day and was ready to head home. I looked down at the tins of gingerbread men that my kids would be decorating this week and smiled. I pulled my phone from my purse and found Dailan's number. I made sure that I had listed him as a contact in my phone after the little mishap from the other night.

I'm thanking you now via text for the gingerbread men and that is the ONLY thanks you will be getting!

I hit the send button, threw my phone in my purse, and headed home. I arrived home, ate a bowl of cereal for dinner, and took a quick shower. I jumped on my laptop to input some grades into the online grading system before heading off to bed. Somewhere in between, my ADHD starting kicking in and I decided to check my e-mail. I was pleasantly surprised to see an e-mail from my brother. I quickly clicked on the little envelope to see what he had to say.

Hey Nic:

How's it going? I can't tell you where I am right now but I just wanted to let you know that I'm still alive and well. Working a lot of long ass days and doing extra training is taking its toll on me, I'm beat.

How's everything going with you? How do you like your job? Have you cheated on me yet...lol. I miss you and can't wait to hang out again. I have to get going. I'll e-mail again when I can.

Love you –
Justin"

The tears began to fall onto my keyboard. I missed my brother so much. Lately he seemed to be the only family that I had left. I sent a quick reply:

Please just be safe!
I love you too! Nicole xoxoxo

I logged off my computer, feeling too melancholic after that e-mail from my brother to concentrate on anything else for the night. I reached into my purse to grab my cell phone. One new text message from yours truly – Mr. Dailan O'Maley.

Suit yourself, I was just figuring we could kill two birds with one stone. You could thank me and get your wish at the same time.

I placed my phone in the charger and headed off to bed. *You won the battle for tonight, Dailan O'Maley, but the war begins on Saturday!*

* * *

Donna and Kara were at my house promptly by five, armed with a bag of make-up, a curling iron, and several different pairs of Donna's shoes. Kara began to get to work right away; first applying make-up to my face, then my eyes, finishing off with lip liner and lip-gloss.

"Make sure you stick this in your purse and don't forget to reapply, especially if there's any kissing going on," Kara said as she handed me the tube of lip-gloss.

Meanwhile, Donna was working on my hair, wrapping big strands around the barrel of the curling iron and choking me with hairspray. When she finished, I got up to look at myself in the mirror.

"No, no, no," Donna shouted. "Wait until you're fully dressed, so you can get the full effect."

Donna and Kara both helped me with my dress, making sure that I didn't mess up my hair or make-up.

"Aren't you wearing pantyhose?" Kara asked.

"No, I never wear pantyhose. I hate them."

"You wear tights all the time," Donna said.

"Tights are different than pantyhose. Pantyhose are uncomfortable," I said.

Donna rolled her eyes at me. "You're going to be freezing."

"No I won't; I've got a long coat."

"Plus it's easier access," Kara chimed in with a giggle.

"Oh no, there will be none of that, Kara," I said playfully.

"Uh huh, we'll see about that," Donna joked.

"Hey, this is war, remember?" I said.

"Yeah, but somehow I see you being the first to surrender," Donna said.

"Never," I said as I walked over to the array of shoes that Donna had brought over, finally settling on the vintage-looking black suede strappy pumps.

I turned around in the full-length mirror to finally take a look at myself, only it wasn't me that I saw in the reflection. My hair had big loose curls and my make-up looked like it was airbrushed on. I was never a big make-up person, so it took me a few minutes to get used to it. Once I did, I was pleasantly pleased with the outcome.

"Oh my God, I wish we could plant a video camera so we could see his reaction when he sees you," Donna said

"Well, if you two don't get out of here soon, you will see it in person," I said, looking at the clock and seeing that it was only 15 minutes till D-Day. Donna and Kara hurriedly made their way out of my apartment, while I sat around with a knot in my stomach waiting for Dailan to arrive. I looked up at the clock that was now flashing 7:16. *What if he doesn't show up? What if he planned this all out to make me get ready and then stand me up?* The sound of the doorbell broke me free from my over-thinking. I took a deep breath, ignoring the butterflies in my stomach as best as I could as I headed to the door. *Okay Dailan O'Maley, let the war begin.*

Chapter 13

I had never seen an actual human being's eyes pop out of their head like they do in cartoons, but Dailan O'Maley's came pretty close to it when I opened up the door. He began to assess me up and down. Normally, his wandering eyes made me uncomfortable, but tonight it was all part of my ambush and he seemed to be falling right into it.

"Wow, I see you're going to make it really hard for me to keep my promise of being a gentleman tonight," he said.

I rolled my eyes as I walked into the kitchen to grab my coat and purse. I accidentally dropped my keys, making sure that I strategically gave him a nice view as I bent over to pick them up. I looked up at him as he ran his hand through his hair and took a deep breath.

I had to admit, he didn't look so bad himself. He was wearing a charcoal gray suit that again looked like it was tailor made for him. His thick wavy brown hair was perfectly tousled and he had that sexy unshaven look that I had grown so fond of.

"Are you ready?" I asked.

"I guess, unless you want to see me in your bed first," he said with a smirk.

Oh God, this was going to be easier than I thought. "Really? Can you please act just a *little* mature tonight?"

He held up his hands as if he were signaling defeat. "It was worth a shot," he said under his breath.

We got into the car and I realized Donna was right; I was freezing. Dailan looked over at me and turned up the heat, seeming to sense that I was cold.

"So where is this Christmas party even at?" I asked.

"Oceanview Terrace," he said.

"Oh," I said, knowing that Oceanview Terrace was one of the most upscale banquet facilities around.

"Oh, and I forgot to tell you. You have to pretend you're my girlfriend," he said nonchalantly.

"What? No way, that was not part of our deal, buddy!"

"I know, but my boss has been on me about taking out his granddaughter. So, instead of telling him the truth, I spared his feelings by telling him I had a girlfriend."

"How did you spare his feelings by not telling him the truth?" I asked, totally confused.

"Because the truth is, his granddaughter looks like she could be on the front of a dog food bag."

My jaw dropped as I gasped. "You know, that's really horrible!"

He shrugged his shoulders. "So you see, now you have to play along. You wouldn't want to hurt the poor old man's feelings, would you, darlin'?"

I shook my head in disgust at him. "Fine, but don't think that gives you any real boyfriend privileges."

"Okay, can we please go over what boyfriend privileges are?" he asked as we pulled up to the valet area.

"Just don't try anything inappropriate. Wait a minute; let me re-phrase that—anything that would be inappropriate to a *normal* man your age," I said as I got out of the car. He was grinning from ear to ear as he handed the valet his car keys. "I mean it, or I'll smack you right in front of everyone," I said.

I noticed the valet snickering as he overheard what I had just said. "If you think that's bad, you should see her in the bedroom," Dailan joked to the valet, causing him to burst out with laughter.

"Keep it up, Dailan, and I will tell your boss that you're just dying to go out with his granddaughter," I said as we made our way into the elaborate ballroom.

Dailan was immediately greeted by two attractive women who looked to be in their mid 40s. "Dailan sweetie, we were wondering when you were coming," one of the woman said as they each gave him a kiss on the cheek.

I had to look away. I was getting nauseated seeing the way these ladies were falling all over him; no wonder he behaved the way he did around women.

"Oh and you must be his girlfriend that he told us about," the brunette said in a sickening sweet voice.

As if their little love fest with Dailan wasn't enough to make me want to vomit, the thought of being his girlfriend was. Dailan wrapped his arm around me and pulled me closer. I shot him a dirty look, but he wasn't paying me any mind.

"Nicole, this is Debbie and Tina," he said. I bit my lip and managed my best smile as I shook each of their hands.

"Well, I hope you won't mind sharing him for a dance tonight?" the blonde who I believed was Debbie asked.

"Oh no, he's all yours," I said, sounding almost too happy.

I waited until they walked away before laying into him. "You said I had to pretend in front of your boss, not in front of everyone here!" I said in a loud whisper.

"Well, don't you think it would get back to him if I introduced you to everyone else as just some pain in the arse that I won a bet with because she stinks at air hockey?"

He went to take my hand, but I pulled it back. "I promise I will be on my best behavior *for now*," he said with a grin as he held out his hand again. I gave him a dirty look and then reluctantly placed my hand in his.

We made our way through the crowd as Dailan was stopped every few seconds to have someone ogle over him, mainly women. I grabbed a glass of white zinfandel off one of the trays that the waiters were carrying around. I didn't have any intention of drinking, but something told me I would need to if I was going to get through this night.

"Dailan!" An older heavyset man exclaimed as he approached us.

I could tell by the way Dailan pulled me closer that this was his boss. I took another sip of wine in an effort to prepare myself for what was to come. Dailan shook the older man's hand. "Judy, Dailan is here," the man yelled as a very classy looking older woman approached us.

"Oh, Dailan, it's so nice to see you again, honey," she said as she gave him a hug and a kiss. Then she looked at me, giving me a warm smile.

"Mr. and Mrs. Allan, this is my girlfriend, Nicole," he said, sounding very convincing.

"Oh dear, it's so nice to meet you," Mrs. Alan said as she took my free hand, wrapping both her hands around it.

"Well, I could see Dailan is not only one of the best employees, but he also has wonderful taste," Mr. Allan said as he shook my hand.

I smiled even though I didn't want to. "Thanks, it's really nice to meet both of you," I said graciously as I took another sip of wine.

"We're hoping that Dailan changes his mind and stays here permanently instead of going back to Dublin," Mr. Allan said.

"How long have you two been dating?" Mrs. Allan asked.

"A year," Dailan blurted out before I could answer.

"Well, it must be hard for you with him being over in Ireland, dear," she looked at me sympathetically.

"Oh no, not at all," I said quickly, taking the older woman a little by surprise.

"That's because she knows how to make up for lost time very well, right, Nicole?" Dailan said, wrapping his arm around my waist, pulling me toward him and kissing me on the forehead. I looked up at him with fire in my eyes. I could see him smirking and enjoying every single minute of it.

Mrs. Allan must have seen the look that I had given Dailan. "Oh, don't be embarrassed dear; we were young once too."

I could feel Dailan's hand moving up the side of my waist and closer to my breast. I squeezed his hand tightly and moved it away.

"Oh Dailan, I have two tickets to Friday night's hockey game that I'm not able to attend. They're excellent seats if you'd like them," Mr. Allan said.

Dailan's eyes lit up with excitement. "Sure, I'll take them," he said enthusiastically.

"Dailan, sweetie, don't you remember we have plans on Friday?" I said in an overly sweetened voice. He wanted me to play the girlfriend role - I was going to play it.

"No, I don't remember making any plans," Dailan said as he gripped my waist tighter.

"How could you forget? We're going to the ballet," I said.

Mr. Allan looked at Dailan as if he were shocked. Dailan began to laugh as he slid his hand down my waist, placing it on my rear end in an effort to get me to stop. But instead of getting angry and removing his hand, I was going to get even.

"He doesn't like to admit that he's into ballet. You know, he used to take ballet lessons as a child," I continued with my assault. I watched in amusement as Dailan nervously ran his hand through his hair and chuckled.

"No, that's not-" Dailan began to say.

"Oh, honey, don't be embarrassed. I think it's sweet that you're in touch with your feminine side," I said, smiling widely and trying my best to hold back the laughter. I knew that I was probably going to get paid back big time for this, but I didn't care. I was having too much fun watching Mr. "Smooth Moves" O'Maley squirm.

"Oh no, dear, don't you dare be embarrassed. I think that's wonderful; you know all the girls at work say he's a wonderful dancer. I guess all those ballet lessons paid off," Mrs. Allan said just as I was taking a sip of my wine, making me almost choke from the laughter that I was trying to stifle.

Dailan had a wry smile on his face. "Well, if you'll excuse us, I would like to dance with my *lovely* girlfriend," Dailan said as he abruptly whisked me away to the dance floor.

He pulled me close as I tried to back away to put a little distance between us. But it was of no use as he just tightened his grip even harder. "What's the matter now; you don't want to play the role of my girlfriend?"

"Well, maybe if you weren't making your obnoxious comments and trying to grope me right in front of them, then you would be going to a hockey game on Friday night."

He looked at me with a mischievous grin. "Oh, Miss Morgan, you think you are so slick but you have no idea who you're messing with. I don't get mad – I get even."

"Bring it on, Mr. O'Maley."

Chapter 14

The rest of the night went rather well and I actually was beginning to enjoy myself after a few more glasses of wine. While Dailan was out on the dance floor keeping his promise to adoring female fans, I was getting to know Mr. Rick Kincaide a little bit better. Rick was another lawyer who worked for Dailan's company, who gave a whole new meaning to tall, dark, and handsome.

"So how long have you been dating O'Maley?" he asked. I could tell right away that there was a little animosity between the two of them just by the tone in his voice.

I looked over at the dance floor to see the two women who had greeted us when we first came in, making a poor attempt at dirty dancing with Dailan. I rolled my eyes and looked back to Rick. "Oh, I don't know, not that long."

"Well, that's kind of rude. He has a beautiful woman like you and he's out there hanging on other women," he said.

I shrugged my shoulders as if I really didn't care. But once I got to thinking, it was kind of rude of him. After all, everyone here *thought* I was his girlfriend and he was making quite a spectacle of himself on the dance floor with those other women.

"So, Nicole, how old are you?" Rick asked.

"Twenty-five," I answered. I was suddenly starting to become very uncomfortable with the way he was looking me over and I was wishing that Dailan would finish up so we could leave.

"Well, O'Maley's a really lucky guy. Here's my card with my cell number, well you know, if things don't-" he was just about to hand me his business card when I felt someone grab me tightly around my waist. I was actually grateful to look up and see Dailan.

"Come on, Nicole, let's go," Dailan said.

"Ah, O'Maley, I was just keeping your beautiful girlfriend here company while you were dancing it up with Debbie and Tina," Rick said with a sarcastic edge.

Dailan had a look of disgust on his face and for the first time since I had known him, he actually looked serious. "I bet you were."

"Nicole, now," Dailan demanded. I shot him a dirty look to let him know that I didn't take orders from anyone. But I could tell by the look in his eyes that there was a reason for his urgency. I didn't put up a fight and even allowed Dailan to take me by the hand as we walked out.

We walked outside to wait for the car. "FYI, if you ever do get a *real* girlfriend, the whole possessive boyfriend act is a real turnoff," I said sarcastically.

"Yeah, well, you should be thanking me right now," he said.

"Oh really, why is that?" I laughed.

"That guy is a total scum."

"Well, just by the way he mentioned your name I would say that the feeling is mutual."

"Yeah, well, he can kiss my fuckin' ass."

"Don't you mean arse?" I began to giggle. Dailan looked at me and smiled, erasing the uncharacteristic serious expression that was on his face just moments ago.

We pulled into the driveway and Dailan walked me to my door. I had decided on the car ride home that I would allow him a goodnight kiss. "Well, thanks for coming with me," he said.

"You're welcome. I had a lot of fun embarrassing you in front of your boss." I laughed.

He shook his head and smiled. "Just remember, I get even."

"Well, good night," I said, looking up at him and hoping that he would read the expression on my face, which was – *kiss me you fool.*

"Good night," he said, waiting for me to turn the handle on my door and walk inside, before he headed down the steps and to his car. I was in shock as I closed the door behind me. *Not even a kiss on the cheek; what the hell? I charged up my credit card for a dress that I couldn't afford and undergarments that I had no business wearing and I didn't even get one lousy kiss out of the deal!* My plan had backfired right in my face. Now it was I who wanted him more than anything. Then I remembered what he said about getting even. This was his way of paying me back for my ballet comment that I had made to his boss. Oh well, I would just have to think of something better to one up him. I kicked off my shoes and I was heading into my bedroom when I heard my doorbell ring. I opened the door and smiled inwardly when I saw it was Dailan.

"Do you always answer the door at this hour of the night without asking who it is?" he asked.

"Tell me about it; look what I just let walk in," I said, raising my eyebrows at him.

"Do you ever just shut up?" he asked.

"Did you forget something, Mr. O'Maley?"

"I believe I did," he said as his lips came crashing down on mine, and his tongue invaded my mouth. I responded back just as eagerly, meeting the intensity of his kiss with each stroke of our tongues. Our lips finally disengaged and he stared down at me with a smoldering look in his eyes that drove me crazy. I rubbed my thumb against the scruff on his face. "Screw getting even," he said as he pushed me up against the wall and began to kiss me again, this time leaving me breathless. His hands began to move up and down my body and unlike earlier, instead of stopping him, I encouraged him, pressing my body into him. I quickly began to remove his already loosened tie. I was waving the white flag and I wasn't ashamed to admit it; I wanted him – now! He lifted me off the ground effortlessly, placing me in his arms. We both began to laugh as I pointed him in the direction of the bedroom. We continued our kiss once in the bedroom as he quickly removed my dress over my head. His hand and mouth began to examine every inch of my body. I had never felt so vulnerable yet so at ease. I began to unbutton his shirt. He helped me out by undoing the last of the buttons and throwing it on the floor. His body was just as I had imagined it underneath his clothes. His chest was rock hard and his arms were perfectly sculpted with a tribal tattoo encircling his left upper arm.

I undid his belt buckle and began to unbutton his pants. I could feel him pressing up against me and I knew he was just as ready as I was. He took my hand and gently guided it away from his pants. "Not so fast." His voice sounded even sexier than it already normally did. He lay me down on the bed and was on top of me as he moved my hair out of the way and kissed my neck, sending chills throughout my body. When he took off my bra, I was a little self-conscious that he was now seeing that real size of my chest and not that overinflated back breaker that I was wearing all night. It didn't seem to bother him as he slowly made his way down to my breasts; he began to graze them lightly with his lips and then his tongue.

"Oh, Dailan, please!" The torture of wanting him so badly made me cry out. He lifted his head up and met my gaze. He gave me that same crooked smile that always made me melt. I was unable to smile back; I was in such a state of pleasurable torture. He ignored my pleas as his lips slowly trailed down my stomach, finally stopping between my legs. His tongue began its delightful assault on my body. I could no longer hold back as I gripped the sheets and let out a scream of pleasure. He finally stopped, looking like he was satisfied with the outcome of his work. He quickly removed his pants and boxers. He reached for his pants from the floor and took a condom out of his wallet. The seconds that it took him to put it on seemed like hours. My body was yearning to have him inside of me. He stood over top of me and I watched as he slowly buried himself in me. My body was still sensitive from the intensity of the orgasm that I just had. I took a deep breath once he was completely inside of me. It felt perfect. I was getting more turned on by the look of pleasure on his face. He began to move slowly at first, making sure that I was comfortable. I pulled him closer in an effort to signal to him that I was fine. He began to move harder and quicker, taking my body by surprise with the intensity of his thrusts. It didn't take me long to adjust and respond positively. He was breathing heavily. I moved my hands up and down his back as he continued to move about inside of me. He took me to my point of pleasure several times before he finally buried his face in my hair and let out a light groan at the same time that my body began to melt around him once again. He quickly pulled himself out of me and my body felt abandoned without the warmth of him inside of me.

I lay in my bed wrapped in Dailan's arms. Even though I knew it was wrong, it felt so right. As he pulled me closer and I started to drift off to sleep, the last thought on my mind was Dailan O'Maley vs. little black dress - tie score.

Chapter 15

Dailan was up and out early in the morning. I had offered him some coffee before he left, but he refused, saying that he had some errands to run before Ryan's Aunt Lisa dropped him off later. He gave me a light kiss on the cheek before heading out the door. There was no future date made, or even *I'll give you a call* - nothing, which made me begin to regret sleeping with him then. I reminded myself that I wanted it to happen last night just as badly as he did. If anything, this is what I wanted, for Dailan to stop making his rude comments and acting like a love crazed teenager around me. So maybe sleeping with him was the cure for this. I tried not to over think it. I certainly didn't want a relationship with him anyway. We just had fun last night and that was it.

I showered and did some laundry, going on with my usual Sunday business. I filled Donna in on all the details of last night in a brief phone conversation as she teased me for being weak and giving in to him. I was all caught up with lesson plans and decided to start wrapping some Christmas presents. I was battling with trying to find the beginning of the scotch tape that I had somehow managed to lose on the roll when my doorbell rang. I was surprised when I opened it up to find my mom and dad standing on the other side.

"Hey," I said, trying to sound excited. I opened the door wider as they walked in.

"Sorry we didn't call first; we were at Ted and Amelia's and decided to just pop in," my mother said as she gave me a kiss on the cheek. Ted and Amelia were our old next-door neighbors who my mom and dad would frequently still come to visit, rarely ever stopping in to see me in the process.

"Oh, no problem, just don't mind the mess," I said, referring to the boxes and rolls of wrapping paper covering my living room floor. My mother waved her hand at me as if it were no big deal.

"Hi, Dad," I said, standing on my tippy toes to give him a kiss. He immediately sat down on the couch. I handed him the remote control as he turned on the TV, drowning out the sound of my mother and me talking.

"Do you guys want something to drink?" I asked.

They both declined as my mother sat on the floor and began to take over my Christmas wrapping, effortlessly finding the edge to the tape that I had been chipping away at for the past fifteen minutes.

"Mom, that's okay. I can do this."

"You know I love wrapping presents," she said.

"Well, I have lasagna in the oven if you guys want to stay for dinner," I said.

"No, we have to get going soon, plus you know that your father won't eat that jarred sauce."

She just couldn't resist getting a dig in and I was half inclined to think that she didn't even realize that she was doing it. Of course, her gift-wrapping services had to come at a cost. I had to listen painfully to her gush about my sister and all the hard work that she had been doing, working on the cancer research foundation at the hospital. I made my best effort to seem interested, even asking questions every now and then. I looked over at my dad, who was a world away, totally engrossed in the football game that he was watching.

"So what's going on with you? I tried calling you last night to let you know we were going to be in the area, but you didn't answer."

"Oh, I was at a Christmas party."

"Where at?" she asked.

"Oceanview Terrace."

She looked at me and her eyes widened. "Wow, that really is an expensive school district that you work for if they can afford to have their Christmas parties there."

"It wasn't for my work," I said, almost regretting the words as soon they were out.

"Oh?" She looked up at me as her brown eyes widened.

"It was a friend of mine's party," I said, not knowing any other way to classify Dailan to my mother.

"And is this a friend a male?" she asked, prying deeper.

"Yes, Mom, he is."

She put down the scotch tape and pushed a strand of her hair behind her ear. She stared at me as if she were waiting for more details.

"What?" I asked as I shrugged my shoulders.

"Well, does this friend have a name?"

"Dailan - Dailan O'Maley," I answered.

"Oh, sounds sexy." She laughed.

She had no idea how sexy. I rolled my eyes. "Relax, Mom, I just went with him as a favor. Don't be picking out your mother-of-the-bride dress."

"How did you meet him?" She was relentless.

"Teresa!" my dad chimed in an effort for her to stop her interrogation. I was quite sure it was because she was interrupting his football game with all of her yapping. Not because he was trying to help me out in any way.

I explained to her how Dailan and I had met and how there was no chance of us ever having a relationship, so she could put any pre-conceived notions that she may have been conjuring up in her head to rest.

"Well, you never know," she said.

"No, Mom, I do know. Trust me!" After Dailan's chilly goodbye this morning, I knew that the chance of that ever happening was slim to none anyway, even if it was what I had wanted – which it wasn't.

She thankfully dropped the subject as we finished wrapping presents. My father got up from the couch as soon as the football game was over.

"Are you ready?" he asked my mother.

"Yeah, I guess," she said as she stood up. I looked up at the two of them standing together. Nick and Teresa Morgan, my parents, were still a very nice-looking couple. They both took such good care of themselves, making sure that they ate right and exercised every day and it showed. My dad was tall and handsome. He wore his gray hair closely cropped to his head and had a demeanor about him that demanded respect.

My brother and I inherited by mother's Italian appearance. We both had her dark hair. My brother also had her big brown eyes. Mine, however, were the same exact shade of hazel as my dad's. My sister resembled no one, with her blonde hair and blue eyes. I always took thrill in that fact. Every time we would get in our knockdown, drag-out fights when we were younger, I would tell her she was adopted. I knew that bothered her more than anything. Of course, she would always go crying to my mom, who in turn would reassure her that she was not.

"Are you guys sure that you don't want to stay for dinner?" I asked.

"Oh no, we have to get going, I'm dreading this two-hour drive," my mom said.

"Okay then, I guess I'll see you guys on Christmas," I said.

"Oh, sweetie, we're going up to Renee's in-laws on Christmas. I'm sorry; I wanted to have it at my house. But she made plans to go up there and that's the only way that we'll get to see the kids," my mother said.

"Of course," I said, trying to hide my hurt at the prospect of spending Christmas all alone.

"Well, you're off that whole week after, so we'll have to pick a day to get together," my mother said as if it were no big deal to her.

I nodded in agreement as I walked them to the door. My mom gave me a hug and kiss as my dad barely grazed my cheek.

I closed the door behind me after I watched them drive away. I took my lasagna with my *jarred sauce* out of the oven and sat down to dinner. I always felt exhausted after spending time with my parents; maybe it was because I was always striving to be the daughter that they wanted when I was in their company. I was feeling unusually down tonight after they had left. I finished eating and wrapping the last of my presents and decided to get into my pajamas early and prepare for the week ahead. I pulled my cell phone from my purse and was a little disheartened to see that there weren't any text messages or phone calls from Dailan. His silence was making me feel like what we shared last night was just a booty call. I had never been the booty call type of girl and I didn't want to start classifying myself that way now. I contemplated for a moment about sending him a sarcastic text, but then quickly dismissed that thought. This is what I had wanted, for Dailan O'Maley to leave me alone once and for all. I put my phone along with any more thoughts of him away for the night, finally falling into a deep sleep on the couch in front of the TV.

Chapter 16

The week was flying by. I couldn't believe that it was already Wednesday. I hadn't heard anything from Dailan. The more I kept telling myself that I was happy about it, the less I believed it. I had a knot in my stomach, knowing that I would have to face him after school today when he picked up Ryan from tutoring. I muddled through the day, feeling a little out of sorts, and by the time 4:00 rolled around, I felt my hands trembling. I was just finishing up the math lesson with Ryan when I heard someone enter the door. I looked up slowly to find Ryan's Aunt Lisa instead.

"Hello." I tried my best to hide my surprise of seeing her and not Dailan.

"Hi. I'm sorry if I'm late, his uncle is stuck in Boston and called me at the last minute to let me know," she said. "So typical," she muttered under her breath.

"Am I staying at your house again, Aunt Lisa?" Ryan asked as he began to pack up his stuff.

"Yupper, kiddo," she answered.

"Has he handed in everything that he's needed to so far for the week? His uncle had a last minute work emergency and had to leave for Boston Monday morning and he's been staying with me."

"No, he's good," I said. I was feeling a little better, knowing that maybe Dailan was busy with work and maybe not totally ignoring me.

"Good, because I'm never given much instruction when it comes to that man; of course that would actually require him to communicate," she said as she shook her head. I gave her an uneasy smile. "I'm sorry to be unloading on you. I just don't know how he thinks he's going to do this on his own when he moves back to Dublin. Chasing women, holding down a demanding job, and raising a child on your own isn't an easy thing. I don't know what my sister was thinking when she let her husband talk her into giving him custody," she continued. "Oh God, there I go again," she said as she stopped herself.

"Well, Ryan finished up his homework and he got a hundred on his spelling test," I said, trying to change the subject as Ryan smiled widely.

"That is awesome, Ryan," Lisa said, giving him a high five.

"Miss Morgan, can you hang out with me and my uncle again? That was fun!" Ryan blurted out of nowhere.

I felt my face start to burn and I was hoping that the floor would open up and swallow me as Lisa looked up staring at me intently. "Oh my God! I'm sorry; are you dating Dailan?" she asked, covering her mouth as if she was in shock.

"No, no, no." I shook my head. "I just went to the tree lighting ceremony with him and Ryan."

"Yeah, and Uncle Dailan killed her at air hockey." Ryan smiled.

"Well, you've done wonders with Ryan. My husband and I always say what a positive influence you are on him."

"Well, thanks, Ryan is a great kid," I said.

Ryan was out the door as Lisa followed behind. She was halfway out the door as well when she poked her head back in. "Now, if you could just work your wonders on Dailan, that would be even better." She raised her eyebrows and gave me a quick smile.

* * *

Thursday was my day for bus duty, which meant I would have to stand outside and wait for all the second-graders to get off the bus and line them up according to class. It had been complete chaos the first few weeks of school. But now, a few months into it, I had it down to a science.

"You do such a good job at this, the other second grade teachers may volunteer you do it every day," Valerie, the school principal, joked. Valerie and I had become very close over the few short months that I had been employed at Pineview Elementary. She was always so supportive and such a positive mentor. I knew that she had played a big part in my employment and I was very grateful for that.

"Oh boy, let me see what's going on over there?" Valerie said upon seeing a group of fifth-graders hovering around, looking like they were up to something. I had most of the second-graders lined up and was just waiting for the last bus to unload. I watched as Ryan made his way down the steps of the bus, greeting me with a huge smile. I smiled back, unable to resist his adorable dimples. I quickly looked behind him to see Cameron Aymes, another student of mine, whispering to another child and laughing, right before he pushed Ryan down the steps, causing him to fall face down on the concrete. I rushed over to help Ryan, but before I could get to him, Cameron kicked him in the back. Ryan quickly got up, with blood dripping from his nose and mouth. He took his best shot at Cameron, hitting him square in the face. Valerie came running over to help me break the two of them up. I looked in my pocket for a tissue to place on Ryan's nose, in order to control the bleeding.

"Oh boy, what happened?" Valerie asked.

I explained to Valerie exactly what I had witnessed and how Cameron initiated the whole thing. "Oh geez, his mother is not going to be happy. I'm dreading this phone call," she said as she rolled her eyes.

Mrs. Aymes, Cameron's mom, was the president of the PTA and under the impression that her child could do no wrong, when in fact, her son was now the most misbehaved and mean-spirited child in my class. Every time I would try to address an issue with her, she would blame it on another student or tell me how I could have approached the situation differently as a teacher. I didn't envy Valerie at all for having to make that phone call.

Valerie called down for one of the other second-grade teachers to come and get the students as she took Cameron into her office. I took Ryan to the nurse's office to get him cleaned up. I could tell that he was upset and trying his best not to cry in front of the other children. Once we got into to the nurse's office, his tears began to fall.

"I didn't start it, Miss Morgan, I swear," he said, trying to catch his breath. "And now, I'm gonna get in trouble with Mrs. Kane."

"No, you're not, Ryan. I saw the whole thing. I know that it wasn't your fault." I rubbed his back lightly, trying to get him to calm down, while Mrs. Towner, the school nurse, cleaned him up. Ryan gasped when he saw Valerie enter the nurse's office.

"Mrs. Kane I didn't -" He started getting upset again.

"It's okay, Ryan, you're not in any trouble," Valerie said in a gentle tone.

"I just got off the phone with Mrs. Aymes and she wants to meet with us after school," Valerie said, rolling her eyes.

"Ryan is your uncle at work?" Valerie asked.

"No, he's still away, I'm staying with my Aunt Lisa," Ryan answered sweetly.

"Oh, okay, I have to get her in here too. I'm sure she wants to ream everyone out." Valerie placed her hand on my shoulder and shook her head. "This should be fun," she said before walking out.

"Are you feeling better?" I asked once I felt like Ryan had calmed down enough. He nodded and stood up, taking my hand in his. I felt sadness looking down at his swollen little lip and bloodstained gloves.

"Thanks, Miss Morgan," he said, his eyes starting to fill up with tears again.

"No problem," I said messing up his hair with my free hand as we made our way back to the classroom.

Chapter 17

The last of my students were gone for the day and I slowly made my way down to Valerie's office, feeling much like a kid who was about to be scolded. But instead of getting in trouble with the principal, it was Mrs. Aymes that I was dreading.

"She's in there, waiting," Valerie's secretary said as she rolled her eyes, having the same opinion of Mrs. Aymes as everyone else did.

I lightly knocked on Valerie's door before walking in. She was seated at the conference room table across from Mrs. Aymes. I immediately took the seat next to Valerie.

"Hi, Mrs. Aymes, how are you?" I asked, trying to sound as pleasant as possible.

"Not too good, obviously," she said rather sarcastically.

"Ryan's Aunt Lisa should be here shortly, but we can begin without her," Valerie said.

Valerie tactfully began to explain the events that transpired earlier in the day as Mrs. Aymes looked at her in disbelief. "Well, clearly there's been a mistake. My Cameron knows better."

"I'm sorry, Mrs. Aymes, but he did push Ryan, I -," I stopped mid-sentence as the door to Valerie's office opened and I found myself looking right into Dailan's eyes.

I quickly looked away as he took the empty seat across from me. My stomach was in knots. I wasn't quite sure if it was over seeing him for the first time since our *booty call* or because I was afraid of how he would react to Mrs. Aymes' superior attitude. Valerie stood up and greeted him with a handshake. Mrs. Aymes and I sat there silently.

"Go ahead and continue, Nicole," Valerie said.

I cleared my throat and was just about to begin to speak when Mrs. Aymes cut me off. "You know what - I really don't care to listen to anything she has to say. I know my son better than anyone and I know that this is not his fault," she said as if she were challenging me.

"But it was his fault, Mrs. Aymes. I witnessed the whole altercation from start to finish and Cameron was the one who initiated it." I quickly looked over at Dailan, who was typing on his phone, seeming very disinterested in the whole thing.

"Oh well, of course you would say it's the other child's fault when Ryan's involved. Everyone knows that you favor him," Mrs. Aymes said with her tone growing louder.

"I do not! I give all of my students equal attention. Yes, I spend time with Ryan after school for extra help, but I would do that for any of my students if they needed it." I watched as Dailan briefly lifted his head from his phone, waiting for Mrs. Aymes' reaction.

"This is exactly why I didn't want Cameron in this class. She is clearly inexperienced!" Mrs. Aymes said to Valerie.

Dailan finally broke his silence. I bit my lower lip, seeing the look on his face. I knew all too well how crude he could be. I had a feeling Mrs. Aymes was just about to find out as well.

"Oh, because your son is a spoiled brat, it's Miss Morgan's fault?"

"Excuse me?" Mrs. Aymes said, looking like her head was about to explode.

"You heard me. I don't think there's a need to repeat myself," he said smugly.

"You know what, you have no business raising a child, just like she has no business teaching!" Mrs. Aymes shouted.

"Oh fuc-"

I didn't know what else to do, so I kicked Dailan under the table, hoping that it wasn't obvious to anyone else. I shook my head at him, signaling for him to stop whatever verbal assault he was about to begin on this woman.

"Oh well, no wonder why you finally speak up when I say something about Miss Morgan. Maybe if you worried a little more about what your nephew was up to instead of trying to get in his teacher's pants, we wouldn't be having this meeting now," Mrs. Aymes said.

Dailan looked at her with that sarcastic grin with which I had become very familiar. I held my breath in angst, waiting for what was going to come out of his mouth.

"Don't be jealous of Miss Morgan, just because no one wants to get in your pants, probably not even your husband," Dailan said very calmly.

"How dare you speak that way to me?" Mrs. Aymes said, looking like she wanted to rip Dailan's eyes out.

"Hey, you started it," Dailan said very matter of fact as he looked down again and started typing away on his phone.

I placed my hands on the side of my head and looked down at the table. I couldn't believe this was happening. Valerie finally interjected. I had wondered what had taken her so long, and part of me was wondering if she was getting some enjoyment out of this. "Mrs. Aymes, that was uncalled for. Miss Morgan is an excellent teacher and I will not allow you to make vicious accusations like that about her," Valerie said.

I just wanted to get out of there. I wanted to end this whole thing now, before Dailan opened his big mouth again and said something we would both regret. I glanced over at him and could tell it was taking everything in him to keep his mouth shut.

"You will switch my son out of her class or you'll be hearing from my attorney," Mrs. Aymes said as she pointed at Valerie.

"Mrs. Aymes, there are no openings in any of the other classes. Cameron is going to have to work through this and adjust," Valerie said. I could tell by the tone in Valerie's voice that she was losing patience with this woman.

"This is absolute nonsense!" Mrs. Aymes stood up and flung her purse over her shoulder.

"Nice to have met you," Dailan said with an obnoxious smirk. She shot him a dirty look and went storming out of the office. Valerie reluctantly went chasing after her, leaving me and Dailan alone.

I stood up and gathered my papers off the table, trying my best to ignore him. "What are you pissed off about? What, does everyone in this room have their period or something?"

"You couldn't just shut up; you had to lead her to believe that we're sleeping together," I said, finally looking into his eyes.

"Well, we are – aren't we?" he asked.

"We *did* once, and it will never happen again!"

"Oh, I see how it is; use me for my body and then cast me aside," he joked.

"No, that would be you; you're the one who went MIA all week!" I regretted my words as soon as they came out. The last thing I wanted was for him to think I was bothered by his absence these last few days.

His grin became a mile wide as he ran his hand down the scruff on his face. "Oh, is that why you're so pissy? Did you miss me, darlin'?"

"No, not at all."

"Well, I wasn't ignoring you. I had to go to Boston last minute. I thought Ryan would have told you. I would have liked to have told you myself, but my cell phone fell into a toilet in Logan Airport and I had no intention of fishing it out. I got a new phone when I was there, but I lost all my contacts."

Even though I tried my hardest, I couldn't contain my laughter as I imagined the inappropriate words coming out of his mouth in the bathroom that day.

"I was hoping that you would have sent me another one of your dirty messages telling me how you couldn't wait to have me in your bed again, so I could get your number," he said with a smirk.

"You're awful sure of yourself, Mr. O'Maley, aren't you?"

"Only at things I'm good at, and sex just happens to be one of them."

I rolled my eyes, trying to disguise that I was in total agreement with him. He stood up like he was getting ready to leave. "Don't forget, we have a date tomorrow night," he said.

"What are you talking about?" I asked.

"'I'm missing out on front row seats to a hockey game because we have a date – remember? So be over at six o'clock; I'm making dinner."

"You – making dinner?" I laughed.

"I know how to cook," he said defensively. "If it makes you feel any better, Ryan will be there. We're going to decorate the Christmas tree." I looked at him, not saying a word. "One other thing, I need your number again."

106

"Hmmm, let me think about that," I said with a smile. "*If* I decide to let you cook me dinner tomorrow, I will text you and let you know, and then you will have my number."

"Well then, I guess I'll be hearing from you later," he said as he moved closer to me, planting a quick kiss on my lips, taking me totally off guard.

"Dailan!" I said as I pushed him away. I couldn't believe how brazen he was, kissing me right in the principal's office of all places.

He laughed at my edginess. "See you tomorrow, beautiful," he said as he walked out the door.

* * *

Donna and I were taking a break from trimming my tree, eating our Chinese food that had just arrived. She had been working the night shift all week and I hadn't talked to her in days, which meant that we had some serious catching up to do. I filled her in on the week's events and what had transpired in the principal's office today.

"Well, I think that was pretty noble of him rushing to your defense in front of the nasty woman."

"Oh, please, Donna, there is nothing noble about him. He has one thing on his mind."

"Well, you did enjoy that one thing – didn't you?" She laughed. I gave her a sarcastic smile and flung a fortune cookie at her. "So are you going out with him again?" she asked.

"I don't know. He invited me over for dinner tomorrow and the only reason that I'm considering it is because Ryan will be there."

Donna looked like she was disappointed. "Oh, I guess that would make it kind of hard for another booty call." She laughed.

"I don't do booty calls," I said as I threw another cookie at her.

After Donna left, I sent Dailan a text, letting him know that I had agreed to come over. I asked him if there was anything he would like me to bring besides Pepto-Bismol. I responded with my usual shake of my head and roll of my eyes when I saw his response.

Just that sexy pair of underwear that you had on the other night.

Chapter 18

The day went by quickly. Cameron Aymes had been more ornery than he normally was. I knew it was probably due to his mother egging him on in her assault against me. I handled it smoothly, even though inside, I was screaming my head off at him.

I arrived home and jumped in the shower. I looked at the week's worth of laundry piling up, knowing exactly how I would be spending my entire morning tomorrow. I searched through my drawers for a pair of underwear. The only two clean pairs I had were an actual pair of granny panties that I only wore during a certain time of the month and the sexy black ones that I purchased to wear with my dress. I decided to go with the granny panties, even though it wasn't that time of the month. I would never give Dailan the satisfaction of wearing the underwear that he had requested. Not that I had any intention of letting him see what underwear I had on under my jeans; it was just the principle of it all.

I stopped off at the bakery on the way to dinner. The smell of freshly baked sweets as I walked in the door was intoxicating. I was overwhelmed and took forever trying to decide on what to bring for dessert. I wanted to make sure that I picked something good, knowing this may be dinner as well, with Dailan cooking. I finally decided on the chocolate fudge cake with sprinkles, adding an adorable snowman cookie for Ryan to the order.

I looked down at my phone to double check the address that Dailan had texted me. I had learned from Dailan the night of the Christmas tree lighting that he had been staying at his brother's house while he was here. His brother had willed the house to Ryan when he turned eighteen. For now, it was placed in Dailan's name until Ryan became of legal age. Since Dailan planned on moving back to Ireland, he would be placing the proceeds from the sale of the house into a college fund for Ryan.

I pulled down the street that the house was on, taking in the elaborate array of Christmas lights on all the prestigious homes. I wondered how many of my students lived in this upscale development. I finally found the house number on the mailbox and seeing Dailan's car in the driveway reassured me that I was at the right house.

I rang the doorbell and immediately heard footsteps of someone running to answer it. "Miss Morgan!" Ryan exclaimed as he opened the door with a huge smile on his face.

"Hey, Ryan."

I was captivated when I walked into the custom brick colonial. I quickly looked around in awe. There was two-story foyer and beautiful hardwood flooring throughout. Ryan walked me through to the gourmet kitchen with beautiful granite countertops and a two-sided fireplace. One side faced the kitchen and the other the great room. I looked around for Dailan, who was nowhere to be found.

"Where's your uncle?"

"Oh, he's taking a shower; he just got home from work."

The delightful aroma of what must have been dinner filled the air. I began to wonder how Dailan prepared dinner when he had just gotten home from work.

"Did your Uncle Dailan cook dinner?"

Ryan looked at me as if he were unsure how to answer. "Mrs. Fairview, my nanny, did. She cooks really good, but don't tell my uncle I told you. For some reason, he wants you to think he cooked it."

I crossed my fingers over my heart. "I promise, I won't," I giggled.

Ryan took my coat and placed it on the chair as we walked back in the kitchen to put the cake away. I showed Ryan the cookie that I had gotten him as well.

"Wow, that's really cool," Ryan said.

I heard footsteps coming down the staircase "Hey, Ryan have you seen –" Dailan stopped himself midsentence when he saw me sitting there. His wavy hair was still damp and he was shirtless. I was hoping what I was thinking wasn't apparent on my face, which was – *wow he looks hot!*

"You're early," he said.

"Um, you did say 'six,' right?" I looked at the clock that was flashing 6:20. "I'd say you're late."

"Oh, sorry," he said as he put the black t-shirt he had been holding over his head.

Seriously, you can leave it off, I said to myself, immediately scolding myself for having such thoughts.

"I just wanted to take a quick shower after cooking all afternoon," he said with a straight face.

"Oh, yeah, of course," I said, trying not to laugh. "Well, it smells really good. What did you make?"

He quickly walked over to the stove and began to remove the lids off the pots. "Umm, chicken and pasta," he said.

"Oh, what kind of chicken?" I asked as I walked over to the stove.

"I don't know what it's called; it's my mother's recipe," he said, sounding like he was trying to get me off the subject.

"Well, what's in it?" I was relentless.

"It's a surprise." He placed his hands on my shoulders and led me out into the dining room.

I looked down at the perfectly set table. "Wow, did you set this beautiful table too?" Ryan stood in the doorway, shaking his head.

"Yup, I do it all," Dailan said from the kitchen.

Ryan and I both began to quietly giggle. I heard the banging of pots and pans in the kitchen. Ryan was still giggling as he sat down next to me. "Oh fuck!" Dailan yelled. I quickly glanced at Ryan.

I got up and walked back into the kitchen. Dailan was holding his hand under the running water in the kitchen sink. "Do you need some help?" I asked.

"No, I'm good, I just burnt my fuckin' hand on that damn fuckin' pan."

I cringed at the obscenities coming from his mouth right in front of Ryan.

"That's because you never use the pot holders," Ryan scolded.

111

"That's because you never use the pot holders," Dailan childishly mimicked Ryan.

"Will you please let me help you? That's the least I could do after you spent all afternoon preparing this nice dinner." I was pouring it on thick.

Ryan shook his head behind Dailan's back. "I know," I mouthed to Ryan as we both began to smirk.

Dailan finally gave in and let me help. Dinner was delicious. I completely agreed with Ryan; Mrs. Fairview was an excellent cook. I was thoroughly enjoying my time spent with Ryan and Dailan.

We were just about done trimming the Christmas tree when I heard an incoming text message. I pulled my phone from my coat pocket and scrolled down to read the message that Donna had just sent:

Hope you're having fun and not having any more booty calls!

I laughed to myself at her message and replied:

Having fun, but not in that way! Trust me, I have no intention of sleeping with Dailan O'Maley ever again!

* * *

"Oh my God, this shouldn't have happened again," I said as I got up and began to dress. I had every intention of it not happening again, until Ryan's friend called at the last minute for a sleepover. Then, I had every intention of leaving when Ryan did, to avoid being alone with Dailan, until I found myself melting in Dailan's sexy smile, ending up in his bed – granny panties and all.

Dailan pulled me back down and kissed me on the lips. "Why not?"

"Because, you're the legal guardian of one of my students. I could probably get fired if anyone ever found out about this."

"Calm down, how is anyone going to find out?"

"I don't know, Ryan could slip, you know seven year olds like to share everything.

"So what if they do find out? I'm not married and neither are you." He paused for a minute. "Wait a minute; are you?" he asked with a laugh.

"Not funny," I said.

"Oh, Nicole, come on. Stop worrying about what other people think – fuck em'."

"Dailan, it's not that sim—" He didn't let me finish. He pressed his lips against mine and it was only in a matter of seconds that I found myself surrendering to him once again - all night long.

I had to admit waking up in Dailan's arms felt pretty good. Waking up to amazing sex was even better. "I seriously have to get going. I have a ton of things I have to get done today," I said.

Dailan pulled me closer, tightening his grip on me. I tried to squirm out of his hold, but it was of no use. "Dailan, come on!"

"Okay, but first I want you to admit something."

"What!"

"I want you to admit that was the most mind-blowing sex that you ever had."

I began to laugh hysterically. "Um, no, I'm not going to say that." He tightened his grip on me. "Well, maybe I didn't think it was," I lied.

"Oh, then you should switch professions because you would make a really good actress." He chuckled.

"All right – it was good," I finally admitted. "Can I go now?"

"Wait. One more thing," he said.

"What?" I asked in annoyance.

"I want you to stop pretending like you don't like me. Stop putting up a fight every time I ask you to go out with me – I know that you really want to."

"Oh, Dailan, I don't do the whole relationship thing very well," I said, being completely honest.

"That's fine; neither do I. So let's just say I'm some guy who you like, that you frequently have sex with."

"Some guy who I *tolerate,* that I *occasionally sleep with,*" I said.

"No, 'frequently' sounds better," he joked.

He kissed me on the top of my head before releasing me from his hold. I got up and began to dress, while he remained lying down, watching me.

"What the heck is up with that underwear?" he asked.

"I wore them just for you," I joked.

"Why don't you let me cook you breakfast?" he asked.

113

"Oh no, I couldn't have you do that, especially after you worked all day in the kitchen yesterday, cooking that delicious dinner," I said with a grin.

He flashed that mischievous smile that made my stomach flip and if I wasn't already dressed and ready to go, I probably would have jumped right back into bed with him. He quickly jumped out of bed and pulled on his jeans, which were lying on the floor. He walked me to the door pausing for a brief second before opening it.

"Are you sure you don't want breakfast?"

"Positive."

"I feel so used," he joked.

I put my hand on his bare chest and playfully pushed him. "Thanks for dinner." "Anytime," he said as he wrapped his arms around me and pulled me closer.

I rested my head against his warm chest as my hands moved up and down his bare back. "You better go while you still can," he whispered.

I pulled away from his embrace. "Well, hopefully you won't be dropping your phone in anymore toilets and I'll be hearing from you sooner than the last time," I joked.

"Oh, darlin' even if I did, I think you're worth sticking my hand in there to get it out," he said, almost sounding sincere as he kissed me on the top of my head.

I got into my car and waited for it to warm up. I couldn't believe that I let this happen yet again, and why did that hug goodbye feel like it meant something to me? The last thing I wanted was to have any feelings for Dailan O'Maley. The only positive that I had in this whole situation I had gotten myself in was that he clearly wasn't the type to let his emotions get in the way. I was depending on that cool, impassive attitude of his to reign me in if my emotions started taking over. I bit my lip and smiled - yes, I could do this!

Chapter 19

I threw a load of laundry in while I eagerly waited for my much-needed cup of coffee to brew. I was so tired from the lack of sleep last night. I smiled and my stomach fluttered just thinking about it. *That's enough Dailan O'Maley thoughts for the day*, I scolded myself. I had way too much to get done and didn't need to be getting sidetracked with thoughts of him.

I looked at the caller ID on my ringing phone to see my sister's number. *Oh no, do I really want to deal with this before I've even had my first cup of coffee for the day?* I took a deep breath before answering it, making sure that I had my cup of coffee in hand.

"Hey, Renee," I answered as cheerfully as I could.

"Hey, Nic, what's new?"

I was just about to tell her when she placed me on hold to yell at her kids. I patiently waited for her to get back to the phone and when she did, it was the same one-sided conversation as usual. Everything was about her, her husband, and her kids. Not that I minded hearing about my nephews, but not every little minor detail in their life.

"What did you get Joey and Christopher for Christmas?" she asked abruptly.

"Oh, Mom gave me a list of DVD's and books that they wanted. I got them each a couple of them and a gift card to Toys R Us."

"Oh, okay," she said, sounding disappointed.

"Why, isn't that what they wanted?"

"No, that's fine."

Whatever, not like I'll be seeing them for Christmas anyway, I thought to myself.

"So Mom tells me you're dating someone?"

I was taken off guard by her question. My sister never really asked me personal questions, because the truth was, she could care less about what was going on in anyone else's life but her own. "I am? That's news to me," I said sarcastically. I was annoyed at how my mother took one little thing and spun it into something that she wanted to believe was true.

"She said that you went to a Christmas party at the Oceanview with some guy."

"I told her he was just a friend – that's all!"

"Oh, well, don't get mad at me, she was the one who said it. I still say you were a fool for breaking up with Drew – but that's just my opinion."

"Well, you know what they say about opinions, Renee."

"Geeze, someone is cranky. Joey, do you want to talk to your Aunt Nicole and cheer her up?"

Oh God, please let him say "no"; the last thing I felt like listening to right now was a three-year-old screaming in my ear.

I couldn't help but smile when I heard my nephew's adorable voice on the other end of the phone. I listened to him as he told me all about his trip to see Santa and as he yammered on about something that was completely incoherent. "Bye, Aunt Cole – I *yove* you," he said sweetly.

"I love you too, Joey," I said as I blew him kisses over the phone. Much to my delight, he hung up the phone before my sister could get back on and torment me with her normal hour-long goodbye.

I threw my clothes in the dryer before jumping in the shower. I quickly dressed and was out the door. I stopped down to see Mrs. Tallone to check if she needed anything from the grocery store to which I was headed. She always would say "no" and I would always pick her up something anyway. The parking lot in the grocery store was packed. With Christmas less than a week away, I wasn't surprised. I began to throw my things into my cart and somewhere down the pasta aisle I decided to be bold. I pulled out my phone and texted Dailan:

Just wondering if I could return the favor and cook dinner for you and Ryan tonight.

My hands were shaking as I hit the send button. A million thoughts raced through my mind. *I shouldn't have done that, I just saw him last night. I don't want him to think I'm getting too clingy. I don't even know how to cook!*

116

I was really starting to feel low when I hit the frozen food aisle and still hadn't heard back from him, causing me to throw two gallons of chocolate chip mint ice cream into my cart. Then I heard the beep of a text message. My stomach did a somersault as I looked at my phone, which I had tightly gripped in my hand.

What time?

A smile stretched across my face that must have been a mile wide. The old man standing next to me picking out his ice cream smiled at my enthusiasm as I said *"yes"* underneath my breath.

Six o'clock –which means six thirty in your time, I texted back.

My phone beeped almost instantaneously after I sent the message.

I promise I will be there on time.

My excitement quickly turned to panic. What the heck was I going to cook? Do I dare run back to the pasta aisle and throw a jar of sauce in my cart after that delicious dinner that *Dailan* had cooked for me last night. My mind began to plot. Mrs. Tallone was an excellent cook, especially when it came to Italian food. I stood in the middle of the frozen food aisle and dialed her number. I walked down each aisle as I was on the phone with her, throwing each ingredient that she instructed me to buy into my cart. I hurriedly checked out my groceries and made my way home. Mrs. Tallone was waiting for me with all of her cooking utensils in hand. She followed me up to my apartment as I carried in the bags of groceries and quickly put everything away.

"Okay, I'm ready," I said, finally putting the last of my food away.

We immediately began to get to work, forming the meatballs, sautéing the garlic and rolling out the dough for the pasta.

My apartment smelled heavenly by the time we were done. Unlike Dailan, I had actually cooked the entire meal, under close supervision from Mrs. Tallone, of course.

"Thank you so much, Mrs. Tallone, you're a lifesaver," I said.

"Anytime, sweetheart. I love to cook and I don't get to do much of it anymore with it just being me. Well, I have to get running so I can finish up my packing," she said. Mrs. Tallone and her man-friend, as she referred to him, were driving up to

Connecticut to visit her family for Christmas. I offered to watch Elmo for her, but she was adamant that he go wherever she went.

"Oh, wait a minute. I have something for you," I said as I ran over to the Christmas tree. I reached under it and grabbed the box with her name on it.

"Oh, Nicole, you didn't have to do this," she said with a huge smile on her face.

"It's just a little something. Open it," I said.

As she slowly opened the box, a smile spread across her face. She pulled out the cream-colored cashmere scarf that she had admired so much on one of our shopping trips.

"You remembered," she said.

I smiled and nodded. "Thank you so much, honey," she said as she gave me a hug.

"I figured you could wear that if you and your man-friend go out on the town while you're away," I said as we both began to laugh.

I walked her to the door, thanking her again for all of her help. "Now remember let that sauce simmer for a few more hours on low. The pasta should be all dried out by then as well. Just throw it in the boiling water for about four minutes right before you're ready to eat," she instructed.

I nodded.

"I hope your fella enjoys it," she said as she walked out the door and we said our goodbyes. I waited until she was down the steps and into her house before closing the door.

Dailan O'Maley as *my fella*? Suddenly, that wasn't sounding so bad after all.

Chapter 20

Dailan kept his promise. My doorbell rang at 5:58. I opened the door and was in complete shock when I saw the purple swollen ring around his eye.

"Oh my God, what happened?" I asked with complete concern.

"Rugby match today," he said nonchalantly.

"Did you get that checked out?" I asked.

"No, it's fine." He laughed as if I were ridiculous for asking such a thing.

"I don't know; that looks pretty bad," I said as I lightly rubbed my thumb under his eye.

"Trust me, this is mild compared to some of the others that I've had."

"It is," Ryan agreed.

"Ryan, do you watch him play?" I was hoping he didn't. I didn't know much about rugby, but from what I had heard, it was a pretty violent sport.

"Yup, I'm gonna play some day too," he said.

"Oh no, Ryan, your face is much too cute to mark up like that," I said, giving Dailan a sarcastic grin.

I took their coats, hung them in the closet, and then walked Ryan into the living room. *Polar Express* was on my TV. "Cool, I love this movie," Ryan said as he sat down on the couch, instantly becoming engrossed in the movie.

"Do you want something to drink?" I asked the two of them.

"Okay," Ryan said, while Dailan declined.

I signaled for Dailan to follow me into the kitchen. "Taste my cooking," I said, feeding him a spoonful of my sauce.

"I've had better," he joked as he pulled me to him and kissed me on the forehead. I quickly looked over to Ryan to make sure he wasn't paying attention.

"Will you relax? He zones out when he's into a movie," he said with his arms still wrapped around me.

119

"Are you hungry?" I asked.

"I'm starving." He pressed his forehead against mine, allowing me a closer look at his eye.

"Okay, that eye is seriously grossing me out," I said.

I handed him a glass of juice to bring into Ryan. "Go sit down and watch TV. Dinner will be ready in a few minutes."

The pasta was cooked to perfection. I carefully drained it and poured the sauce over top. I smiled at my beautiful creation that was on the big pasta platter, which I had bought several months ago and was using for the very first time tonight. It looked like it belonged on the cover of a cookbook. I walked into the living room to announce that dinner was ready. Ryan was still absorbed in his movie and Dailan looked like he was about to fall asleep.

Once we sat down to dinner, the two of them started to liven up. Ryan began to tell me all about Dailan's rugby match. It was so apparent how much he looked up to his uncle just by listening to him talk.

"You're going to work with that black eye?" I asked.

Dailan nodded at me and laughed as if I were ridiculous for asking such a question.

"Well, don't you have to meet with clients and stuff? What are you going to tell them happened?" I asked.

"I don't have to tell them anything. Fuck 'em."

Ryan gasped and shook his head. "That's another one that goes on the list, Uncle Dailan."

Ryan finished his dinner and went back in the living room to finish watching his movie.

"When the hell did my nephew become the curse word police?" Dailan asked.

"I told Ryan to remind you every time you say a word that belongs on the inappropriate list."

Dailan began to laugh. "Darlin', don't you know there's no hope for me?"

"Somehow, I'm beginning to believe that. It worked for him; he hasn't said an inappropriate word in months," I said.

"You're emasculating my nephew." He laughed.

"I am not. It's not nice for a young boy *or* a grown man to be using those words."

"So would it be more appropriate to say, 'I'm banging the teacher,' instead of 'I'm fucking the teacher'?"

I looked at him with disgust. "Why do you have to be so vulgar?"

"Okay, how about this: I'm having sexual relations with the teacher?"

I tried my best not to laugh, but I couldn't hold it anymore. "Keep it up and I'll make both your eyes match!"

I got up from the table and began to clear the dishes. Dailan was trying his best to help me, but I could tell that he clearly wasn't comfortable in the kitchen. I told him to go sit down about a million times but he refused. So instead, he kept me entertained with his sarcastic comments as I loaded the dishwasher.

"Hey Uncle Dailan, this is Miss Morgan's brother, he's a soldier," Ryan said as he walked into the kitchen with the picture of me and my brother. I smiled at how impressed Ryan still was over that picture and the fact that my brother was in the military. My smile soon turned to panic when I realized Dailan thought my brother was my boyfriend. *Oh shit, another thing he's never going to let me live down. Maybe he won't realize that the guy in the picture is the same one that I introduced him to as my boyfriend that day. He did only have one good eye tonight, after all.*

I watched in angst as he examined the picture closely and I could tell immediately by the expression on his face that the one good eye worked perfectly, so I admitted defeat.

"No, I'm not some sicko that dates her brother," I said. He raised his eyebrow at me, waiting for an explanation. "I lied when I introduced you to him as my boyfriend."

"Well, I hope so, or I'd say you belong on one of those trashy talk shows," he said, laughing. I rolled my eyes at him. "So tell me, why did you lie?"

"I don't know, because I didn't want you to think that I was really interested in you after how I behaved at the bar that night. So, I figured if you *thought* that I had a boyfriend, then maybe you would—"

"That I would what? Believe your hokey story that it was really the alcohol and that you really didn't want to..." I was amazed that he stopped himself before something crass came out of his mouth in front of Ryan.

I nodded.

"Yeah, well it didn't work." He laughed.

The rest of the night was spent in front of the TV watching Christmas movies. Ryan and I were shocked that Dailan had never seen *A Christmas Story,* so we made him sit through it. Ryan fell asleep about a half hour into it.

The movie ended, and Dailan looked over at Ryan. "I better get him home." He moved over to where I was sitting on the couch, taking me totally off guard as he kissed me with great intensity. I was a little reluctant at first, but when I heard Ryan snoring, I knew it was safe. So I kissed him back with the same vigor.

"You better get going," I said as I ran my thumb along his face. Even though my body was screaming for him to take me into the bedroom, I controlled myself. I knew that would be at the top of the inappropriate list, with Ryan just a few feet away.

Dailan must have been thinking the same thing. He quickly stood up from the couch. Even though I scolded myself for thinking this, I was so hoping that he would give me some indication of when I would see him again.

"I have to go to Texas on Monday for three days," he said.

"Texas? What the heck is in Texas?"

"That Fuck-head Kincaide screwed up the paperwork for one the firm's major accounts and now it's got to get fixed before the end of the year or they'll lose them as a client. It just pisses me off that I'm stuck fixing that jerk-off's mistake." When Dailan spoke about him, it was more than his usual crass tone; there was a sound of pure loathing for this man in his voice. It was apparent from that night at the Christmas party.

I stood up and he took my face in his hands. "I promise I won't be droppin' my phone in anymore toilets," he said as he kissed me gently on the forehead.

I was hoping that meant I would be hearing from him, but I wasn't quite sure; he was always so vague. I instantly began to sympathize with Ryan's Aunt Lisa when she said he didn't know how to communicate. *Why did I even care anyway? This was just supposed to be a casual thing.*

I was impressed at how he had gotten Ryan's coat, hat, and gloves on without ever waking him. He easily picked him up and walked to the door, while Ryan remained sound asleep, draped over his shoulder.

"Thanks for dinner," he said, sounding so sincere.

"You're welcome."

"I'll talk to you this week." He leaned in and gave me a quick kiss on the lips.

"Have a safe trip."

"Don't fuckin' remind me."

I opened the door as he repositioned Ryan to his other shoulder. I waited until he was down the stairs and in his car before I shut off the light and closed my door. It was bitter cold outside and there was nothing that I had wished for more than for Dailan to be in my bed, keeping me warm. *Must stop with these crazy thoughts,* I said to myself as I locked the door behind me.

Beth Rinyu

Chapter 21

It was the last day of school before Christmas break. Tomorrow was Christmas Eve. The kids were bouncing off the walls during our class Christmas party. Of course, our lead room mom, Mrs. Aymes, was there being obnoxious as usual and going out of her way to ignore me. I just killed her with kindness, not falling into her trap.

I tried my best not to think of Dailan. It was easier than I thought. I had been super busy this week, preparing for this party and doing last minute Christmas shopping. I did get one text from him that said, *"hi, beautiful."* He didn't tell me exactly what day he would be home, but if my calculations were right, it would be tomorrow.

I looked over at Ryan sitting alone; all of the other children had a parent or grandparent here with them joining in on the festivities. I walked over to his desk where he was quietly coloring his Christmas tree and eating a cookie.

"Your Christmas tree came out awesome, Ryan!" I sat down in the empty desk next to him.

"Thanks," he said, never lifting his head up.

"So your Aunt Lisa couldn't make it?"

"No, she couldn't leave work."

"Oh, well, I'm sure she would much rather be here with you than working."

"I guess," he said.

"Well, just think, tomorrow Santa will be here!" I said in an effort to cheer him up.

"Yeah," he said, still not showing much enthusiasm.

"What's wrong, Ryan?"

He shook his head like he didn't want to answer, and I could tell that he was about to cry. I quickly took him into the hallway, letting the other room mom know where I was going along the way.

"Do you want to talk about something?" I asked, once we reached the hallway.

He nodded as the tears began to fall, "I wish my mommy was here."

"Oh Ryan, it's okay," I said, giving him a hug.

Valerie was walking down the hall, paying each of the classes a visit. She came rushing over when she saw Ryan crying. Ryan tried quickly to wipe away the tears.

"Is everything okay?" she asked. Ryan nodded as he looked down at the ground.

"Miss Morgan, why don't you and Ryan go down to my office and talk? I'll watch your class for you," Valerie said, giving Ryan a sympathetic smile.

"Thanks," I whispered to Valerie as Ryan and I made our way down to Valerie's office.

"Am I in trouble?" Ryan asked as he took a seat in Valerie's office.

"No, Mrs. Kane just thought you would be more comfortable talking in her office instead of the hallway."

"Oh," he said.

"Do you ever talk to Mrs. Brewer about how you're feeling?" Mrs. Brewer was the school guidance counselor. Ryan had been seeing her once a week at lunchtime.

"Sometimes, but most of the time we play games."

"Well, maybe you should start telling her about everything that makes you sad. She's a really good listener."

He shrugged his shoulders and looked like his mind was a million miles away. "Miss Morgan?"

"Yeah?"

"Will you come and see me for Christmas?"

"Oh, sweetie, I don't think so. I'm sure you have plans with your family."

He shook his head quickly. "No, I'm staying with my Aunt Lisa for Christmas Eve and then my Uncle for Christmas. So you could just come over, I think my uncle likes you a lot," he said.

"We'll see what happens, Ryan." I didn't want to get his hopes up, but at the same time, I didn't want him feeling any worse than he already was.

He forced a smile. "Well, I'm going to tell Santa that's what I want for Christmas, more than anything."

"What's that, Ryan?" I asked in confusion.

"For you to spend Christmas with me and my uncle." He smiled.

I smiled back at him and messed up his hair. "Are you ready to go back before all the good cookies are gone?" I asked.

"Yup," he said, much happier than when we had first arrived at Valerie's office.

* * *

I curled up on my couch under my warm fuzzy blanket. Seven o'clock on Christmas Eve and I was already in my sweats and watching TV. What an exciting life I led. I was flicking through the channels, trying to find something funny to lighten my mood. I became annoyed at the ringing of my cell phone. I was so comfortable and I didn't feel like getting up to get it from my purse. I knew that it was probably Donna calling for the hundredth time to make sure I wasn't suicidal with spending the holidays alone. She was in New York, spending Christmas with Michael's family. I reluctantly got up to answer it and fumbled through my purse to find it. The butterflies unleashed in my stomach when I looked down and saw Dailan's name.

"Hey," I answered, trying to contain my excitement.

"Merry Christmas," he said. "Are you at your parents'?"

"Oh no, they actually were going away this year."

"Oh, you're home?" he asked, sounding surprised.

"Yup, already in my sweats and ready for bed."

"Well, how long will it take you to get ready?" he asked.

"Ready for what?

"I'm meeting my friend Tommy and his new girlfriend at the Irish pub up the street from you. You want to go?"

I looked at the warm fuzzy blanket on the couch and then imagined Dailan's sexy smile. *Hmmm, what should I do?*

"Twenty minutes," I blurted out.

Twenty minutes to Dailan was more like forty-five, so I had plenty of time to get ready. I changed into my skinny jeans, wearing my warm black boots overtop. After trying on five different tops, I finally decided on my red boucle knit turtleneck sweater. I jumped off the couch at the sound of the doorbell. When I opened up the door, I was instantly happy with my choice of Dailan over my warm fuzzy blanket.

He looked absolutely adorable; his eye was healing and was now a light shade of purple. He had on a grey button-up shirt untucked over his jeans and a black ski jacket that looked just like the one Ryan wore, but in a bigger size. He smiled and my stomach flipped. He moved closer and wrapped his arms around me tightly as he pressed his mouth against mine, parting my lips with his tongue. He ran his hands up my shirt and was starting to unhook my bra.

"Wait, wait, wait," I said as I released my lips from his. "I thought we were leaving."

"We will, in a little bit," he said as he kissed my neck.

"Mr. O'Maley, let's save that for later, *if* you're a good boy, that is," I joked.

"You're killing me, Nicole."

"Remember, patience makes the outcome so much better," I teased.

I grabbed my coat and gloves and we headed out the door. Dailan walked over to the passenger's side of his car to get the door for me.

"Let's walk," I said.

He looked at me strangely. "Are you nuts? It's freezing out!"

"I love going for walks in the winter. Okay, maybe it is a little crazy, but I do," I said.

He was still looking at me with hesitation. "Zip up your coat, put on your gloves, and stop being a wimp."

He rolled his eyes at me and closed the car door. "If I die of hypothermia, make sure you tell everyone it was your fault."

I zipped his coat up for him, much like I would do for one of my students, and kissed him lightly on the lips. "You'll be fine."

"You just love to torture me, don't you?"

"No, if anything, I'm helping you."

"How are you helping me?" he asked in confusion.

"Think of this as a cold shower," I said, unable to contain my laughter.

"You're just wrong." He put his arm around me and we began our short walk down the street.

Chapter 22

The walk to the pub allowed me time to talk to Dailan about what happened with Ryan yesterday. I could tell that it pained him to listen, especially since it brought up memories of his brother. I felt bad for even bringing it up, but I felt that it was important for him to know.

"Dailan, he just needs someone to talk to about it. He's still really upset and it's not good for him to keep it all inside." Dailan became quiet and nodded. I stopped walking for a second and took his hands in mine. "It's okay to be upset, Dailan, and it's okay to talk about it." I wanted him to know that I would be there to listen if he ever needed me to. I stood on my tippy toes and kissed him on the lips. "So, have you turned into an icicle yet?" I asked, trying to change the subject and lighten the mood.

"No, and your whole cold shower theory – it's not working." I was happy when I saw that crooked smile of his appear on his face once again.

We walked into the pub and he led me over to where his friend Tommy and his girlfriend were sitting. "Nicole, this is Tommy and Rhonda," Dailan said. I shook hands with the blond-haired man whom I vaguely remembered from the awkward night that Dailan and I had first met.

"Ah, Nicole, it's really nice to meet you," Tommy said with a smile.

His girlfriend Rhonda, who was hanging all over him, took a break from kissing his neck to look up and smile at me. "Hi, Nicole," she said.

I gave her a smile back and said hello, right before she grabbed Tommy by the face and kissed him on the lips. *Get a room*, I thought to myself. I took a seat on the other side of Dailan as the two of them continued putting on a show for everyone in the bar.

"I think those two should go step outside in the cold for a while," I joked.

Dailan turned around and looked at Tommy. "What the hell, Tommy, why did you even bother coming out if you're just going to sit here and make out all night?"

Rhonda shot Dailan a dirty look as she wrapped her arms around Tommy's neck. "Babe, let's dance," she said, pulling Tommy off the barstool and onto the dance floor.

I was trying not to rush judgment on her. I could get past all the tattoos, piercings, and the fact that she wasn't afraid to show her affection for others in a very public forum. The thing that I couldn't get past was when she called him "babe." For some reason, that term of endearment annoyed me to no end.

While Tommy and Rhonda were out on the dance floor groping each other, Dailan and I sat and had a beer. Dailan quickly looked over at the two of them and shook his head. "He falls in love so quick," he joked. "I don't even bother getting to know them anymore because chances are, he'll have a new one next week."

He told me that he and Tommy had been friends since he was he was a child. Tommy's family had lived down the street from Dailan's dad. Growing up, Dailan would spend his summers visiting his dad, and he and Tommy would get into all kinds of trouble. I laughed as I imagined the mischief that the two of them must have gotten into together.

"You were probably a teacher's worst nightmare." He flashed me a mischievous smile that indicated to me that I was right.

"So why aren't you with your family for Christmas?" Dailan asked.

I began to explain to him where my parents were spending Christmas. I continued, giving him just a little insight into my relationship with my family. By the time I had finished, I had taken my last sip of beer and probably told him more than he really wanted to know.

He took my hands in his. "Well, since you don't have any plans for tomorrow, would you like to spend it with me and Ryan?" he asked. "Oh, and my dad and his wife," he added.

I smiled, as I remembered Ryan's request from Santa. "I'd love to."

"Good." He pulled toward him and kissed me. He rubbed his thumb over the top of my hand and stared at me briefly. The music changed and Van Morrison's "Tupelo Honey" began to fill the air.

"I love this song," I said.

Dailan grabbed my hand and took me to the dance floor. He wrapped his arms around my waist as I wrapped mine around his neck. I rested my head on his chest. I closed my eyes and listened to his heart beating, feeling so at ease as he kissed me on the top of my head.

The music began to come to an end. "Nicole?"

"Yeah," I said, not wanting to remove my head from his chest.

"Have I been patient enough?"

I looked up at him and nodded as I rubbed my thumb over the remnants of what was once a black eye.

* * *

Dailan and I lay on my living room floor in front of the fireplace, wrapped in my warm, soft, fuzzy blanket. I was so sleepy from the last two hours of *mind-blowing* sex, as Dailan referred to it. I would never admit it to him, but I was in total agreement. I didn't want to fall asleep. I didn't want this perfect night to end. I began to have my normal conflict within, the same way I would after each time I would sleep with him, telling myself that it was wrong and it shouldn't be happening. I quickly silenced that voice inside my head that was scolding me. I reminded myself that I had this all under control. I wasn't going to let myself get emotionally attached to him. Dailan wouldn't let that happen anyway. He made it very hard to keep that thought when he kissed me on my head and whispered, "Happy Christmas, beautiful." I rested my head on his chest and closed my eyes, unable to fight the sleepiness – yes, it was a very happy Christmas.

Beth Rinyu

Chapter 23

The bright morning sunlight was shining through my living room window. I slowly opened my eyes and smiled as I looked up at Dailan, still sound asleep, lying next to me. I nuzzled closer to him and placed a soft kiss on his chest. I lay in comfortable silence, listening to him breathe. He kissed me on the top of my head as he began to awaken.

"Good morning," I said, looking up at him.

"What time is it?" He sat up, trying to see the clock.

"Eight thirty. What time do you have to get Ryan?" I asked.

"Eleven o'clock, Lisa wants him there for some stupid family breakfast she has every year," Dailan said as he rolled his eyes.

"Good, then you have time for me to make you breakfast." I sat up and began to dress. "Oh, and Merry Christmas!" I leaned in and gave him a kiss before heading off to the kitchen.

I was much more comfortable with cooking breakfast than dinner. I took out the carton of eggs and was whisking away when Dailan came walking into the kitchen. He ran his hand though his messy wavy hair, still looking like he was half asleep. I quickly poured him a cup of coffee while he sat down at the breakfast bar, rubbing his eyes.

"Somebody looks like they're still sleepy," I joked.

His cell phone began to ring from the pocket of his coat, which was hanging on the back of the chair. He fumbled around, trying to find it. He pulled out an envelope and held it up, giving me a quick smile as if he had forgotten something. I looked at him in confusion as he answered his phone and went walking off into the living room, along with the envelope. From the brief exchange that I heard going on in the living room, I realized that it was his mother, calling to wish him a Merry Christmas.

He came back into the kitchen just in time. I placed the plate containing my picture-perfect omelet in front of him. "Perfect timing," I said as he sat down.

He waited until I sat down before handing me the envelope that was is in front of him. "Here, this is for you."

135

I looked at him strangely before taking it from his hand. "What is it?"

He shrugged his shoulders, "I don't know. Open it."

I slowly ripped open the envelope, wondering what kind of joke would be awaiting me. I pulled out what looked to be two tickets. I looked them over to find they were to tomorrow night's showing of *The Nutcracker*. I smiled, remembering how I had told him the night that he was over for dinner that *The Nutcracker* was my favorite Christmas story and how my mother would always take my sister and me to see it the day after Christmas.

"Thank you," I said as I looked up at him with a warm smile.

"You're welcome."

"Does this include a date with you?"

"No, I don't do ballets – remember?"

"Oh, this is so much more than ballet; it's a classic."

"Well, that's okay. I'm sure one of your friends will enjoy going to see that classic with you a lot better."

I stood up and leaned over to give him a kiss on the cheek. "Well, now, I just got to one up you."

I walked over to the Christmas tree and grabbed the small box that I had labeled for him. He had a look of surprise when I handed it to him.

"Merry Christmas," I said placing it in his hand.

"Nicole, why did you do this?"

"Because I wanted to, so just shut up and open it."

He took the wrapping paper off and slowly lifted the lid. His eyes lit up when he saw two tickets to a hockey game. From what I was told, they were very good seats, but since I knew nothing at all about hockey, I was unsure.

He looked at me in disbelief, "These are great but you really – "

"You're welcome," I said, cutting him off. "Besides, I owed you after what I did to you at your Christmas party."

"Nicole these seats are expensive, let me –"

"Will you stop? I have connections." I laughed. I wasn't lying; one of Michael's co-workers had season tickets and gave me a really good deal on them. "I'm just glad that they really are good seats," I said.

"Thanks," he said as he leaned in and kissed me on the head.

We finished up eating breakfast as Dailan prepared to leave. He wanted to go home and take a shower before he picked Ryan up from his Aunt Lisa's.

"Come over as soon you're ready; I might need your help," he said with a grin.

"With what?" I asked.

"Cooking a turkey."

I shook my head. "I don't know the first thing about cooking a turkey and besides I have a phobia of raw poultry. I never touch the stuff."

He looked at me as if I were crazy.

"I do!" I laughed. "You mean to tell me that you cooked that delicious dinner last week and you don't know how to make a stinkin' turkey," I teased.

He ignored my sarcasm, still refusing to admit that he didn't cook dinner that night. "Okay, if you want to disappoint Ryan. He loves turkey, you know."

"Fine, I will *try* and help you but I'm not making any promises and if anyone ends up in the hospital with salmonella – it's not my fault."

I walked him to the door and gave him a kiss goodbye. I walked back into the kitchen and cleaned up the breakfast dishes. I sent Donna a quick text wishing her a Merry Christmas. I decided to get it over with as I punched my mom's cell phone number into my phone. I was both hurt and relieved when I got her voicemail. Hurt, because I couldn't believe that she couldn't even bother to answer the phone to wish me a Merry Christmas. Relieved, because I knew that talking to her and my dad would only bring me down from the great mood that I was in this morning. I waited for the tone after my mother's long-winded message.

Hi, Mom, just wanted to wish you and Dad a Merry Christmas. Hope you guys have a great day. I'll talk to you soon. Love yas!

"Okay, I did my dutiful daughter part," I said to myself before heading off to take a shower.

I was showered and dressed by eleven. I knew that Dailan was sill picking up Ryan, so I didn't want to leave just yet. I decided to kill some time checking my e-mail and was given the best Christmas present ever when I saw a new message from my brother. I was smiling from ear to ear as I anxiously waited for my computer to load up the message.

Merry Christmas, Nic! I wish I could be home with you guys instead of here! Try and survive the day with our crazy family! Wish I could be there with everyone! Love and miss you lots!
Justin

Leave it to my little brother to make me cry on a morning where I was feeling totally fantastic. I wiped the tears as I typed out a reply.

I wish so bad that you could be here instead of wherever the heck you are! I'm not spending Christmas with our crazy family this year. I actually am spending it with a really great guy – I believe you met him already...lol. Oh, and don't worry, I explained to him that you're not some sicko who likes to date his sister! Please stay safe and I can't wait until we can talk in person instead of e-mail. Merry Christmas!
Love you xoxoxo
Nicole

I closed the lid to my laptop, hoping that I would actually be able to spend next Christmas with my brother or at least have the comfort of knowing he was somewhere safe. I took a moment to gather my thoughts before grabbing the Christmas present that I had gotten for Ryan, just in case I did see him for Christmas. I grabbed my coat and headed out the door, realizing that Ryan wasn't the only one getting his wish today. I was pretty happy to being spending Christmas with him and Dailan as well.

Chapter 24

I arrived at Dailan's by noon. I was surprised when I wasn't excitedly greeted by Ryan at the door like the last time I had visited. Still, I wasn't disappointed to see Dailan behind the door, looking just as handsome as ever. He opened the door and took my hand. "Shh," he said as he led me through the house, back into the great room. Ryan was sitting in front of the TV, playing a video game.

"Hey, Ryan," Dailan said, causing Ryan to look up from his game.

My heart melted at the sight of Ryan's smile, which stretched across his face. He dropped the controller to the ground and came running over to greet me. "Miss Morgan, you came!" he exclaimed, giving me a hug.

"He told me you weren't coming," Ryan said as he playfully pushed Dailan. I smiled and handed Ryan his Christmas present. "Thanks!" he said as he sat down on the floor to open it.

I took a seat on the couch to watch him as Dailan sat down next to me. "Wow!" Ryan exclaimed as he tore away at the paper, revealing a buildable racetrack that seemed to be all the rage with the boys in my class this year. "Thanks, Miss Morgan, this is cool."

The enthusiasm on his face was all the thanks that I needed. "You're very welcome," I said.

Ryan walked over to the Christmas tree and returned with a small box for me. "Ryan, you already gave me a present," I said, remembering the yummy vanilla candle he had given me the day of our class party.

"That was really from my Aunt Lisa," he said. "This is from me. Well, I mean my Uncle D paid for it, but I picked it out."

I laughed as Dailan shook his head at Ryan. "Ryan, you never tell a girl that someone else paid for a present that you gave them," Dailan said, playfully smacking Ryan on the head.

"Just like you never tell a girl that someone else cooked dinner for her." I couldn't resist as I started to giggle. I watched as a grin stretched across Dailan's face. I slowly removed the wrapping paper and the lid from the box as Ryan looked on anxiously. I immediately smiled upon seeing the beautiful sterling silver necklace with a whimsical heart charm dangling from it.

"Oh, Ryan, I love this."

Ryan's smile was a mile wide. "I told you she liked hearts," he said to Dailan.

"Yup, hearts are my favorite thing," I said.

"They had all different kinds of hearts that you can add to it. But I liked this one best," Ryan said proudly.

"This is an awesome heart, Ryan," I said as I gave him a hug.

I lifted my hair as Ryan clasped it on my neck. I looked down at the heart hanging from my neck. It truly was one of the best presents I ever received because I knew how much it meant to Ryan to give it to me.

Ryan excitedly showed me all of the presents that he received from Santa before returning to his video game and then falling dead asleep in the middle of it.

"Huh...that game must not be very interesting," I said, looking at Ryan passed out on the floor.

"Lisa said he went to bed late and he got up really early. Ah, shit!" Dailan said as if he suddenly remembered something. "I was supposed to have him call my mom." He looked at the clock and was calculating the time difference in his head. "Oh well, she should still be up by the time he wakes up."

"Does it bother you not being able to spend the holidays with your family and friends in Ireland?" I asked.

He shrugged his shoulders. "No, not really. I mean everyone pretty much has their own lives and families. My mom spends Christmas with her sisters and her *friend*."

"Oh, do you mean *man-friend*?" I laughed.

He looked at me in confusion and I explained to him how I had gotten so much amusement out of Mrs. Tallone and her reference to her man-friend.

"So, am I your man-friend?" he asked with a grin.

I shook my head. "Nope, I think I like you better as my 'fella,'" I smiled.

"Oh, so are you finally admitting that you like me?"

"Hmmm….ever so slightly."

"Well, I am humbled, Miss Morgan," he said as he kissed me playfully on the lips. He stood up and pulled me off the couch. "Now, we've got work to do in the kitchen."

"No, *you've* got work to do; I'm supervising. I don't touch raw poultry, remember?"

He led me into the kitchen. I watched as he pulled a large turkey out of the fridge. "Doesn't that have to cook forever?" I asked, looking at the clock and seeing that it was almost one.

He shrugged his shoulders. "I don't know."

I watched as he punched something into his phone. "What are you doing?" I asked.

"You can do anything as long as you have the internet," he said with a triumphant look on his face.

I shook my head, hoping that I wouldn't be spending my night in the hospital with salmonella poisoning. He read his phone quickly before sticking his hand inside the turkey. I actually felt myself gagging as I watched. He looked over at me and rolled his eyes.

"It seriously grosses me out," I said in my defense. I watched in silence as he wrestled with the turkey. "Can I just ask one question? Why do you have your hand up a turkey's ass?"

"It says that there's supposed to be a bag or something in here." He said as he pulled with all his might, finally coming out with something.

"Here, hold this," he said.

I was half paying attention when I looked down to see that I was holding the decapitated neck of what was going to be tonight's dinner in my hand. "Ewww!" I screamed as I dropped it on the counter and ran over to the sink to wash my hands.

Dailan couldn't control his laughter from my reaction. I scrubbed my hands vigorously as he came over to wash his. "Okay, Nicole, you're not performing surgery," he said, waiting for me to get done. I grabbed a paper towel and dried my hands. I immediately took the anti-bacterial gel from my purse and squirted some on my hands. I waited for Dailan to finish drying his hands before giving him a squirt as well.

"That was mean," I said as I punched him lightly on his arm.

"You punch like a girl," he joked.

"I was just taking it easy on you. I can punch much harder than that."

"Go ahead and take your best shot," he said.

"No, I'm not going to do that, I don't want to hurt you."

"Trust me, there is no way that you would hurt me."

"Are you challenging me?" I asked.

"I believe I am, little girl."

I curled up my fingers, making sure they were positioned properly. Dailan smirked when he saw me move my thumb from under my underneath to overtop. I clenched my fingers tightly, closed my eyes and took my best shot. He didn't even flinch as my fist met his rock hard muscular arm.

"Ouch," I said as I shook off the stinging in my fingers.

Dailan began to laugh at my reaction. "Aww, did you hurt your hand?" he teased as he came closer.

"No, I did not, I'm just out of practice," I played it off.

"I don't know; looks like it hurts to me." He took his hand in mine, lifted it to his lips, and kissed me softly on the knuckles. He slowly released my hand from his and wrapped his arms around my waist. He pulled me into him and kissed me tenderly on the lips. I was a little hesitant at first as I thought about Ryan just in the next room. I quickly dismissed that thought, remembering Ryan was sound asleep. I wrapped my arms around Dailan's neck and stood on my tippy toes to kiss him back. Who would have thought that cleaning a turkey could be so romantic?

Chapter 25

Dailan's nice romantic kiss went from tender to passionate at warp speed. I was just about to pull away and get it under control, knowing this wasn't the time or place for that when I heard someone clearing their throat loudly. I broke free from his embrace to find a tall, handsome, gray-haired man with the most striking blue eyes standing in the doorway.

"Honestly, Dailan, have I taught you nothing? You should always lock the front door before you kiss a pretty girl in the kitchen," the gray-haired man said with a smile. He immediately extended his hand to me "Jack O'Maley," he said. It took a minute for me to realize that he was Dailan's father. It was hard to make the connection at first because his father didn't have any accent at all; then, I quickly remembered that his dad was American.

"Dad, this is Nicole Morgan," Dailan said.

"Oh, as in 'Miss Morgan'?"

I nodded with a smile.

"Well, my grandson is quite taken with you," he said. "And given what I just walked in on, I'd say my son is quite taken with you too," he added with a smile. I knew that I liked this man within the first few minutes of meeting him. He had a presence about him that immediately made me feel comfortable.

"Jack, do you think you could get the rest of the bags out for me?" a short blonde woman who had just entered the kitchen asked. "Oh, hi, I'm Annette," she said, looking at me as if she were surprised, even as a smile stretched across her face.

"Annette, this is Nicole Morgan, as in '*the Miss Morgan*,'" Jack O'Maley said, making it sound like I was some type of celebrity.

"Oh, Miss Morgan, Ryan has told us so much about you! Oh, and I'm Jack's wife, by the way, just in case you haven't figured that out."

"Nice to meet you," I said.

She gave me another smile before giving Dailan a kiss on the cheek. "What the heck? Oh God, Dailan, please don't tell me *you* were trying to cook?" she asked upon seeing the turkey still sitting on the counter.

Dailan shrugged his shoulders. "Hey, it's not my fault that my helper here refuses to touch raw poultry."

Dailan's father began to laugh. "Or that the cook obviously got distracted by his beautiful helper."

I felt myself begin to blush; I was hoping that Dailan's father didn't form an unfavorable opinion of me based on what he walked in on. I quickly put that thought out of my mind; he somehow didn't seem like the judgmental type to me.

"I'll finish this, Dailan, please stay out of the kitchen," Annette said as she quickly began tending to the turkey.

I spent the rest of the afternoon listening to Jack O'Maley recollect on Dailan's childhood. Some of the stories he told brought tears of laughter to my eyes, listening to all the mischief Dailan got into as a child. I was given a whole history of the O'Maley clan. Dailan's dad met his mother when he was over in Ireland visiting family. They married and had Dailan's brother Jerry and Dailan wasn't born until seven years later. I was surprised, not realizing there was such a big age difference between him and his brother.

It seemed therapeutic for Jack O'Maley to talk about his son. But I could see the pain on Dailan's face at the mention of his brother's name. I placed my hand in his and squeezed it tight. He looked at me with a quick smile of gratitude as his father continued reminiscing about Jerry.

"I always said that's why Jerry came back here to live once he got older. He was always more American than Dailan. He lived here for nine years before moving to Ireland. Dailan was just a baby when he left and I still haven't been able to convince him to move here permanently since," Jack said.

Dailan rolled his eyes at his father. I could tell by the look on this face that it was a topic he didn't want to discuss. Ryan had woken up somewhere in between, probably from all the laughter. He sat on his grandfather's lap, unable to wipe the smile from his face.

Jack O'Maley teased his grandson. "Ryan, how come you didn't tell me your teacher was so pretty?"

Ryan laughed and shrugged his shoulders, looking like he was embarrassed.

"Awww, Ryan, do you have a crush on Miss Morgan?" Dailan teased.

"No, but you do," Ryan blurted out, causing Jack O'Maley to spew with laughter at his grandson's observation.

"Me? Are you crazy? I don't even like her," Dailan joked.

Ryan jumped off of his grandfather's lap and came walking over to the couch where Dailan and I were seated. He playfully punched Dailan in the arm. "Yes, you do, silly," he said, sounding as if he were getting upset.

"Oh, you think you're tough," Dailan said as his got up from the couch and playfully wrestled Ryan to the floor where he began to relentlessly tickle him.

Ryan squirmed around, trying to catch his breath from the laughter and break free from Dailan. I smiled as I watched the two of them interacting.

"Dinner's ready," Annette said as she walked into the living room, shaking her head at Dailan and Ryan.

The turkey was delicious, thanks to Annette, and the conversation even better. We finished up the night playing *Clue*, with Ryan and I having more fun trying to teach Dailan how to play. I looked up at the clock; I was disheartened to see that it was already nine. I was sure I had twenty plus missed calls from my mom and I wanted to call her back before it got too late.

"I have to get going," I said.

"Aww," Ryan said with a frown. I looked over at Jack and Annette, who had the same look of discontent as Ryan.

Dailan got up to get my coat as I gave Ryan a hug goodbye. "Thanks for inviting me over, Ryan. I had lots of fun," I said as he squeezed me tight.

Jack and Annette both stood up at the same time. I went to extend my hand to Jack, but he instead wrapped his arms around and gave me a hug, "I hope to see you again real soon, Nicole. It's not very often that Dailan brings girls around to meet his old man – you must be special." He winked.

Annette followed suit, giving me a hug and placing a kiss on my cheek. "It really was nice to meet you, Nicole. I can see everything Ryan's said about you is true."

"Hey, thanks, it was really nice meeting both of you too," I said sincerely. I truly enjoyed their company.

Dailan walked me to my car. He took the keys from my hand and started my car to warm it up for me. We stood outside my car as he wrapped his arms around me and pulled me closer. Suddenly, it wasn't feeling so cold anymore.

"Did you have a good Christmas?" he asked.

"I did, thank you very much." I stood on my tippy toes, placing a gentle kiss on his lips. He responded back with much more intensity, placing his hands on my face and kissing me hard.

"Can you please just text me and let me know that you made it into your apartment safely, since I know you didn't leave that front porch light on."

"It was light out when I left my house. Why in the world would I have turned my porch light on? I will," I said appeasing his wishes.

I was waiting to see if he would make any future plans before I got into the car, but he didn't. He was always so vague and it drove me nuts! He had told his dad over dinner that he had a busy week at work ahead, trying to get contracts wrapped up before the end of the year. Maybe that's why he wasn't so quick to make plans. I told myself I wasn't going to overthink it.

I arrived home and waited until I was safely in my apartment before pulling my phone out of my purse to text Dailan. I was surprised to find only one text from Donna, agreeing to go see *The Nutcracker* with me tomorrow night and no missed calls from my mom.

I'm home safe and sound. I had a lot of fun today – thanks!

I quickly ran to check my home phone to see if my mom had left a message, but there was nothing. I took a deep breath and fought the tears.

Dailan's text back helped in halting them. *You're very welcome, beautiful. I'll see you this week, sweet dreams.*

146

I smiled as warmth overtook my body. I looked down at my phone again that was vibrating with a text message from Donna. *Open your door; I'm freezing*! I ran to the door and opened it as Donna was making her way up the stairs. She was carrying her overnight bag, a tray of cookies, and a bottle of wine.

"Hey, what are you doing here?" I asked as a smile stretched across my face.

"Well, Michael got called in to work. So I'm having a Christmas sleepover with my best friend," she said as she made her way inside.

I couldn't remove the smile from my face. I threw my arms around her and hugged her tightly. We made our way into the living room, where we would spend the rest of the night watching chick flicks, drinking wine, and eating cookies. It had been the perfect Christmas – even without a phone call from my mom.

Chapter 26

The weeks were flying by and turning into months and my best friend was becoming nonexistent, taking on extra shifts at work to help pay for her wedding. But Dailan was the perfect fill-in. We were growing closer with each passing day. We were still having mind-blowing sex, but I found something else was happening. I was confiding in him and turning to him on a daily basis to share my day, ask his opinion, or just to vent. Exactly what I told myself I wasn't going to do when we started this whole thing. But Dailan had a way that made it so easy to do. I knew that he didn't have any intention of falling in love with me. I would never have to worry about him talking about getting married or having kids someday. He just wasn't that type of guy and I was okay with that. I had that with Drew and it had scared me away. Every time I found myself starting to get those feelings of thinking that I could possibly fall in love with him, I cast them aside and reminded myself that this romance was just a temporary thing, Dailan would be moving back to Ireland soon. Still, I couldn't deny the heaviness in my chest every time I reminded myself of that fact.

Donna and Michael had instantly liked Dailan when I finally decided to introduce them. I knew that deep down inside Donna was hoping that I would overcome my fear of relationships and take the plunge with Dailan.

I couldn't believe that it was already the end of February. I was headed to Dailan's office to pick up Ryan. Normally, Dailan didn't have to work on Saturdays, but today he had to go in for what he thought would be a short period of time, so he brought Ryan with him. He called and asked me if I would mind picking up Ryan up and watching him for a few hours, since he was starting to get restless. I gladly obliged since I had no other plans.

I pulled into the parking lot and made my way into the large, upscale office building. I hit the Number 3 button as the elevator ascended to the third floor. I got off the elevator and took in the suite numbers on each door, finally finding Suite 8. I opened up the door and was immediately greeted by Rick Kincaide dressed casually in a black turtleneck and jeans. I felt a little guilty noticing just how handsome he was, because I knew how much Dailan despised him.

"Oh, Nicole? Right?" he said.

I nodded. "Well, I see you're still slumming with O'Maley," he said with a sarcastic edge.

I didn't respond and was happy when I heard Ryan's footsteps running down the hallway with Dailan following close behind. Dailan once again had an out-of-character serious demeanor in Rick's presence. He placed his arm around my waist and kissed me with a little more passion then I cared to display in public. I knew that it was clearly for Rick's benefit. He knew that I didn't like to openly display our affection for each other in front of Ryan. I still didn't get why he felt the need to lay claim to me in front of this man.

"Well, it was really a pleasure to see you again, Nicole," Rick said in a very flirtatious voice.

I nodded as he walked away. I gave Dailan a look of disdain. "Why do you two hate each other so much?" I asked once Rick was out of earshot.

"Because, he's total scum. Ryan, be good for Nicole," Dailan said, totally changing the subject.

"She's not Nicole, she's Miss Morgan," Ryan corrected him.

"Hey, Ryan, do you know how to ice skate?" I asked.

Ryan smiled and nodded. "Then that's where were going!".

"Cool!" Ryan exclaimed.

"I'll call you as soon as I'm done. I should only be a couple more hours," Dailan said.

"That's fine."

"Thanks, beautiful," he said, giving me another one of his intense kisses. This time I didn't care because Ryan was already out the door. I walked out the door, catching up with Ryan at the elevator. He was anxiously pressing buttons, waiting for the door to open.

"Miss Morgan, I don't have ice skates," he said as we stepped into the elevator.

"We can rent them there," I said.

We got into the car and took the short drive to Ice World, an outdoor skating rink that was one the most popular attractions in the winter. Ryan looked over at the large ice skating area in awe. "Wow, this is really cool," he said with a huge grin.

We stood in line and waited our turn for the skate rentals. "Ryan, do you know what size your foot is?" He shook his head. "Take off your sneaker and let me see," I said. He removed his sneaker as I looked inside, locating his size, before handing him back his sneaker. We sat down on the bench and laced up our skates. I double checked Ryan's to make sure they were tight enough.

"Are you ready?" I asked.

Ryan nodded as we awkwardly walked on the ground in our skates, finally making our way to the ice. It had been a few years since I had last been ice skating, so it took me a minute to adjust to the ice. I grabbed onto Ryan's hand as the two of us made our way around the rink like two pros.

"Wow, you skate really well, Ryan."

"My dad taught me," he said proudly.

We spent the next hour gliding around effortlessly as I listened to Ryan talk about his mom and dad. He seemed to be happy this time when he mentioned their names, telling me all about the happy times he had spent with them. I learned that his mom loved to cook, she was an animal lover, and that she had long dark hair like mine. I could hear the love and admiration in Ryan's voice when he spoke about her. He also told me that she stayed home with him until he started kindergarten and then she started working part-time for the same company that Dailan worked for.

"Oh, did your Uncle Dailan get her the job?" I asked.

"I think so. My daddy didn't want to her to work, but she was always home to get me off the bus."

"So are you excited about going to Ireland?" I asked.

"Not really. I like it there; I used to go all the time to visit my Nan and Uncle Dailan. But I'm going to miss it here," he said sadly.

"Well, I heard it's beautiful there."

"You've never been there?" he asked as if he were surprised.

I shook my head.

"Well, you will get to see it when you come to visit me and my Uncle Dailan," he said sweetly.

It finally occurred to me that Dailan and I weren't the only ones whose emotions were involved in this arrangement that we had. Ryan was clearly a big part of it. I didn't know how to respond, because I didn't know what Dailan's and my relationship would be once he moved back to Ireland. I felt my heart sink, thinking of how this would affect Ryan.

I quickly changed the subject. "I think we just burned off a billion calories with all that ice skating. How about some hot chocolate?" We were taking off our skates when my phone began to ring. "It's your uncle," I said to Ryan.

"Perfect timing," I answered. "Ryan and I just got done skating."

Dailan agreed to meet us at the ice skating rink and then we were going out to dinner from there. Ryan and I handed in our skates and sat down to some hot chocolate, waiting for Dailan to arrive.

"Nicole!" I was hoping that very familiar voice wasn't who I thought it was.

I turned around to see my sister and her older son, Christopher, right behind me. "Renee, what the heck are you doing here?" I asked as I got up and gave my nephew a hug and a kiss.

"Oh, well, Mark is away on business, so Mom and Dad invited me to come down with them to visit Ted and Amelia."

Oh God, please don't tell me my mom and dad are here too. "Oh, are Mom and Dad with you?" I asked.

"No, they're out with Ted and Amelia. They took Joey with them, so I told Christopher I would take him to one of my favorite places growing up."

"Christopher, did you get the Christmas presents I sent you?" I asked.

He just nodded and smiled.

"Oh, sorry, yeah, they got them. Things have just been so busy, I haven't had a chance to even call you and let you know."

"No big deal, I wish I knew Mom and Dad were coming down. I still have their presents as well," I said.

"Oh, well, it was a last minute thing," she said as if she were trying to defend them for their actions.

"Well, whatever. Maybe I'll just drop them off at Ted and Amelia's, since they always make it a point to visit them once a month," I said sarcastically.

My sister finally focused her attention on Ryan and looked at me as if she was waiting for an explanation as to who he was. "Oh, Ryan, this is my sister, Renee," I said. I wasn't going to get into the details of exactly who Ryan was, even though I knew she was dying to know.

"Oh, hello," she said in her sickening sweet voice.

There was an awkward silence just as Dailan approached us. *Oh, shit, shit, shit, now I'm going to have to introduce her to him!* Ryan's smile was a mile wide when he saw his Uncle. Dailan walked right past my sister and planted a kiss on my lips before sitting down next to Ryan. *There goes my just friends excuse.*

My sister raised her eyebrows at me, waiting for an introduction. "Dailan, this is my sister, Renee."

Dailan stood up to shake her hand and I watched as she checked him out from head to toe. I smiled inwardly as I thought, maybe, just maybe, my sister was jealous of something that I had or at least *she thought* I had.

"I want to show you all these cool hockey sticks they have," Ryan said to Dailan as he stood up and took him by the hand.

"It was nice meeting you, Renee," he said with that crooked smile that made me melt. I hoped that it was having the same effect on my sister.

"You too," she said again in her sickening sweet voice.

"I'll be right there," I said to Dailan as he was quickly whisked away by Ryan.

"Well, he's certainly good looking, but he has a kid!" she said with disgust in her voice. "Honestly, Nicole, why would you break up with someone as level-headed as Drew to go out with someone with baggage? Oh, let me guess – because he's hot," she said as if she was mocking me while she rolled her eyes.

"You are unbelievable, you know that, Renee?"

"Oh, come on, Nicole, we all know you're not mother material. It takes a lot more to being a parent than taking a kid ice skating," she said in a very condescending tone.

"First of all, Renee, that's not his son; it's his nephew. His brother and sister-law died last year, so he's taking care of him."

"Oh, I didn't know." She became quieter and I could almost see some regret wash over her face.

"No, you wouldn't know anything about that, would you? Because that's what brothers and sisters are *supposed* to do for one another – be there for you when you need them the most, something you know *nothing* about."

She stood there speechless as I bent down to give my nephew a kiss goodbye. "See ya, Christopher; give your brother a hug for me." I walked away, saying nothing more to my sister.

I knew she was probably on the phone already telling my mother all about Dailan and how I was so *mean* to her. For the first time in my life, I had stood up to my bossy older sister and it felt good!

Chapter 27

I awoke with a smile on my face when I took my phone from my nightstand to read a text message from Dailan that said, *Happy Birthday, beautiful.* He had been in Boston for the past four days. I only had brief conversations with him while he was gone because he was super busy. I stretched out in my bed and smiled upon thinking he would be back tomorrow. I was mad at myself for missing him, but I couldn't help it. I knew that I had feelings for him, but I planned on keeping them inside and never to let him know. My heart sank when I thought that this was how it would be in a few months anyway – Dailan would be gone for good.

I flung my legs over the side of the bed, grabbed my phone, and replied, *Thanks! Miss you.* I instantly regretted my words after I sent the message. I didn't want him to know that I missed him. I didn't want him to think that I needed him, even though deep down inside I was beginning to feel like I did. I got out of bed and jumped into the shower. The warm water relaxed me and helped to clear my head. I stayed in for a little longer than I should have, causing me to have to rush around to get ready for work once I had gotten out. I planned on ignoring my ringing phone as I ran around my bedroom in search of the matching shoe to the one that was already on my foot. But I decided that I would risk being late when I saw Dailan's name flashing on the caller ID.

"Good morning," I answered, finally finding the shoe I was looking for.

"How's it feel to be another year older?"

"No different; catching up to you!" I walked into the bathroom to put on my make-up while I was talking to him. I realized just how hard it was to apply blush when you were unable to stop smiling.

We talked for a few minutes longer. I filled him in on the last few days and gave him an update on Ryan.

"Well, I have to go into a meeting. Have a good day," he said.

"Thanks, I'll try."

"I'll see you tomorrow," he said.

"Okay." Another huge smile stretched across my face just thinking about tomorrow.

"And, Nicole?"

"Yeah?"

"I miss you too."

I hung up the phone and beamed. *He missed me too!* That was the first time that Dailan had ever given me any type of insight as to how he felt toward me. I was going back on my plan of not wanting him to express any feelings for me, but I figured today was an exception - it was my birthday after all!

The school day was uneventful. We eagerly worked on our class bulletin board for the spring fling, even though it was a month away.

Ryan's Aunt Lisa was coming to pick him up from tutoring. At this point Ryan was doing so well, he really didn't need to be staying after school anymore. But he looked forward to it every week and I found that I did as well. So, we continued our Wednesday schedule just like we had in the beginning of the year. Ryan would spend that time finishing up homework or helping me out around the classroom. Ryan excitedly told me about his skiing trip that he was leaving for tomorrow morning with his Aunt Lisa, her husband, and his cousin. He was even more excited because he was missing two days of school to go.

"Do you like to ski, Miss Morgan?"

"Umm, kind of, I'm not really good at it, though," I said as I stapled shamrocks to our March bulletin board.

"Well, you should have my Uncle Dailan teach you; he's really good," Ryan said proudly.

"Is he?" I asked with a smile. Somehow, just hearing his name made me smile today.

Ryan nodded. "Him and my daddy used to go all the time. My daddy always said that he was better at it than Uncle D, but I really think my Uncle D was better," he whispered like there was someone else in the room. We both started giggling.

"Well, it sounds like you guys are having way too much fun," Lisa said as she walked through the door. Ryan got up and started gathering his papers.

"Today's Miss Morgan's birthday," Ryan said.

"Oh, happy birthday!" Lisa said with a warm smile.

"Hey, thanks." I smiled back.

"Are you doing anything special?" Lisa asked.

"Going out to dinner with my best friend and her fiancée."

"Well, enjoy! Once you get to my age, you don't want to celebrate anymore!" Lisa said.

I looked at Lisa trying quickly to gauge her age. I knew that she was older than her sister. If her sister was the same age as Dailan's brother, I was guessing Lisa to be somewhere around forty, hardly old at all.

"Are you all ready, Ryan?" I asked.

He smiled and nodded. I let Lisa know he had worked on the assignments that he would be missing over the next two days, so he'd be pretty much caught up when he got back on Monday.

"Have a great time, Ryan," I said, messing up his hair.

"Oh, Nicole, if you *happen* to talk to Dailan, would you mind telling him that we'll be home around eleven on Sunday? He had asked me if he could pick up Ryan early, since he hasn't seen him all week," Lisa said.

I nodded, still feeling a little uncomfortable with her knowing about mine and Dailan's relationship. But I didn't try to deny it. I knew that Ryan probably told her everything.

"Have a great time," I said.

"Thanks and have a great birthday!" Lisa said as she and Ryan headed out the door.

I arrived home and quickly checked my e-mails before jumping in the shower. Five new messages, but the only one I cared about was from Justin Morgan.

Happy Birthday to my favorite sister (don't tell Renee or I will deny it...lol). Hope you are doing something fun for your birthday! How are things going with your, do I dare say – boyfriend? I can't wait to be properly introduced to him and set the record straight on whose idea it was for the sick lie...lol. Well, I hope you have a great day and have a drink for me.

Love your favorite and only brother,
Justin

Dear Justin,
Thanks for remembering! You are the best! I will have two drinks for you!!
Love and miss you lots!! xoxo
Nicole

I hit the send button and closed my laptop. It amazed me that the only family member who wished me a happy birthday was probably a million miles away. I shook my head and fought off the sadness, thinking how my mom hadn't even bothered to call me today.

I quickly took a shower and dressed in my favorite boot cut jeans and a gray turtleneck. Donna texted me that she and Michael were a few minutes away. I walked outside and sat on my bottom step, waiting for them to arrive. It was a chilly March night, but there was still a hint of springtime in the air. I breathed it in, never able to get enough of that scent. As I listened closely, I could hear the faint sound of the spring peepers that were beginning to sing their yearly tune. I got up and jumped in the car when Michael and Donna pulled in the driveway.

"Happy birthday!" Michael said in his normal cheerful voice.

"Thanks," I said. I was so appreciative of Donna and Michael; because of them, I wouldn't be spending my birthday alone.

We entered the restaurant and Donna led us right to the bar. "We have to have one drink before dinner, this is the one and only day you will be turning twenty-six, you know," Donna said.

"Okay, but just one, I have to go to work tomorrow and somehow I don't think dealing with twenty-one kids and a hangover would be that much fun!"

"Fine, party pooper," Donna said.

Michael ordered himself a beer and Donna and I each a glass of wine. I excitedly listened as they told me all about their honeymoon to Italy that they had just booked. Michael was ordering another round of drinks before I could stop him, as

Donna continued talking about the honeymoon. I felt my phone vibrating from my coat pocket and pulled it out while still trying to stay focused on what Donna was saying. I totally tuned her out when I saw that it was a text from Dailan and opened it up to read it.

Getting older suits you; you look beautiful tonight.

"What?" I said out loud.

"What's the matter?" Donna asked.

I quickly turned around and was unable to contain the smile that stretched across my face when I saw my fella, Dailan O'Maley, right in front of me, looking just as handsome as ever.

Chapter 28

I stood up and threw my arms around him. "I thought you weren't coming back until tomorrow."

"Well, I figured you were worth rearranging my schedule for," he said.

Donna was smiling in delight. "You see, Michael, I was able to keep a secret from her." I was quite sure that she had orchestrated this whole thing.

"Dailan, we almost got her drunk waiting for you," Donna joked.

"Sorry, there was a lot of traffic coming from the airport," he said as Michael handed Dailan a beer. *He had come straight from the airport just to celebrate my birthday with me.* That thought made me want him even more than I already did tonight.

Donna and Michael were deep in conversation with the bartender, who had just returned from a trip to Italy and was giving them all sorts of tips.

"Thank you so much for being here," I said

"No problem." He took my hand in his and kissed it.

"Dailan, you are alive! My God, I haven't heard from you in ages." I looked up to see a skinny, familiar-looking redhead with a very handsome man. She leaned down to give Dailan a kiss on the cheek and it finally dawned on me where I had seen her before. She was the girl that Dailan was with the day I was having lunch with my brother.

"Hey, how are you?" Dailan said, not sounding as enthusiastic about their meeting as she did.

"I've been good," she said, finally looking over at me.

"Oh, Jenna, this is my girlfriend, Nicole," Dailan said, taking me a little off guard with the word *girlfriend.* Sure, we were seeing each other quite a bit over these past few months and it was probably perfectly safe to assume that I was his girlfriend. But to hear him actually say it to someone sounded weird.

161

"Oh," she said as she raised her eyebrows, looking surprised as if to say she finally got why she hadn't heard from him.

"It's really nice to meet you," she said. It was hard for me to gauge if she was being sincere or not.

"Jenna, come on, our table's ready," the man she was with said.

"Well, it was nice seeing you again, Dailan," she said. She gave me a quick smile and headed off to her table.

"Who was she?" I asked.

"Just some girl," Dailan said, sounding as if he didn't want to talk about it.

"Some girl who you use to –"

"Some girl I use to know and let's just leave at that," he said as he pulled me close and gave me kiss on the cheek.

I couldn't believe I was finding myself getting jealous over coming face to face with some girl who was clearly one of his ex - whatever you call someone that you have casual sex with.

Dailan was quick to jump in the conversation that Donna and Michael were having with the bartender. I wasn't quite sure if it was because they were now talking about the bartender's trip to Ireland or because he just wanted to change the subject of his recent encounter.

We sat down to dinner and talked non-stop, or should I say Donna and Michael laughed non-stop at the stories Dailan was telling. I grabbed his hand under the table and stroked the top of it with my thumb. I just couldn't wait to be alone with him. I missed him so much these past few days, and I wanted to show him just how much. I couldn't control myself any longer. I made sure that my hand was discreetly covered by the tablecloth as I began to slide my hand up his leg and slowly unzipped his pants halfway. He stopped talking mid-sentence, being caught off guard by my uncharacteristic behavior. He looked at me out of the corner of his eye and smiled slightly, continuing with his story. I slid my fingers under the flap of his boxer shorts and began to caress the shaft of his penis. I was impressed with the way that he maintained his composure even as I felt his erection beginning to form. He took a sip of his beer as I continued with my pleasurable assault. He finally removed my hand when it must have become too much for him. Donna and Michael were clueless as to what had just transpired, as they both were talking over each other with their playful bickering.

I finally got myself temporarily under control, but I was counting the minutes until I could be alone with Dailan. I was so happy when the check finally arrived. Dailan graciously paid for everyone, ignoring Donna's protest that she and Michael pay for half.

We walked out to the parking lot and I gave Donna and Michael a hug and kiss goodbye. Dailan wrapped his arm around me as we walked to his car. "What did you do with this girl Nicole that I use to know?" he joked.

"Well, I thought that you of all people would like the new version better."

"Oh, don't get me wrong; I loved that girl inside the restaurant, but I'm quite fond of the old version as well."

"Well, then, maybe tonight, you'll get a little bit of both."

He stopped walking for a brief second and looked at me with his sexy crooked smile. "Don't look at me like that," I said.

"Why?" he laughed.

"Because I may just have to tear your clothes off right here and do some things that I'm sure would be at the top of the inappropriate list."

"I don't know what the hell got into you, but I like it." He waited for me to get into the car, closing the door once I was in.

He got into the car and started it up. "Hey, Dailan?"

"Yeah?"

"When you introduced me to that girl tonight as your girlfriend, did you mean pretend girlfriend like at your Christmas party or did you mean real girlfriend?"

"Whatever kind of girlfriend you want to be."

I smiled and pretended to be deep in thought. "Hmm...I think I like real girlfriend better," I said with a smile.

He smiled back at me. "I was hoping that's the one you'd pick."

And just like that.....Dailan O'Maley had gone from being my fella to my boyfriend.

Chapter 29

We arrived at my apartment. I felt like I couldn't get out of the car quick enough. I took off my seatbelt and had my hand on the car door. I looked at Dailan, who was still sitting there with the car running.

"What are you doing?" I asked.

"Would you be really pissed off at me if I just went home? I'm really tired."

"Are you serious?" I was feeling myself becoming even more sexually frustrated by the second.

"Yeah, I am. I'm sorry, Nicole. I promise we'll get together tomorrow."

Tomorrow? What the hell? Tomorrow my body wouldn't be aching for him uncontrollably. Okay, maybe it would, but I'm sure it wouldn't be nearly as bad as tonight.

He kissed me goodbye, but I pulled away before it became too intense. I didn't want to make my situation any worse. "You won't be mad if I don't walk you in, will you? I'm just exhausted." I shook my head and got out of the car.

"I'll call you tomorrow," he said.

I nodded and shut the car door. I couldn't believe he was choosing sleep over sex. If he thought there was a new version of me tonight, there was definitely a new version of him as well!

I was halfway to my steps when I heard his car door slam. He came running up behind me. "Ha, I got you," he laughed as he effortlessly picked me up and flung me over his shoulder.

"Dailan, put me down, you're going to drop me," I said as I hung over his shoulder while he carried me up the stairs.

He finally put me down once we reached the top. I dug around in my purse, looking for my keys. Dailan looked up at the unlit porch light and shook his head.

"Be quiet," I said. I finally found the key and opened the door.

"The look on your face was priceless." Dailan laughed as he closed the door behind him.

"Yeah, well suddenly I'm not in the mood anymore," I said.

"Okay, that's fine. Let's go watch TV." He took off his coat and began to walk toward the living room.

I wasn't able to pretend, even for a second! I quickly removed my coat and pulled him toward me. I grabbed his face and began to kiss him mercilessly. He held up his hands, signaling for me to calm down but I couldn't. I wanted him so badly. I ran my hands up and down his body, longing for him with each passing second.

"Okay, I know this is probably a really bad time to mention this, but I don't have anything with me. Don't kill me," he said.

"Have you been with anyone else since we started sleeping together?" I asked.

"Nicole, you have your hand two inches away from a very sensitive area on my body. How am I supposed to answer that?" he joked.

"With the truth, Dailan." I was almost afraid of what the truth would be.

"No, Nicole, I swear, you have been the only girl I've been with for the past four months," he said, sounding much more serious.

"Okay, we're good then. I'm on the pill." I pulled him hard by the hand and led him into my bedroom.

"Please be gentle with me," he joked once we reached my bedroom. I removed his shirt and threw it on the floor. I began to run my tongue around his neck, then up and down his chest. His skin tasted delicious. He lifted my shirt over my head and removed my bra. He moved my hair out of the way and began to kiss my neck vigorously. My hand slid down to his pants and unbuckled his belt. I removed his pants with a sense of urgency. I pushed him down on my bed, climbed on top of him, and began to kiss him softly on the lips, then his neck, making my way down to his stomach. I dropped to my knees and took him in my mouth. He was so hard, so ready, that a rush of excitement came over me.

"Oh, Nicole," he whispered. He ran his fingers through my hair as I continued to take him in with ease. I found myself becoming more aroused over his heightened sense of excitement. He began to breathe heavier as my tongue cascaded over the skin of his penis. I sensed that he was almost there when he quickly pulled me up and removed my jeans and underwear. "I want to be inside of you." He cupped my breast with his mouth and ran his hands up and down my body. He pushed me down on the bed as he continued kissing my breasts. There was a look of longing in his eyes that made me want him even more. I whimpered with delight as I felt the fullness of him inside of me for the first time without a condom. I could tell by the look on his face that he was feeling the same way that I was, being together in this way without any barriers. It was so new and intimate, making me yearn for him even more. I raised my hips to meet him as he continued to take me with each move. I was enjoying every single second. I smiled inwardly, seeing the pleasure that washed across his face. At this particular moment, I knew that I was all that he wanted, all that he needed. I had never felt so in control. My body was providing him everything that he desired. I ran my hands through his thick wavy hair and up and down his back. I gently pressed my fingers into his back, raising my hips one last time to meet him as I let out a gentle cry of sheer pleasure. He began to move quicker and harder now.

"Oh, Nicole, you feel so fuckin' good," he whispered. My insides tingled at the sound of his voice. He continued for a few more seconds before he buried his face in the pillow, trying to catch his breath as I felt the warmth of his release filling me up.

I kissed him gently on the cheek. "That was perfect," I said as I caressed his face. He shook his head in agreement, still trying to catch his breath. He rolled over and wrapped his arms around me. I rested my head on his chest while he played with my hair.

"This was the best birthday ever. Thanks to you and Donna," I said. "Oh, and my brother." I explained to him how my brother had sent me an e-mail from wherever he was to wish me happy birthday when no one else in my family bothered.

He looked at me sadly and kissed my forehead. "Why don't you get along with your mom and dad?"

My stomach dropped at that question. "It's a long story that I'd just rather not get into right now."

I was so grateful that he had just dropped it, not asking any more questions. "Oh, I forgot something," he said as he jumped up and pulled on his boxers. He walked out of the bedroom as I sat up and reached over to turn on the lamp.

I covered myself with the sheet and wondered what the heck he was doing. He came back in with a small box wrapped in birthday wrapping paper and a card. "I wanted to give this to you earlier, but then I was attacked," he joked.

I playfully punched him in the arm. I opened up the card and laughed. It was a very fitting humorous Dailan-type card signed, *Love always, Dailan*. I stood it up on my nightstand and began to unwrap the present.

I removed the lid from the box and found a silver bangle-type bracelet that matched the necklace that Ryan had given me for Christmas. It had a heart charm dangling from it, similar to my necklace.

"I love it!" I said as I clasped it on my wrist.

"Ryan approved of that heart, so I figured you would like it," he said.

I was so happy I wanted to cry, but instead I took his face in my hands and kissed him deeply.

I finally released my lips from his. "Thank you so much," I said as I hugged him tightly.

I smiled as I looked down at the bracelet sparkling on my arm. My smile became wider when Dailan whispered, "Happy birthday, beautiful."

Chapter 30

Dailan spent the night. He got ready for work at my place. Being forced to leave the warmth of his arms at the sound of my alarm was a little bit difficult. A round of morning sex and being able to shower with him before work helped make up for it.

I walked into work unable to wipe the grin from my face. I had met up with Sarah, one of the other second grade teachers, in the parking lot. "Well, someone looks like they had a happy birthday," she said.

"It was my best one yet," I said.

She took my arm in her hand and looked down at my bracelet. "Pretty! Is that from someone special?"

I nodded. "Very special!"

"Oh, to be twenty-six and in love," she said with a smile. I smiled back and wondered if all of these feelings that I was beginning to have for Dailan were love. It's not what I had wanted to happen, but the more I was with him, the stronger the feelings became. I reminded myself once again that Dailan had this under control. He wasn't the type to express his feelings, which would allow me to conceal mine. Still, I found myself getting a little upset knowing that I wasn't going to see him tonight; he had made plans a while ago to go to a basketball game with his friend Tommy. I was thoroughly impressed when he actually made plans to go to the movies with me tomorrow night. For the first time since I had met him, he had actually planned something ahead of time.

To my delight, the next two school days whizzed by and in a just a few short hours, I would be seeing Dailan. The kids were lining up for bus dismissal when out of nowhere Cameron Aymes turned around and roughly pushed the child behind him, causing a chain reaction. Victoria, the tiniest girl in the class, ended up at the bottom of that pile, slamming her head hard on the desk along the way. I ran over to help her off the ground. She had tears rolling down her face. I felt a large goose egg instantly

Beth Rinyu

forming on the back of her head as her best friend came over to console her.

"What a baby," Cameron said to Victoria, who was hysterically crying.

"Cameron, that's enough," I said.

"My mom says I don't have to listen to anything you say," Cameron shouted.

I listened as all the kids gasped at Cameron's disrespectful behavior. I never wanted to think that I could actually dislike a child, but at this particular moment, Cameron Aymes was making me re-think that.

"Cameron, get out of line and go sit down – now!" I said. What I really wanted to say was, *You're a brat, and your mom is a bitch!*

"If you make me miss my bus, my mom's gonna be mad," Cameron said as he stomped back to his desk.

I quickly called down to the office to see if Valerie was available. I knew that she was probably running around somewhere. She was always crazed at dismissal time.

I grabbed the ice pack from the first aid kit and held it on the back of Victoria's head. I rubbed her back as she tried to catch her breath from crying.

I looked up to find Valerie in the doorway. "What happened?" she asked.

I explained to her what had occurred. She looked at Cameron, signaling for him to get up from the desk.

"Cameron, this is totally unacceptable behavior. Look what you did to Victoria," Valerie said.

"I don't care; she's a baby," Cameron said.

"I am not," Victoria cried.

Mrs. Towner, the school nurse, came down to get Victoria. She told me that she would call Victoria's mom and let her know what happened and see if she could come and pick her up since the buses were leaving in five minutes.

"Cameron, you're coming with me," Valerie said.

"No, I'm not. I'm going home," he said, blatantly defying Valerie.

"No, you're coming to my office and your mother will have to pick you up from there." I could hear the frustration in Valerie's voice.

"No, I'm not. I don't have to listen to you or her," he said, pointing at me. "My mom says you're both idiots," he said, causing more gasps from the class.

Valerie took Cameron by the hand as he reluctantly walked out the door with her. I tried to restore order as best as I could as I walked my class down to the buses. I waited until the last bus loaded up, and then walked back to my classroom to gather my things. I stopped in Mrs. Towner's office to check on Victoria. She was sitting on the cot and her mother was in the chair next to her.

"Are you doing okay?" I asked.

She nodded and smiled, continuing to hold the ice pack on her head.

"Mrs. Towner said that she doesn't think we have to worry about a concussion, but to just keep an eye on it," Victoria's mother said.

"Good, well just go home and try to have a good weekend," I said with a smile.

"I will." Victoria smiled sweetly. She jumped down from the cot and wrapped her arms around me. "Thank you, Miss Morgan," she said as she looked up at me.

Even though I didn't want to, I stopped in Valerie's office on my way out. I knocked lightly on her door. Cameron was sitting at the conference table with his head down, never looking up. Valerie got up and came walking out of her office when she saw me.

"Hey, do you need me to stay until his mom gets here?" I asked. *Please say no, please say no.*

"No, no sense in both of us starting out the weekend dealing with that dreadful woman," she whispered.

"Are you sure?" I asked, feeling a little guilty, like I was throwing Valerie to the wolves.

"That's what I get paid the big bucks for," she said. "Now go and have a good weekend."

"Thanks, you too, Valerie, and good luck."

171

She smiled and shook her head as she headed back into her office.

I got into my car and cringed when I saw Mrs. Aymes pulling in the parking lot. I thought about poor Valerie, and what she probably had in store for her. I decided not think about it anymore. I pulled out my phone and texted Dailan. *Do we still have a date tonight?*

I was halfway home when he replied. *Since my other girlfriend cancelled, I guess you'll do......see you at six, beautiful.*

I pulled into the driveway before texting him back. *Okay, so that means seven.* I could never resist taking the opportunity to tease him about perpetually being late.

I got out of my car and realized what a beautiful spring-like afternoon it was. I looked down at my watch. It was only 4:15, so I had plenty of time to go for a walk and be home in time to get ready for my *date*. I ran upstairs and threw my stuff inside, quickly changing into my sweats and sneakers. I began the short walk up to the bay, taking in the warm sunshine when Dailan replied to my text. *One of these days I will surprise you....I'll see you at six, I promise.* I walked a little way along the beach before sitting down to people-watch. The bay beach was pretty active for a March day, but given the beautiful weather, it wasn't hard to see why. I was thoroughly entertained by a black lab running tirelessly in and out of the water to retrieve the stick that his owner would throw. I watched as an older couple walked hand and hand, looking like they were two teenagers in love. I looked out at the water and realized just how much I had yearned for something like that; to grow old with someone I love, and still be so in love after all those years. Of course, that would mean letting my guard down and ridding myself of the guilt that I harbored inside. I felt a knot in my stomach and tears in my eyes, knowing that I would probably never be able to, no matter how hard I tried. But that little voice inside my heart was whispering, maybe, just maybe Dailan was worth taking that risk for.

Chapter 31

I opened up the door and pointed to my watch as Dailan made his way up the stairs. "It's not my fault; I would have actually been here early if it weren't for that asshole Kincaide," he said.

I gave him a quick kiss as he walked in the door. "Okay, let's make a deal, I won't talk about Mrs. Aymes tonight, and you don't talk about Rick Kincaide."

"Oh, you're on a first names basis with that jerk-off now, are you?" he asked, sounding like he was actually offended.

"No, I'm not on a first name basis with him, silly," I said as I planted a kiss on his cheek. "I ordered us pizza, if it's not cold by now, that is," I teased.

"Well if it is, you can blame it on *Rick*," he said, this time sounding a lot less serious.

"I thought we agreed no more talk of *Mr. Kincaide*."

"Fine by me," he said as we sat down to eat our pizza.

* * *

"That was the worst movie ever," I said as we walked out of the theater.

"It wasn't that bad," he said.

I rolled my eyes in disagreement at him. "I guess blood and gore just isn't my thing."

He pulled his phone from his pocket. I watched as a smile lit up his face from a text message he received. He handed me the phone and showed me what he was reading. It was a text from Lisa. It was a picture of Ryan getting ready to go down the hill. Clearly, Ryan had typed the message that was included when I saw all the misspelled words.

Uncle D next time we go skying I will be beter than u I will see u on sonday. I miss u love u.

I smiled as well. I loved the special relationship the two of them had. Ryan loved Dailan so much and vice-versa.

He took his phone back and scrolled down to read another text. "Do you feel like meeting Tommy at PJ's?" he asked.

"I don't care," I said as I shrugged my shoulders. If it was anything like last time we had met his friend Tommy, it would be just Dailan and me hanging out alone anyway.

We walked into PJ's and I began to laugh, remembering the last time I had been here was the first night I had met Dailan and made a complete fool of myself. So much had changed since that night. Tommy was sitting at the bar with another guy who looked to be the same age as he and Dailan were. I looked around for Tommy's girlfriend, but she was nowhere in sight.

"Hey, Nicole," Tommy said with a smile.

"Hi," I shouted over the music.

"Bryce, this is Dailan's girlfriend, Nicole," he said to the guy that was sitting next to him. A rush of excitement overtook me whenever I was referred to as Dailan's girlfriend.

He extended his hand to me. "Nice to meet you, Nicole."

Tommy quickly ordered Dailan and me drinks and began to chat. He was much different without his girlfriend around and I found that I really did like him. He reminded me so much of Dailan with his sense of humor and I could instantly see why the two of them were such good friends. I found out through his endless chatter that he and his girlfriend broke up.

"Dailan, I need to get some legal advice," Bryce said when he finally was able to get in a word. He began to talk to Dailan about some legal mumbo jumbo that I didn't care to listen to.

"I love this song," Tommy said as some dance tune that I had never even heard of filled the air. "Dailan, I'm borrowing your girlfriend," Tommy screamed over the music as he pulled me onto the dance floor. Tommy began to flail about aimlessly to the music as I tried to contain my laughter. I began to dance with him and by the time the song had ended, my stomach muscles were hurting from laughing so hard.

Tommy took me by the hand as we walked back to where Dailan and Bryce were standing. Dailan was shaking his head and laughing. "Dude, you suck at dancing."

"That's not what Nicole said; she even slipped her number out there," Tommy teased. I laughed and walked over to Dailan, and gave him a kiss on the lips with a little more passion than I normally displayed in public.

"Wooooooo," Tommy screamed loudly, causing the people who were standing next to us at the bar ordering drinks to look over. I had just removed my lips from Dailan's, when I noticed that one of those people who had focused their attention on us was Mrs. Aymes.

Shit, shit, shit, I said to myself. *Maybe she didn't realize it was me; it was dark in here. Even if she did, she surely wouldn't have remembered who Dailan was.*

"Dailan, I think we need to leave," I said.

"Oh okay, only if you promise a repeat performance from the other night," he joked. I managed a smile, even though my stomach was in knots.

"We're going," Dailan shouted over the music to Tommy and Bryce.

"What's the matter, Dailan, are you afraid I'm gonna steal your girl?" Tommy teased.

"Not a chance," Dailan said.

We walked out the door hand in hand. I kept my head down the whole time in an effort to avoid Mrs. Aymes again. I was happy when we finally made it to the car unnoticed.

"What's the matter?" Dailan asked

"That freakin bitch Mrs. Aymes was there tonight and I think she saw me kissing you."

"I thought we had an agreement to not talk about her."

"I know, but now she's going to make my life a living hell after seeing that."

"Fuck her," Dailan said. "What you do with your personal life is your business."

"I know but....you're right. Okay, I'm not going to talk about her anymore." I tried my best to put it out of my mind.

After a couple hours of incredible sex, Mrs. Aymes was completely out of my mind. I moved closer to Dailan and rested my head on his chest. "That was really good," I said.

I looked up at him as he nodded and I realized that he was half asleep. He pulled me even closer to him. "I think I could fall in love with you, Nicole," he muttered. My jaw dropped as panic ensued. I looked up at him again and he was already fast asleep.

My stomach fluttered as tears began to fall from my eyes, onto his bare chest. The one thing that I had depended on this whole relationship was now gone. Dailan O'Maley had opened his heart to me. Now I had to decide if I wanted to enter.

Chapter 32

I stood outside the mall, waiting for Donna. Dailan had to go into work for a few hours and then made plans ahead of time *again* to take me out to dinner. I was starting to like this new Dailan, who actually planned things out ever so slightly, instead of leaving with just a goodbye or I'll talk to you later. I didn't mention anything to him about what he had said in his sleep stupor last night. Once I thought about it, I realized he was probably just talking in his sleep anyway and didn't really mean it. Dailan was sweet and charming in his own sort of way, but he was not a mushy I'm-so-in-love-with-you type of guy.

I smiled when I saw Donna walking from the parking lot in the far off distance. "I had to park a mile away. I can't believe all these crazy people out shopping this early already," she said as she got closer.

We walked into the mall and Donna immediately gravitated to the bathing suits that were out already. She had wanted to do some shopping for clothes to take on her honeymoon, which was now only three months away. She held a plum-colored two-piece up to her body. "How do you think this would look?" she asked.

"Well, I think it's pretty, but you can't buy a bathing suit without trying it on." She hurried up and grabbed some others that she liked from the rack and went into the fitting room.

"Come in with me," she said. I sat down on the chair inside the fitting room as she began to try on the bathing suits. I shook my head as she finished putting on the plum-colored suit.

"Yeah, I don't like it either," she said as she handed it to me to hang back up. She grabbed the next one off the rack and began to try it on.

"I like that one," I said somewhat expressionlessly, looking at her in a very flattering royal blue tankini.

"What's wrong?" Donna asked as she turned from the mirror to look at me. Sometimes she was so in tune with my emotions it scared me.

I shook my head, not really wanting to unload my issues on her today, but she was insistent. I told her about running into Mrs. Aymes last night, and how I was terrified of what she would now do. Donna's reaction was similar to Dailan's, but in a more polite manner, she told me to tell her to mind her business. I went on to tell her how I had never heard from my parents on my birthday – well, actually, my mom. I never expected phone calls from my dad for my birthday.

"When was the last time that you talked to them?"

"About a month ago. My mom called me to ream me about hurting my sister's feelings when I ran into her at the ice skating rink. I'm sure my sister left out the nasty things she said to me that day."

"Oh, Nicole, I'm sorry. But that's their issue, not yours, and you have to stop letting it affect your life. If that's how they choose to behave over something that happened years ago, then let them. You did nothing wrong."

Donna's words put me at ease. I was so glad that I had someone else that knew about my past that I could confide in.

"Hey, Donna?"

"Yeah," she said, turning around from the mirror again.

"What does 'I think I could fall in love with you' mean?"

The serious look on Donna's face suddenly turned into a full-fledged grin. "Oh my God! Did he tell you that he loved you!"

"No, not exactly, he said 'I *think* I could fall in love with you,'" I clarified.

"Well, how did you respond?"

"I didn't; he fell asleep right after he said it. I think he may have actually already been asleep when he said it."

"Well, then, it was his subconscious talking. Which means he really does love you," Donna said with a smile.

I knew that this was what any *normal* girl would love to hear from a guy that she couldn't get enough of, but I was far from normal.

"Nicole, what's the matter?"

"I don't know. I don't do the whole relationship thing too well. Even if I did, he's going to be leaving in a few months."

"Well, do you love him?" Donna asked.

I was silent for a brief second. "I think I do and that's what scares me. It just feels so much different than it did with Drew. I feel like I need him, Donna."

Donna smiled. "That's okay, Nicole. It's okay to need someone. Dailan is a great guy."

"I know he is, but that still doesn't change the fact that he's leaving."

"Even that's something you guys could probably work out if you really wanted to make it work."

"Really, how?"

"I don't know, but I'm sure there's a way," she said as the hopeless romantic side in her was out in full force.

I shrugged my shoulders, not being able to see any way of maintaining a relationship that was an ocean apart.

Two shopping bags full of clothes later – all Donna's – and we were done. I helped her carry them to her car and gave her a hug goodbye, then made my way back to my car. I sat in my car for some time, thinking about the conversation I had with Donna earlier. For the first time, I began to realize just how much I was going to miss Dailan when he was gone. Yet another mess I had gotten myself into with him. I remembered the comment that his boss had made at the Christmas party about him changing his mind and staying here permanently. In the back of my mind, I was hoping that he would, even though I would never let him know that. That would be a decision he would have to make on his own. I started up my car to head home as my phone began to ring from inside my purse. I quickly answered it. I smiled upon seeing Dailan's name on the caller ID.

"Hey, sexy! Guess who's at your apartment and who's not?"

I looked at my clock; it was only 2:45. "You said five o'clock."

"I told you one day I'd surprise you."

"I will be there in fifteen minutes. There's a front door key under the doormat. Just let yourself in."

"Nicole, you know you really shouldn't just leave a key to your house out on your front porch. Anyone could just break in," he said with concern.

"Yeah, well, if you locked yourself out as many times as I had, then you would keep a key out too! Besides, it's not like I live in a bad neighborhood."

"That doesn't matter, anyone could -"

I cut him off mid-sentence. "I will see you in fifteen minutes, Dailan!" I hung up the phone and threw it into my purse. I backed out of the parking spot and began the short drive home. I smiled, thinking about Dailan's concern for my safety. It was nice to have someone who cared - even if it was just temporary.

Chapter 33

I threw my keys on the kitchen table and wrapped my arms around Dailan, who was standing in my kitchen, talking on his phone. I could tell right away that he was talking to Ryan just by the way he was joking around.

"Well, I'll still kick your butt," Dailan teased.

He pulled me close and kissed me on the head. "She's right here; do you want to talk to her?" Dailan asked.

Dailan handed me his phone. "Hey, Ryan, are you having fun?" I asked.

"Yeah, it's lots of fun. You should see the big hill I went down this morning."

"Well, you better be careful."

"I will," he said. "I'll see you on Monday, Miss Morgan."

"Okay, here's your Uncle Dailan back," I said as I handed the phone back to Dailan.

Dailan finished up his call and sat down next to me on the couch. "What a nice surprise, to have you actually show up two hours early," I said as I moved closer and rested my head on his shoulder. I hit the remote control and turned on the TV. I gave Dailan the remote and he instantly became engrossed in the March Madness basketball game. I moved my head to his chest, listening to his heartbeat. I closed my eyes while he gently played with my hair. I felt so relaxed that I slowly fell into a deep sleep.

I woke up to the touch of Dailan's lips on my forehead.

"Wow, sleeping beauty's awake."

"What time is it?" I asked as I lifted my head off his chest, still feeling half out of it.

"Five-thirty," he said.

"Why didn't you wake me up?"

"Because you were tired and I wanted to finish watching the basketball game, even though it was a little hard to hear through your snoring," he teased.

"Shut up," I said as I playfully punched his arm.

181

"Are you hungry?" he asked.

"Starving," I answered. "Can I just get myself ready before we go?"

"Take your time," he said as he became absorbed in the new basketball game that had just started up.

I went into the bathroom, washed my face, brushed my teeth, and reapplied my make-up.

"I'm ready," I said as I came out into the living room while Dailan was screaming at the TV.

I grabbed the remote and turned the TV off. "You're going to get high blood pressure watching that," I said.

He got up from the couch and put his coat on and we headed out the door. We decided on the new Thai restaurant that had just opened up a couple of weeks ago. I had never tasted Thai food before and was hoping I would like it. Dailan assured me that I would, but I was still a little apprehensive.

The restaurant was very welcoming, decorated in white and pink orchids. We were immediately greeted by a hostess dressed in traditional Thai dress. She had her hands pressed together at her chest and said something in her native language that I assumed was a hello. She took us to our seats and I sat down taking in all the Buddhist images scattered among the restaurant. After scrutinizing the menu forever, I finally decided on some dish that I couldn't even pronounce. I just knew that it was stir-fried sweet and sour sauce with pineapple, onions, scallions, bell peppers, tomato, and carrots. Dailan kept me thoroughly entertained by telling me his experience that he had with eating Thai food for the very first time.

"You know you're not making me feel any better about trying this with these stories."

"You'll like it; I promise," he said.

The waiter came out with the soup that Dailan had insisted that I order. He stared at me waiting for me to take a spoonful.

"Go ahead, try it," he said with a smile.

I picked up my spoon and put some in my mouth. My face didn't know what expression to make when the soup hit my taste buds. It was a mixture of sweet, salty, sour, and spicy all rolled into one. I hurriedly took a sip of water as Dailan was unable to control his laughter from my reaction. By the time I had taken my third spoonful, I actually kind of liked it. My entrée was even better, still flooding my taste buds with different sensations, but it was really good.

We finished and got up from the table. "Well, that was fun, to get to experience a first with you," I said.

Dailan took my hand and we began to walk out, when I looked over at a table in the far off distance, noticing my mom and dad with their friends Ted and Amelia. My mom and dad had their backs toward me. I could have made it out unnoticed and I almost did until I heard Amelia shout, "Nicole?"

Shit, shit, shit. I was having a great night too. I took a deep breath, gripped Dailan's hand tighter, and walked over to where they were sitting.

"Hi," I said nonchalantly.

"Nicole!" my mom said with a smile that grew bigger as her eyes moved to Dailan.

"Dailan, this is my Mom, Dad, Ted, and Amelia," I said, pointing each one out to him.

"Oh, Dailan, it's nice to finally meet you," my mom said, sounding as if I talked to her all the time about him.

I watched my dad's reaction and was surprised that he was unusually quite pleasant as he shook Dailan's hand and actually smiled.

"I'm surprised you were able to get Nicole to try Thai food; you know she never likes trying anything new. Lasagna with jarred sauce, that's her specialty," my mom said as she and Amelia both laughed. What she failed to recognize was that her poor attempt at humor was just pissing me off. "We just came down last minute to celebrate Ted's birthday, a little early, but better early than never," my mom said. "Oh, and speaking of birthdays, Nicole, please don't forget your nephew's is next week. I'm still hearing about it from your sister because you mailed the kids' Christmas presents two weeks late."

I couldn't take it anymore. My jaw dropped. I felt my insides raging and I knew that I couldn't control what was about to come out of my mouth. "Well, since you're the birthday police, then maybe you should have someone reminding you as well."

"What are you talking about?" my mom asked with a look of confusion.

"I don't know, Mom, but my birthday was three days ago and I didn't get a phone call from anyone in my family. Oh wait, I got an e-mail from my brother who's a million miles away, but still took the time to wish me a happy birthday."

My dad looked down at the table as if he were embarrassed to be having this conversation in front of Ted and Amelia.

"Oh my God, Nicole, I am so sorry!" my mother said. "The kids had that awful stomach bug and I was trying to help Renee out -"

"Of course, it's always about Renee," I started.

"Nicole," Dailan said gently in an effort to get me to stop.

"It's okay, Dailan, this is how my so-called family is." If I hadn't known better, I would have sworn that he somehow made his phone ring right at that particular moment to get out of a very awkward situation.

"I have to take this call. I'll meet you at the car," he said, giving me a look that was basically telling me not to go any further with my verbal assault on them.

"It was nice meeting you," everyone said to Dailan in unison.

"Yeah, you too," Dailan said as he answered his phone and walked out the door.

"Well, it was good seeing you all. Happy birthday, Ted," I said as he nodded with gratitude.

"Nicole!" my mother shouted with desperation in her voice. I said nothing to her or my dad as I walked towards the door, almost making it completely out until my dad caught me in the vestibule.

"Nicole," he shouted.

"What?"

"You have your mother in tears in there; you go in and apologize to her."

"For what? For insulting me any chance that she can get or because she couldn't even pick up the phone and say happy birthday, because she's so far up Renee's ass that she'd probably have to ask her permission to do it."

"Nicole, I mean it, if you don't go in there and apologize, you are no longer part of this family." My dad was using his usual bullying tactics that would normally work on me.

"Oh really – well, then, I guess now it will finally be official, because for the past eight years you have been doing everything in your power to make me feel like I wasn't part of this family anyway. So this should be a big weight off your shoulders, now you don't have to *pretend* to even tolerate your fucked up daughter."

"You watch your mouth, young lady."

I rolled my eyes at him and gave him a sarcastic smile. "I am a grown woman and no longer your concern. I will say what I want, when I want. Enjoy the rest of your dinner." I looked into my dad's hazel eyes, for the first time not feeling afraid to stand up to him. I flung my purse over my shoulder and walked out of the restaurant. I finally confronted big bad Nick Morgan, even though I might have lost my family in the process – it strangely felt good.

Beth Rinyu

Chapter 34

"Are you okay?" Dailan asked as I got in the car.

"Yup, I'm fine," I said, trying to play it off coolly. He looked at me in disbelief. "Really, I'm good," I said.

He started up the car and I was grateful that he didn't ask any more questions. We arrived back at my house and rented a movie on demand. I cuddled on the couch with Dailan as he held me tightly. Even though I didn't tell him what happened, he seemed to sense that I needed the comfort of his arms around me. This time it was Dailan who had fallen asleep somewhere in the middle of the movie. I was still wide awake from my little nap that I had taken earlier. I looked up and watched him sleep as the tears began to form in my eyes. Strangely, I wasn't crying over what had happened tonight with my dad. It was because at that moment, I knew I was in love with Dailan O'Maley and there was nothing I could do to change that. I rested my head back on his chest as the tears streamed down my face. I hugged him tightly and closed my eyes, wishing I could freeze time and never have this moment end.

I woke up Dailan when the movie was over and led him into my bed in his sleep stupor. I took off his shoes and climbed in next to him. I pulled the covers over us and wrapped my arms around him, this time falling into a deep sleep as well.

I woke up to the bright sunlight shining through my bedroom window. Dailan was already awake and laying silently as he played with my hair and kissed me on the head.

"Good morning," I said.

"How did I even get in your bed last night?" he asked.

"I carried you," I joked. "You walked in, silly, with a little help. You were pretty out of it."

"Yeah, I must have been," he said, running his hand through his hair.

"Are you hungry?" I asked.

"No, I actually got to get going soon. I want to take a shower and get changed before I go get Ryan. Do you want to come with me while I get him?" he asked.

"Oh, I would love to, but I have to get caught up on laundry and lesson plans," I said regretfully. I would much rather be spending the day with Dailan and Ryan, but I had been ignoring all my other responsibilities these past couple of days, being so caught up in spending time with Dailan.

Dailan had a quick cup of coffee before leaving. I hugged him tightly at the door as we said our goodbyes. "Thanks for the great weekend," I said.

"Anytime," he said kissing me on the forehead. "I'll talk to you later," he said as he walked out the door. I watched him pull away with heaviness in my chest. He wasn't even gone for a minute and I already missed him. *Snap out of this, Nicole, you can't be feeling this way. Soon he will be gone for longer than that,* I reminded myself.

I put a load of laundry in and poured another cup of coffee. I pulled my planner from my bag and did my best to try and concentrate on my lesson plans.

The ringing of my phone broke my concentration. I felt a knot in my stomach when I saw that it was my mother. I reluctantly answered, even though I wasn't in the mood to deal with it.

"Nicole, I'm so sorry about your birthday," she started out right away.

"Mom, just drop it. It's over and done with."

There was an awkward silence before she began to talk again. "Well, your friend certainly is handsome," she said. This was so typical of her. She always skirted around the issue at hand by changing the topic

"Mom, just stop!" I couldn't take it anymore.

"Stop what?"

"Trying to sweep everything under the carpet like it doesn't exist."

"Nicole, I don't know –"

"Oh, Mom, come on! I'm surprised you're even allowed to call me. Didn't your husband forbid it? I'm not part of your family anymore - remember?"

"Your father doesn't dictate to me who I can and cannot talk to, Nicole."

"Mom, you've always teetered when it came to me; almost like you were disobeying your husband by having a relationship with your daughter. Well, I'm going to make it easy for you. You made a commitment to him till death do you part. I'm just your daughter; you have no obligation to me."

"Oh, Nicole, stop with the drama and start considering other people's feelings. Your father never got over the hurt that you caused him."

"The hurt that I caused him! Please tell me that you really did not just say that to me. Do you have any idea how scared and alone I felt, Mom? Did you even care or were you just too busy stroking your husband's ego because his fucked up daughter humiliated him so bad?"

"Nicole, stop it; that's not true!"

"Just leave me alone, Mom, all of you. I'm trying to get over my past and it seems like every time I'm around you and Dad, it's just a constant reminder. Now you don't have to feel like you're going against anyone." I hung up the phone before she had a chance to respond.

I did my best to finish up my lesson plans. I put them away once I was finally somewhat satisfied with them. I pulled the spelling tests out that I needed to grade and, before I knew it, they were all done and already entered into the online grading system. I found myself to be quite productive when I was angry. I looked outside to what seemed to be a beautiful afternoon. I quickly changed and decided to go for a walk. I stopped at the end of the driveway to talk briefly to Mrs. Tallone and her man-friend, who were just getting back from church. I continued, listening to my iPod. It was a beautiful spring afternoon. The temperature was already feeling like it was in the 70s. I walked up onto the bay beach and looked out at the water, trying to clear my head. I wondered what Dailan and Ryan were doing on this beautiful afternoon and briefly contemplated calling them, but quickly changed my mind. They hadn't seen each other in almost a week; they didn't need me tagging along with whatever plans they had. I closed my eyes and took in the warm sun while Bruce Springsteen blared through my headphones.

I looked up when I felt someone standing over top of me. I used my hands as a visor to block out the sun. I pulled my headphones out of my ears and immediately stood up, noticing that it was my ex-boyfriend Drew. He must have been out for his daily run, which he always took along the beach.

"Hey!" I said with a smile, being taken a little off guard when he wrapped his arms around me to give me a hug.

"How have you been, Nic?"

"Good, really good," I said. "Still running every day, I see."

He nodded. We both sat back down and began to talk. "So how are things with Heather – right?" I asked.

Drew shook his head. "Pretty good; we're engaged," he said, sounding like he was almost afraid to tell me.

"That's great. When is the big day?"

"Not until October. I never knew so much went into planning a wedding," he said.

"Yeah, tell me about it. Donna is almost nonexistent with planning hers."

"How have you been? Did you ever get that job?" he asked.

"I did and I love it."

"That's great. I'm sure all the kids love you."

I smiled and shrugged my shoulders.

"So, are you seeing anyone?" he asked.

I was silent for a moment before answering. "Yeah, I am."

"Well, he's a lucky guy."

"Thanks," I said quietly.

The look in his eyes seemed to reflect mixed emotions. He was silent for a moment as he gazed into my eyes. "I still think about you a lot," he said.

I took a deep breath. "Congratulations, Drew. I know you will make a great husband."

He nodded. "Well, I better get back to my run. It was good seeing you, Nic," he said as he stood up.

"You too."

I watched as he ran off, slowly becoming just a small speck in the distance. I was truly happy for him and his new life that he was planning. I realized that although I had once loved Drew very much, the love I felt for Dailan was so different. It was much more intense, like none I've ever known, and it scared me half to death.

Chapter 35

As much as I tried to avoid it, Monday morning had arrived. I stopped in Valerie's office on my way in to find out the outcome of her meeting with Mrs. Aymes on Friday afternoon. It was just as I suspected; she accused Valerie and me of ganging up on her son. She refused to listen to anything that Valerie had to say. I cringed as I thought of the new ammunition that she might have against me.

I left her office and arrived at my classroom, savoring the last few minutes of silence. My stomach flipped when I pulled my phone from my purse and read the text I had just gotten from Dailan: *I missed waking up with you this morning....have a great day, beautiful.* This was the first I had heard from him since he left my house yesterday morning. I quickly texted him back: *Me too and you too.* I was just about to put my phone away when another text came through: *See you tonight?* I quickly replied: *Perhaps....call me after 3.* I threw my phone in my purse and mentally prepared myself for the chaos coming down the hallway. The day went by smoothly, partly because Cameron Aymes was absent, much to my delight. Ryan was so excited to see me. I spent my whole recess duty listening to him tell me about his ski trip.

I almost forgot about my "up in the air" plans with Dailan that night until my phone began to ring on my way home from work.

"Hey you," I answered.

"Well, I just happened to get out of work early so I wanted to see if you wanted to come over and hang out with me and Ryan?"

"Hmmm.....sure, why not? What time?"

"Whenever, come over now, I'm here."

"Okay, I just want to run home and get changed really quickly," I said.

I hung up the phone and finished driving home. I ran into my apartment, quickly changing into my jeans and a t-shirt before heading back out the door. It was another beautiful spring-like day. I rolled down the windows and let the fresh air in on the drive over. Dailan opened the front door before I had even got to the porch. I was greeted with one of his deep passionate kisses that made my stomach drop. I tensed up the way I always did whenever I knew Ryan was around and Dailan would kiss me. "Will you relax? He's in the backyard with my dad," he said just as I noticed that there was another car besides Dailan's in the driveway. "Sorry, he just stopped over unexpectedly," Dailan said.

"Why are you apologizing? I think your dad's great." I followed Dailan into the backyard where Ryan was having a baseball catch with his grandfather.

"Hi, Miss Morgan," Ryan said excitedly.

I smiled and waved, not wanting to break his concentration.

But it was too late, Jack O'Maley took off his baseball glove and came walking toward me. "Nicole, it's so nice to see you again," he said giving me a quick kiss on the cheek.

"You too, Mr. O'Maley," I said with a smile.

"Please call me 'Jack.'"

I nodded. He had such a way of making me feel instantly comfortable around him. I found myself secretly wishing that my own dad could be that way.

"Grandpop," Ryan whined as he waited anxiously for him to throw the ball back.

Jack handed the glove and ball to Dailan. "I'm taking a break; have a catch with your nephew."

Dailan immediately began to tease Ryan before throwing him the ball. "Okay, Ryan, try not to throw like a girl."

"I don't throw like a girl, you do, fool," Ryan teased back.

Jack and I both laughed at the way Dailan and Ryan playfully bantered back and forth.

"I have to say, I was a little apprehensive about Dailan taking on such a big responsibility with Ryan. I didn't think he had it in him, but he's doing a great job. His brother would be proud of

194

him." Jack said as he kept his eyes on Dailan and Ryan having a catch.

I nodded in total agreement.

"A little selfish part of me was wishing he didn't get the court approvals so quickly; or maybe not at all. I like having my son and grandson just a car ride away instead of a plane ride," Jack said.

"Dailan got the approval to take Ryan out of the country?" I asked, trying to hide the surprise in my voice.

"Yes, just today," Jack said with a little sadness in his voice.

"Oh," I said, biting my lip and trying not to look how I was feeling, which was disheartened.

"Well, I guess there's still time for him to change his mind. His boss was going on and on about him when I picked him up for lunch a few weeks ago. I know he's hoping that he decides to stay."

I listened closely as Jack O'Maley continued. "Of course, there's always the chance that you could get him to change his mind."

"Oh, Mr. O' - I mean, Jack. If there's anything that I've learned over the years, it's that you have to let people make their own decisions on what's best for them, even if it's not what I want."

He smiled warmly at me. "I really like you, Nicole, and I know that my son really does too. I just hope that he makes the right decision."

I smiled back. *I hope he does too,* I thought to myself.

Jack's wife Annette was away visiting family so Jack was insistent that he take us to dinner. Jack began his endless stories about Dailan throughout dinner and I found that I never tired of listening to them. Dailan just rolled his eyes and endlessly tried to change the topic.

We finished up with dinner and said our goodbyes. Ryan hugged his grandfather tightly before jumping in the backseat of Dailan's car.

"Thanks for dinner, Mr. O'Maley," I said. He raised his eyebrow at me. "I mean, Jack."

"Anytime, Nicole."

"See ya, Dad," Dailan said as Jack patted him on the shoulder and made his way to his car.

Ryan chattered non-stop the whole car ride home and before we knew it, we were pulling into the driveway.

"Miss Morgan?" Ryan asked, taking off his seat belt.

"Yeah."

"I was thinking, would I still have to call you 'Miss Morgan' if you and my uncle D get married?"

I looked over at Dailan, who was looking straight ahead, expressionless, almost acting like he hadn't heard what Ryan had just asked. I didn't know how to answer that question, so I did the best that I could. "Umm Ryan, I'll make a deal with you. You can call me 'Nicole' outside of school, but in school you have to call me 'Miss Morgan.'"

"Cool," Ryan said with a smile. "But then you would be my Aunt Nicole if you guys got married."

I laughed it off, not knowing what else to do. Dailan quickly got out of the car and opened Ryan's car door, not adding to the conversation in any way. Ryan stepped out of the car and looked up at Dailan. "Uncle Dailan, can she be my Aunt Nicole one day?" Dailan picked up Ryan and turned him upside down. "Ahhh, put me down," Ryan said as he hung over Dailan's shoulder. And just like that, Dailan had diverted the question - a question that I strangely wanted to know the answer to.

Chapter 36

"Ryan, it's nine-thirty," Dailan said.

"Aww," Ryan pouted as Dailan pulled him off the couch. "Good night, Miss Morgan – I mean, Nicole." Ryan smiled and flashed me his adorable dimples.

"Good night, sweetie."

"I'll be right back, I have to make sure that *somebody* brushes their teeth," Dailan said, messing up Ryan's hair as the two of them went up the stairs.

I got up from the couch and looked around at the photographs that lined the walls and fireplace mantel. I focused my attention on Dailan's brother's wedding picture. He looked a lot like Dailan, but with darker hair. His wife was beautiful. She had long dark hair just like Ryan had described her. They looked so in love in that picture. I felt immediate sorrow thinking about how their love story ended. I took in all of the baby pictures of Ryan that covered the walls from birth right on up to his school picture from last year. I picked up the beautiful black and white portrait of Ryan and his mother. Ryan looked to be about three years old. She was leaning behind him with her arms wrapped tightly around him as their cheeks pressed up against each other. It exuded the love of a mother for her child perfectly. My chest tightened thinking that this woman that Ryan loved so much was now gone from his life forever. I put the picture down and stood in silence. Dailan came back down the stairs and I turned around from the mantle.

"Your brother looked a lot like you," I said.

He nodded and I watched, as the smile that was just on his face disappeared.

I moved closer to him and wrapped my arms around his neck. "I have to get going."

He moved my hair out of the way and kissed my neck. "Stay," he whispered in my ear. His voice sounded so sexy that my insides instantly longed for him.

I looked up at him as if he were crazy. That was a definite no-no when Ryan was here. "You know that's not possible tonight," I said.

"Nicole, Ryan is already out like a light and once he falls asleep, he's done. It takes me forever to get him up in the morning."

He continued to kiss my neck, making my resistance even weaker. "Dailan, we can't –"

He ignored me and kissed me on my lips to stop me from talking. He picked me up and carried me up the stairs, ignoring my feeble protest. It took me a while to relax and stop thinking about Ryan, who was asleep in the next room. But Dailan helped to relax me; quite a few times, making me happy that I had let him talk me into staying. Once Dailan was *satisfied* that I was *satisfied*, his movements became a little more intense. I responded eagerly to each thrust.

"Oh, Nicole, baby," Dailan whimpered in delight. I pulled him closer, feeling like I couldn't get enough of him, as we both found our release at the same time. "I love you," he whispered. His words were barely audible. He lay on top of me, trying to catch his breath as I tried to think of how to reply. I ran my hands through his disheveled hair. I was just about to respond when the bedroom door flung open and I saw Ryan standing in the doorway. I gasped and quickly pushed Dailan off of me. I pulled the sheet over my head in my best attempt to hide.

Dailan sat up and threw on his boxers. "He's sleepwalking," he said. I stayed hidden under the sheet until Dailan walked Ryan back to his room. I sat up, waiting for Dailan to come back in. I decided I was going to leave. I should have listened to the logical side of me and this wouldn't be happening right now.

Dailan finally came back in. "Oh my God, Dailan, he just walked in on his uncle having sex with his teacher. We just caused him to be lying on a couch talking to a shrink one day years from now."

Dailan laughed at my assessment of the whole situation. "He sleepwalks from time to time. Trust me, he didn't really see anything; he was sleeping. Technically, we weren't having sex anyway – we just finished," he said with a grin

"I should really go," I said as I started to grab my bra from the floor.

"No, you're not going anywhere, it's almost midnight, and you're not going home this late." He pushed me down on the bed and hovered over top of me so I couldn't go anywhere. "Besides, I like waking up with you," he said, turning on his side and pulling me toward him. I didn't put up any more of a fight, because I knew I wouldn't win anyway. As I began to feel myself drift off to sleep, the last thought on my mind was the response that never got said to Dailan – I love you too.

I was wide awake before the alarm on my phone even went off. I hurried up and turned it off, not wanting to take a chance of waking Ryan. I looked over at Dailan, who was still asleep. I was about to get up and get dressed when he pulled me toward him.

"Where are you going?" he asked as he began to tickle me.

I was laughing as I tried to break free of his tickle assault. "I have to go home and get ready for work. Remember, it's Tuesday and Ryan will be awake in a few short hours."

I had my back turned toward him as he hugged me tightly. He began to kiss my bare back while gently caressing my breasts. As perfect as it felt, I had to tear myself away, if I planned on getting out of there unseen by Ryan and getting to work on time.

I turned around to him, "Dailan, as much as I would love to spend the day in bed with you, I have to get going."

He sighed, giving me one last kiss on the cheek before releasing me from his arms.

I sat up and began to dress while he watched me. "What are you staring at?" I asked.

"You're just so beautiful."

"Oh, I'm sure I look really beautiful right now," I joked, knowing that I probably looked like a mess after just waking up.

"You do," he said with a serious expression on his face.

"You are too kind." I leaned down and gave him a kiss.

He got up and started to dress. "I can see my way out; go back to sleep," I said. He ignored me as he pulled up his pants and followed me out of the bedroom. I tiptoed past Ryan's bedroom and headed down the steps to the front door.

"Geez, I feel like I'm having an affair, sneaking around like this. Are you sure he was sleepwalking?" I was still on edge over what had happened last night.

"I'm positive." He wrapped his arms around me and hugged me tightly. I hugged him back, thinking that maybe he would say those three little words again – but he didn't. So I decided to keep my feelings in for now as well, even though I wanted to shout it from the rooftop at that particular moment.

Chapter 37

I called Donna on my drive to work, filling her in on what had transpired last night. "Well, did you say it back?" her voice radiated from the speaker of my phone.

"I was going to, but then Ryan walked in," I said feeling myself tensing up at my words.

"What!" Donna exclaimed.

"He was sleepwalking. Dailan swears that he had no clue what was going on."

"Oh, Nicole, this could only happen to you." She laughed.

"The thing is, I don't know if he really meant it or if it was well you know –"

"If it was what?"

"In the heat of the moment – if you know what I mean?" I couldn't believe that I was actually getting embarrassed talking about this to my best friend, with whom I shared everything. But my relationship with Dailan was so different than any other I had been in. I felt like I wanted to keep our intimate moments between just him and me.

"Nicole, he said it. It doesn't matter when or how – he loves you. Now the question is, are you going to love him back or are you going to run away?"

"Oh, Donna, it's so much more complicated than that."

I pulled in the school parking lot and parked my car. I remained in the car and told her about my conversation with Jack O'Maley last night, and how Dailan had gotten approval to take Ryan out of the country.

"Wait, Dailan didn't mention to you that he got the approval? His dad did?" I could tell by the tone in her voice that she felt it was wrong on Dailan's part to have not said anything to me.

"Yes," I said.

"Well if you really do love him and want to continue your relationship, then I think you guys need to sit down and figure out what's going to happen once he leaves. Just remember you two aren't the only ones involved in this. There's a little boy who seems to be growing quite attached to you too!"

I hung up the phone feeling disheartened. I had grown quite attached to Ryan too. I thought about the picture of him and his mother sitting on the mantle. Would I soon be someone else that he grew to love that he would have to say goodbye to as well?

I pulled myself together and prepared myself for the school day. I realized that I was super early when I walked in and the only other person who had greeted me was the school janitor. I walked down to my classroom and decided to get working on my April bulletin board. I jammed my finger with the stapler and I wasn't very pleased. Just when I thought my mood couldn't have gotten any worse – Mrs. Aymes was standing in my doorway. I was glad that I had opted to skip breakfast because I was quite sure my stomach would have been churning ten times worse than it already was.

"Hi, can I help you with something?" I asked, trying to sound as professional as possible.

She walked closer to where I was standing. "Well, actually, I came in to get Cameron's work from yesterday and today – he has the flu," she said rather snidely. I knew that this was not the real reason for her visit. She knew better than anyone did what the proper protocol was for collecting missed assignments. Still, I went to Cameron's desk and began to pull out the books that he needed in an effort to get her out of my classroom as soon as possible.

"You know, the flu is still going around really bad," she said. I didn't lift my head from Cameron's desk, although I did find her attempt at small talk a little odd. "So you should really watch kissing guys in bars – wouldn't want the teacher getting sick now," she added once I finally looked up.

I wasn't sure how to respond. I knew what I *wanted* to say, but if I wanted to keep my job, I needed to re-think that response. "Here are all the books Cameron will need. Yesterday's assignments are on my webpage. I will be updating it with today's assignments this afternoon," I said as I tried handing her the books.

"You know, come to think of it, that guy you were kissing looked very familiar. Almost like the uncle of one of your students," she said, finally taking the books out of my hand.

"If you don't need anything else, Mrs. Aymes, I have some work I need to finish up."

"Actually I do have something else for you. I want you and Mrs. Kane to stop singling out my son for everything that goes wrong in this classroom and maybe I won't have to tell my friends on the Board of Ed that sweet little Miss Morgan was making out with Ryan O'Maley's uncle."

I never wanted to smack someone so badly in my life. But I refused to let her get the best of me and stayed calm. "You do what you have to do, Mrs. Aymes. But my job while I'm in this classroom is to teach the kids right from wrong. So if a child is misbehaving or doing something inappropriate, then I'm not going to ignore it just because his mother thinks she has something to hold over my head. What I do with my personal life is nobody's business but my own." I was so proud of myself for the way that I handled her, even though on the inside my stomach was in knots.

"Well, clearly it is my business when you're favoring his nephew over the other students." She was relentless with trying to egg me on, but I wasn't biting.

"I'll have today's assignments on the webpage at the end of the day. Have a nice day." I went back to my bulletin board and started stapling as if she weren't even standing there. I could still feel her standing there for a few seconds. I heard her finally leave when she must have realized that I wasn't going to play her game.

I sat back down at my desk and realized that my hands were shaking. I decided that I needed to come clean with Valerie. I didn't want her being caught off guard by hearing a twisted version from someone else. I called down to the office to see if she was there. She told me that she would take a walk down to see me. I waited anxiously for her to arrive.

"Hey, that bulletin board looks great!" she said as she entered.

"Thanks," I said, trying my best to muster a smile.

"What's wrong?" she asked, apparently seeing the apprehension on my face.

I held nothing back. I told her that I had been seeing Dailan for the past four months. I continued, telling her about my visit from Mrs. Aymes and her threat that she had made if I didn't abide by her wishes.

I waited in angst for her response. "You did the right thing," she said. "Don't even entertain anything she says."

"Valerie, you know that I would never let my outside relationships interfere with my job."

"Nicole, you don't have to prove yourself to me. I know what a great teacher you are and so do the people that matter. She does know a few people on the Board of Ed, but for the most part, everyone pretty much knows what she is all about. Just ride out these next few months as best as you can and then next year Cameron and his mom will be some poor third grade teacher's problem."

I felt better that I had confided in Valerie, but I was still on edge for the rest of the day. I checked my messages at the end of the day to find a text from Dailan:

I have to go on a last-minute trip to Boston, be back tomorrow. I'll call you later.

I was hoping that I would hear from him soon, I felt like I needed to talk to him about what had happened with Mrs. Aymes. Even though I knew his response would be something very inappropriate, I still felt better every time I talked to him about something that was bothering me.

I put my phone back in my purse, relishing the thought of an early night in my pajamas in front of the TV. I was going to try my best to put Mrs. Aymes and her threat out of my mind. There was no use worrying about something that was out of my hands. I was just about to leave for the day when my classroom phone began to ring.

"Hello," I answered anxious of who it could be.

"Nicole, it's Valerie, can you come and see me on your way out?"

Somehow, from the sound of her voice, I knew that my worries about Mrs. Aymes weren't going to rest as easily as I had hoped.

Beth Rinyu

Chapter 38

I walked into Valerie's office, apprehensive of what my presence was needed for. Valerie sat at her desk, signaling for me to shut the door behind me. I sat down at her desk as my stomach began to churn.

"Well, our *friend* got a hold of Dr. Joyner," she said.

I looked down at the floor, not knowing what to say.

"I'm so glad that you told me everything, Nicole, so I wasn't blind-sided."

"What did she say?" I asked.

"Oh, basically that you and I are picking on her son. And she made sure that she told him about your relationship with Mr. O'Maley."

"Valerie, that is my personal life. I don't see why she has to drag that into anything."

"I completely understand, Nicole. I explained to Dr. Joyner and he seems to understand as well. I just want you to be prepared in case she shows up at the Board of Ed meeting tonight and tries to rip you up."

"Great," I sighed.

"Nicole, I support you on this. I've seen what a difference you've made this past year with your class –*with all of the children*, not just Ryan."

Valerie's backing on this meant a lot to me. "Thanks, Valerie."

"You're welcome. If it makes you feel any better, I think she may hate me just as much as she hates you."

I gave her a quick smile and got up to leave.

"Go home and get a good night sleep," she said.

I arrived home and immediately changed into my pajamas. I could feel my head actually throbbing as I began to surmise what was taking place at the Board of Ed meeting right now. I knew that it was only a matter of time before all of the other parents would be hearing about whatever distorted story Mrs. Aymes would be spinning. Stories spread around that school like wildfire. I still hadn't heard from Dailan and I was unsure if even hearing his voice would put me at ease at this particular moment. I dialed his number and patiently waited for him to answer. After the fifth ring, I realized that he was probably tied up with work and waited for his voicemail message to end.

Hey, Dailan, it's me. Give me a call when you get a chance. I really need someone to talk to. I miss you lots....bye.

It was only 8 p.m., but it felt like midnight to me. I was so tired; I went into to my bedroom to lie down, taking my phone with me in case Dailan called, soon falling into a deep sleep.

I woke up extra early from all the extra sleep I had gotten. I immediately checked my phone; no calls from Dailan. I felt heaviness in my chest and stinging in my eyes. Last night of all nights, I needed to talk to him.

I jumped into the shower, trying to prepare myself for what lay ahead today after the drama from yesterday and the meeting last night. I left for work a half hour earlier than normal. My stomach was in knots. Caffeine always helped me feel a little better, so I decided to stop at the coffee shop on my way in. I pulled into the parking lot and was half tempted to text Dailan, but I found that I was a little angry with him for not calling me last night. I knew I was being a little silly and there was probably a good reason for it, but still I put my phone away, deciding not to text him.

I walked into the coffee shop, feeling a little better as I breathed in the heavy aroma of coffee beans. I looked up at the menu, finally deciding on a raspberry eruption. I stood off to the side, waiting to pay.

"Hi, Nicole." I turned around to see Rick Kincaide, who had just finished ordering his coffee.

"Oh, hi," I said, feeling like a traitor for even talking to him.

"I had to get my double dose of caffeine. I had an early flight from Boston this morning."

Suddenly my ears perked up. I felt a little sneaky trying to get information about Dailan from his worst enemy. I nodded, hoping that he would offer some up – which didn't take too long.

"Are you and O'Maley still together?"

I nodded. "Yes, we are." I couldn't get the words out quickly enough.

"Oh, I just assumed that maybe you weren't. Well, with all the women that he had hanging on him at the client party last night. Of course, he was a little drunk."

I looked at him expressionlessly. I didn't want to give him the satisfaction of knowing that he was pissing me off.

The cashier rang me up as Rick nudged me out of the way. "I got this," he said.

"Oh no, that's okay," I said, but it was too late. He was already collecting his change from the cashier.

"Well, thank you, Mr. Kincaide." I was feeling very uncomfortable, knowing that Dailan wouldn't be very happy if he knew that I allowed him to buy me coffee. But then I remembered right now, I wasn't very happy with Dailan either, if what I was just told was true.

"Please call me 'Rick.' Have a good day, Nicole."

I tried my best to force a smile as I walked out the door, feeling worse about the day already and I hadn't even gotten to work yet. No wonder why I never heard from Dailan last night. I cringed, thinking about what might have happened. But then I reminded myself of the source of this information.

I was backing out of my parking spot when I heard my phone ringing. I quickly looked down to see that it was Dailan and immediately sent it to voicemail. I didn't want to take a chance of getting into it with him before I had to go to work. I had enough on my mind and I needed to save my energy for the day that lay ahead. I told myself on the drive to work that I wasn't going to listen to his voicemail until the end of the day. I was unable to keep that promise. I was typing the password for my voicemail as fast as I could by the time I pulled into the school parking lot.

Hey, Nicole, sorry I didn't call you last night. I'll talk to you later, beautiful. Have a good day.

Whatever, I said to myself. This was exactly why I didn't want to be in a relationship. Because right now I could be focusing on other things like my job, instead of what Dailan did or didn't do last night. Not to mention, I wouldn't have to be worried about my job right now if I weren't in this relationship.

I poked my head into the main office to see if Valerie was in yet. I knew that she attended the meeting last night and even though I didn't want to know what happened, I couldn't help myself. Her secretary was on the phone, but shook her head, signaling that it was okay to go in. I lightly knocked on her door, which was half open, and walked in.

"Well, am I going to be burned at the stake?" I asked, trying my best to make light of the situation.

Valerie smiled. "Well, she got up and spoke, bashing you and me," she said, trying to make the blow seem a little less harsh.

"Did she mention anything about...?" I could feel the coffee churning in my stomach as I waited for Valerie's reply.

Valerie gave me a sympathetic smile and I could tell just by the look on her face that I didn't want to hear what she was going to say. "Well, she said that she witnessed you outside of work acting very inappropriately with a man. Then she didn't mention any names, but she asked what the rules were for a teacher dating a legal guardian of one of her students."

"Acting inappropriately? I kissed him, Valerie, that was it!"

"Nicole, you don't have to explain to me. I think I know you well enough to know that you wouldn't go around doing something tasteless with random men in bars."

"Yes, you know that, but everyone else at the meeting probably now thinks I'm some floozy who goes around groping the parents of my students in bars," I said, getting more disheartened by the minute.

"Well if it makes you feel any better, Ryan's Aunt Lisa was there. Her daughter was getting an award. She got up and spoke very kindly on your behalf."

"What do you think is going to happen now?" I asked.

"Honestly, nothing. I could tell you right now there's nothing in the handbook that addresses parent-teacher relationships. Just give it a few more weeks and she will be on some new crusade."

"I guess I'm just going to have to try and ignore the whispers and speculation behind my back." I said, worrying about the perception that was now out there about me.

"Nicole, when you've been in the education business as long as I've been, this will seem like nothing. Just hold your head up high. You did nothing wrong."

* * *

I went through the day completely on edge, feeling much like one of my students, afraid that I would be called down to the principal's office at any given moment for some other tale that Mrs. Aymes was spinning. I was thankful that Cameron was out sick again today, which was one less problem I had to deal with. Ryan stayed for his Wednesday after school tutoring. I wasn't sure if Dailan would be back from Boston to pick him up or not.

I was both happy and disappointed when I saw Lisa come walking through the door. Happy, because I was still annoyed with Dailan and disappointed because as annoyed as I was - I missed him.

"Hey, Ryan, we got to get moving," Lisa said in a hurried voice.

Ryan quickly gathered up his things. Lisa finally looked at me giving me a warm smile. "There are days when I feel like I'm going crazy, and this is one of them!" she said, looking a little frazzled.

"Thank you," I said, letting her know I appreciated her kind words at the meeting last night.

"No problem; I speak the truth. Some people are just so miserable with their own lives that they feel the need to destroy others and that woman is clearly one of them."

I smiled and helped Ryan load his books into his backpack. "Am I sleeping at your house tonight, Aunt Lisa?" Ryan asked.

"No, your uncle will be home later to pick you up."

They both said their goodbyes and hurriedly made their way out of the classroom.

So, I guess Dailan would be home tonight. I hated how I had to always find out details of his life through third parties. His lack of communication was right up there with his lack of planning on things that drove me crazy. I finished up the day thinking that if I could just make it to June without any more drama – I would be golden. But as long as Cameron Aymes was in my class, that would be very hard to do.

Beth Rinyu

Chapter 39

I arrived home and ate peanut butter and jelly sandwich for dinner while checking my e-mails, in an effort to distract me from texting Dailan. A flash of excitement would always overtake me whenever I saw my brother's name in my inbox. I opened up his e-mail the same way as usual – with a smile.

Hey, Nic-
How's everything? Are you married yet? Any kids? lol. I feel like I've been here for an eternity and can't wait to come home. Am I missing anything good? If you do plan on getting married to your new man, you better wait for me to get home first! Gotta run, just wanted to send you a quick note to let you know I was thinking about you and miss you.
Love,
Justin

No matter how hard I tried, I always found myself wiping tears from my keyboard after one of my brother's e-mails. I felt that he was all I had left in my family and I hated that fact that he was so far away.

To my little Pooh-
I love and miss you more than you will ever know!
PS. If I were to get married…..which I am not! I would never have a wedding without you there…..who would be my flower girl?
Nicole xoxoxo

I scrolled down further to find an e-vite from my sister for my nephew's birthday party. I quickly scanned it over. I had no intention of attending, but I made a mental note that I did have to send him a card. I closed the lid on my laptop and was digging around in the drawer for a pen, when I heard a knock on my door.

I ran to open it hoping that it was who I thought it would be. I flung the door open, pleased to see that it was. His smile almost made me forget that I was annoyed with him; his hug only added to the amnesia.

"Is your phone broken?" he asked.

"No," I said, quickly removing myself from the state of oblivion I was in as I released myself from his embrace.

"I've sent you three texts."

"Oh, sorry my phone is on vibrate and it's in my purse."

He went to kiss me on the lips and I pulled away. "What's the matter?" he asked.

"Nothing," I said, shaking my head and walking away to sit on the couch.

He sat down next to me. "Okay, obviously you're pissed at something, but I can't try to fix it if I don't know what it is," he said calmly.

"Just a bad couple of days."

"What happened?"

"You know what, Dailan? I don't want to talk about it now. I needed someone to talk to last night. But you weren't around."

"I'm sorry that I didn't call you last night. What happened yesterday that got you so upset?"

I unloaded everything that I wanted to tell him last night. I included the information that I had uncovered about the Board of Education meeting as well. I made sure that I let him know that Lisa jumped to my defense, hoping that maybe he would somehow lighten up and change his opinion of her.

"Who cares what those assholes say," he said.

He kissed me again. This time I gave in and kissed him back. He pushed me down on the couch and grazed his lips along my neck. "I couldn't stop thinking about you all day, Nicole. I want you so fuckin' bad," he whispered in my ear. My stomach was doing double flips for him, but I knew I had to stop. We needed to talk and having sex with him tonight would just make that talk even more difficult. I pushed him away taking him a little off guard. "What is your problem?" I could tell he was annoyed.

"Dailan, we need to talk."

"What the fuck, Nicole? Can we talk after?" he said as he placed his lips on mine, kissing me again.

As much as I wanted to continue the kiss and go into the bedroom, I knew that I had to clear things up that were weighing heavily on my mind with him first. "Dailan – no," I said sternly.

He sat up and ran his hand through his hair, "Okay, what's so important that you need to talk to me about?"

"Why didn't you tell me that you got the approval to take Ryan to Ireland?"

"What? I don't know; I didn't think it was that big of a deal."

"Well it is, kind of; because that means that you have a definite timeframe of when you're moving back, right?"

"Probably in the summer. I have to finalize everything still," he said as if it were no big deal.

"What's going to happen with us once you move back?" I had no intention of asking this question to him just yet, but I was on a roll and felt like it had to be addressed.

"I don't know, Nicole, I guess I really haven't thought that far in advance," he said. *Of course, he hadn't; he couldn't make plans from one day to the next. Forget about planning out months in advance.*

"Well, I think it's kind of important that we think about it. I mean, unless you don't want to continue this relationship once you leave."

"Nicole, do we really have to talk about something that's probably not going to happen until months from now?"

I found it ironic that I was now the one wanting to make plans for a future, when I was so scared of having that with anyone before. I had changed over these past few months. Dailan had made me see that maybe I deserved to be happy and there was nothing I wanted more than to have that happiness with him. All I wanted to hear was that he was possibly entertaining the idea of staying, even if he didn't mean it. That was all I needed at this particular moment to keep me going. But he didn't give me any indication of that happening, even in the slightest.

"I don't know, Dailan, maybe we should just cool it." I felt like someone had kicked me in the stomach at the sound of my words. "It's just getting to be too much. We're not the only ones who are involved in this relationship. You do realize that Ryan is affected by every choice we make as well. Then I have to worry about my job," I said

"Why do you care so much about what those assholes at work think?" I could tell that he was beyond annoyed with me at this point.

"I don't care what they think. But I do care about my job."

"What do you think is going to happen with your job? What, you're going to get fired because some bitch has a vendetta against you?"

"I don't know. She knows a lot of people, Dailan."

He rolled his eyes at me as if I were overreacting.

"I realize this isn't a big deal to you, but it is to me. Next year, you will be back in Ireland *with a job*. I don't want to be left here unemployed because we decided to start something up that should have never happened in the first place." I instantly regretted my words when I saw the hurt in his eyes.

"Is that really how you feel?"

"Dailan, I'm sorry, I didn't mean to sound so harsh. It's just that it seems to be getting really complicated now."

"That's because you're making it complicated," he said with anger in his voice.

"Me? How am I making it complicated? I'm the one who's been sick to my stomach at work for the past two days, having horrible accusations made about me. While you're out at parties getting drunk and doing God knows what with God knows who. I'm not asking for a marriage proposal, Dailan, I just need to know if I'm enduring all of this humiliation for nothing."

"What did you just say?" I could hear the anger in his voice. I looked at him blankly. "About me getting drunk at parties," he clarified.

Oh shit, how the hell was I going to get out of this one? He stared at me intently, waiting for an answer. I took a deep breath and decided to be honest. "I ran into Rick Kincaide in the coffee shop this morning," I said, feeling a little ashamed of myself.

"What the fuck did that bastard tell you, Nicole? Because the only thing that happened last night was I got drunk off my ass."

"Nothing." I was sorry that I had even said anything to him.

"No, Nicole, you started this. Now you're going tell me what that asshole said."

"I don't know, just that you were drunk and had women hanging on you."

"First of all they weren't hanging on me and did he bother telling you that it was two girls that I work with who were there with their *husbands*?"

"No, he didn't," I said, feeling a little relief sweep over me.

"Really, Nicole, is this what it's come to? You go behind my back and try to get information about me from some fuckin' asshole who I can't fuckin' stand and actually believe the made-up shit he tells you."

"I didn't go behind your back. I just happened to run into him in the coffee shop."

"Well, you know what, you're right, maybe we should just cool it."

He stared at me with coldness in his eyes that I had never seen before. He got up from the couch and headed for the door. I immediately got up and followed him.

"Where are you going?" I asked.

"It's done, Nicole."

My heart was racing and I felt myself becoming frantic. I didn't expect this to happen. All I wanted from him was some sense of commitment for the future and somehow, hearing Rick Kincaide's name sent him over the edge.

I grabbed his arm in an effort to make him stay. "Dailan, I didn't go out with him behind your back, I swear to you. I ran into him at the coffee shop and he just happened to mention it."

"And you just happened to believe it without even asking me first."

"No, I wasn't even going to say anything. It just came out because you make me feel like I'm being ridiculous for wanting to know if there's a chance for us to continue our relationship once you're gone."

"Maybe you should have asked Rick that this morning when you were having coffee with him, since he seems to know so much about me." He yanked his arm from my grip.

I couldn't let him walk out that door. I knew if I did, he would probably never be walking through it again. I was desperate and I wasn't ashamed to let him know it. I didn't care if I had to use sex as a weapon to get him to stay. If that's what it took, then I was willing to sink to that low. I took his face in my hands and tried kissing him, but he just pushed me away. "Dailan, don't go." I was begging him. He ignored me as he opened the door. I could feel the moisture building up in my eyes.

He had the door half opened before he turned around. "I'll answer your question for you right now. No, there's no chance of us continuing this relationship. So you don't have to worry about what those assholes at school say anymore and you're free to see Rick Kincaide anytime you'd like."

I shook my head, fighting back the tears. I couldn't breathe. "Please don't do this." My voice was cracking with emotion.

"I didn't do anything. Nicole; you did," he said as he slammed the door behind him.

Chapter 40

I awoke from a horrible night's sleep, not even recognizing the girl looking back at me in the mirror. My eyes were practically swollen shut from crying all night, making it hard to even see. I made a cup of coffee and took two Tylenol to try and control the pounding in my head. I contemplated calling out sick, but quickly changed my mind. I didn't want anyone from school to think that I was calling out just to hide from the humiliation over what had happened at the Board of Ed meeting the other night. I jumped into the shower, hoping the warm water would aid in making me feel better – to no avail.

My head was spinning and I was still trying to grasp what exactly had happened last night. Dailan was by no means the jealous type, but for whatever reason, Rick Kincaide set him off, and I had to be the stupid one to press that button last night. I had wondered if there was a chance I would hear from him once he cooled down, but something told me by the look in his eyes last night that I wouldn't.

I did my best to try and make myself look somewhat human. I gave myself one last look in the mirror, realizing that it was useless. I would just have to tell everyone my allergies were acting up and hope that they believe it. I checked my phone in hopes that there would be some type of message from Dailan, but there was nothing. I decided to make the first move and send him a text to try and break the ice. My hands were shaking as I typed it out.

I am so sorry for whatever happened last night. I would really like to talk to you about it. Please call me.

I went into work with a few stares from others. The allergy excuse seemed to be working. Sarah, the teacher next door to me, came in with two of her prescription allergy pills. I was forced to take them as she stood there watching me. What she didn't realize was that there wasn't a pill to help what was ailing me. The only medicine would be to hear from Dailan. I found myself checking my phone constantly throughout the day and my stomach would turn upon seeing nothing. Ryan seemed to be his normal self, seemingly unaware that anything had happened between Dailan and me. It pained me to look at him - he was a constant reminder of Dailan.

The last of my kids were dismissed and I had made it through the day. My head was still pounding and my stomach was in knots. Tomorrow was the last day before spring break and suddenly I wasn't looking as forward to it as I was before. I found that I wasn't looking forward to anything, just a phone call from Dailan, which clearly wasn't going to come.

I was at the back of my classroom when I heard my cell phone ringing on my desk. I tripped over one of chairs as I ran to answer it. I got disheartened and my eyes burned with tears when I saw that it was only Donna.

"Hello," I answered, trying to disguise the despair in my voice.

"Hey, don't forget we have a fitting tonight," she said.

Shit, shit, shit, I had totally forgotten and it was the last thing I wanted to do tonight. I just wanted to go home, put a cold rag on my head, and wallow in my sorrow.

"Oh yeah. What time again?"

"Seven. Did you want to grab a bite to eat first?"

I suddenly realized that I didn't eat anything at all. I had no appetite whatsoever. My stomach was in knots. I wasn't sure if food would help or make it worse, but I quickly obliged, agreeing to meet her at 5:30 for dinner at the restaurant located right across from the bridal shop.

I ran home to change quickly and popped two Tylenol. I headed back out to my car, breathing in the warm spring air, admiring Mrs. Tallone's beautiful daffodils, which were in full bloom. I instinctively looked down at my phone, hoping by some chance that there would be some form of communication from Dailan – but there was none.

I pulled into the restaurant parking lot. Donna was standing outside waiting for me.

"What the heck happened to you?" Donna asked, no doubt still seeing the puffiness of my eyes.

Do I dare see if the allergy excuse works on my very best friend, or do I tell her the truth? I went with the truth, knowing that she was going to find out soon enough anyway.

"Dailan broke up with me last night."

I watched as her face dropped. "Oh, Nicole, what happened, sweetie?" She wrapped her arm around me and we walked into the restaurant.

I waited until we were seated before I began to unload the whole story on her. She listened closely, asking questions every now and then.

"So, he got jealous because he thinks you were having coffee with this guy?" Donna asked.

"I don't know what happened, honestly. For some reason, he despises this guy and it just threw him over the edge when I mentioned what he had told me about him."

"Well, do you know why he hates him so much?"

"I have no clue. Dailan isn't much of a communicator."

"Well, what was his response when you asked him about going back to Ireland?"

"Before or after he found out that I was talking to Rick Kincaide?"

"Before."

"Nothing. He said that's it's not going to happen until months from now and I shouldn't be worrying about it. Then he made me feel like I was being paranoid for worrying about my job. That's what pissed me off and made me mention what Rick had said. If I had known it was going to get that type of reaction, I would have just kept my mouth shut."

"Well, Nicole, regardless of what happened with that guy from his work, he still owed you some type of explanation about what's going to happen with your relationship once he leaves."

"Well, he did now – it's over." I felt myself begin to choke up.

Donna reached across the booth, taking my hand in hers. "Nicole, I realize that you really care for him, probably more than any other guy you've been with. But maybe this was for the best, if he was planning on leaving anyway."

I shook my head, "I don't know, Donna. For the first time, I felt like I wanted to build a future with someone. I wasn't afraid and this is what happens."

Donna looked at me sympathetically. "Well, that's a good sign. At least you know that you don't have to be afraid in future relationships."

I couldn't think of any future relationships with anyone else. The only person I wanted to be in a relationship with was Dailan. We ordered our food and by the time we were done eating, I didn't feel the slightest bit better.

I tried on my dress as the seamstress poked and prodded at me, sticking pins where it needed to be taken in. I honestly wasn't even paying attention when she asked me questions. I just kept my fingers crossed that it would fit me on the day of the wedding. I tried my best at feigning excitement at the sight of Donna in her dress. I was hoping that I was able to pass it off as genuine. I patiently waited for her to finish up and was relieved when we finally were making our way out the door.

Donna hugged me good-bye and I quickly got in my car. The tears I had been holding in all night long began to flow down my face when I pulled my phone from my purse to find no messages from Dailan.

I arrived home, trying my best to keep my mind occupied. I felt so alone. I wished now more than ever that my relationship were different with my mom and my sister. I got on my laptop and began to type out an e-mail to my brother. I wasn't sure when he would receive it, but it made me feel better just to type the words and confide in someone else besides Donna.

Hey, Justin,

Wishing you were here more than ever. I feel so alone. I totally distanced myself from Mom, Dad, and Renee. You're all I got left, Pooh. I could really use your shoulder to cry on right now. I finally know what it feels like to have a broken heart and it really stinks! So for now, I will send you a virtual hug until I see you again and could give you a real one. Love and miss you so much!! Nicole xoxo

I picked up my phone and dialed Dailan's number. My hands were shaking as it began to ring. I felt like I was kicked in the stomach when he didn't answer. Just hearing his voice on his voicemail made my heart sink.

Dailan, it's Nicole. Please don't do this; I need to talk to you. I swear to you that I didn't have coffee with him. I didn't talk about you at all to him. Please, Dailan, just call me, I miss you.

I realized that I was sounding pretty pathetic, but I didn't care. I just needed to understand why he was so angry with me over something that I didn't even do. I headed off to bed, tucking my phone in beside me, hoping for a call that never came.

Chapter 41

Four days into spring break and six days without hearing from Dailan, and I was going stir crazy. I had left several messages for him without a response. I felt like a crazed stalker as I pulled into his work parking lot. I didn't care though; I needed to talk to him. I couldn't go to his house because I didn't want Ryan to know anything that was going on. I saw his car in the parking lot so I knew he was there. My legs were shaking as I got out of the car. I took a deep breath before entering the elevator. I began to second-guess myself as the elevator door opened, letting me off on the third floor. *You can do this, you can do this,* I repeated over and over to myself as I made the long walk down the hallway. I walked into the lobby and I was greeted by a familiar-looking woman. I quickly recognized her as one of the women Dailan was dancing with at the Christmas party.

"Nicole, right?" she said with a smile, sounding very upbeat.

I bit my lip and nodded, too nervous to smile.

"You're here to see Dailan?"

"Yes," I was able to get out in a loud whisper.

"Okay, I'll take you down to his office."

She got up and led me down a long corridor. I looked straight ahead and tried to ignore the churning in my stomach. I wanted to turn around and run out, but it was too late. She stopped and knocked lightly on the door of what I presumed to be Dailan's office. Dailan lifted his head from his computer screen, looking unpleasantly surprised to see me standing there. I felt the burning in my eyes, seeing him for the first time in almost a week and coming to the realization of just how much I missed him.

"Shut my door, Debbie," he said as she exited the room, leaving just him and me.

"What are you doing here?" he asked.

"I need to talk to you and you won't return my phone calls."

"Well, I'm really busy," he said, turning his attention back to his work.

"What is wrong with you, Dailan? Why are you acting this way?"

"Acting what way? This is who I am, Nicole, who I always was. Not that guy that you tried to turn me into. I never let my guard down with any girl before and now I know why. So if you don't mind, I have work to do."

"I just want to talk to you, I miss you, Dailan," I said with desperation in my voice.

He looked back up with coldness in his eyes and a sarcastic smile. What do you miss, Nicole, the sex? Because we can do it right here, right now, if you'd like."

"No, I miss *you*. I miss talking to you every day, hearing your voice." I was on the brink of tears.

"Well, Nicole, I'm sorry, but I can't offer you anything else. I don't need another friend. I can show you where Rick's office is; maybe he'd be willing to listen to what you have to say, especially if it's about me."

I shook my head in disbelief at him. Why was he tormenting me for something I didn't even do? "Dailan, I swear to you I *ran* into him that day, that was it, you have to believe me."

"I don't have to believe *anything* because I really don't care. It's over and done with. But I guess this is my fault too, for confusing a good fuck with something else."

His words sliced through me like a jagged knife. I bit my lip and tried my hardest to hold back the tears, but I couldn't. They gushed from eyes and ran down my face like a waterfall. This had been the first time in years that I had ever let someone see me cry. I couldn't believe the pain in my heart or the coldness in his eyes. It was as if I wasn't even looking at the same man I had grown to care about so much.

"Why are you crying, Nicole? That's what you wanted. Just sex, no emotions involved. You should be happy. Remember, this shouldn't have even happened in the first place. Those were your words, right?" He was expressionless, unaffected in any way by my tears.

I felt myself trembling and I was quite sure that he noticed it as well. I didn't know what else to say. I stared into his cold eyes one last time before he looked away. I took what little pride I had left and walked out the door, wiping the tears that were rolling down my face along the way. I made my way into the lobby with my head held down. I looked up just in time to see Jenna, the redheaded girl that Dailan had introduced me to on the night of my birthday. If I had any doubt as to why she was there, it was quickly erased as I heard the receptionist on the phone. "Mr. O'Maley, there's a Jenna Crawford here to see you." I looked at the girl and immediately put my head back down so she wouldn't see the tears that were beginning to fall once again.

I briskly walked down the hallway, relentlessly slamming the elevator button so the elevator would hurry up. My stomach was burning and I was thankful that I didn't eat breakfast because I was quite certain that it would be coming up right about now. I decided to take the steps. The last thing I wanted was to get stuck in the elevator with Dailan and his friend. I ran down the steps two at time, not able to get out of the building quickly enough.

I was breaking out into a cold sweat when I finally made it to my car. I was fumbling through my purse for my keys when I heard someone calling my name. I quickly turned around to see Rick Kincaide approaching me.

Oh, God not now, I said to myself as I wiped the tears from my eyes, knowing that I probably looked like a mess with mascara all over my face.

"Hey, are you okay?" he asked, clearly being able to see that I had been crying.

"Yeah, I'm fine," I said, rubbing my eyes once more.

"Well, I know it's none of my business, but if you're crying for the reason I think, then you're probably better off," he said, almost sounding sincere. I didn't respond as I opened up my car door. "Listen, I know now isn't a good time but, I'd really like to take you out for a drink sometime."

I thought about the coldness in Dailan's eyes and the gut-wrenching pain of knowing that he was probably going out to lunch with some girl that he had a history of having casual sex with. It was all too much for me to take. I wanted Dailan to feel the pain that I was going through right now. To feel like his heart was being ripped from his chest and torn into a million pieces. I knew that the only person who could help make sure that he felt that pain was standing right in front of me.

"Sure, when did you want to go?" I responded.

Chapter 42

By the time Friday rolled around, I was beginning to second-guess my decision about meeting Rick Kincaide for a drink. I knew that this would be the final nail in the coffin once Dailan found out about it, not that I had any hope that we would be getting back together anyway after the way he responded to me the other day at his office. I felt a heaviness in my chest every time I thought back to that day. I began to realize that maybe both those times that he told me that he loved me weren't genuine. I couldn't see how you could treat someone that you supposedly loved the way that he did. I decided that I wouldn't speak of Dailan at all to Rick tonight, even though I was curious to know exactly what had happened between the two of them to cause Dailan to have so much animosity toward him.

I sat in my car, giving myself one last look in the mirror before entering The Terrace, a very upscale restaurant, located right around the corner from my school. I was beginning to look more like myself again. The puffiness under my eyes had finally gone down and the churning in my stomach had subsided, but the pain in my heart was still as strong. I was so thankful to have had off this past week. It gave me time to regroup my thoughts and pull it together somewhat. I took a deep breath and got out of my car, making my way into the restaurant. I was immediately greeted by the hostess. I informed her that I was meeting someone as I quickly scouted the bar area and saw Rick Kincaide, sitting off by himself. I made my way over, feeling a little ashamed of myself for agreeing to this.

He smiled widely upon seeing me and I made my best effort to form a smile back that seemed somewhat genuine. "Nicole, how are you?"

"I'm good, thanks," I said, taking the empty seat next to him.

He ordered me a glass of wine and wasted no time jumping into conversation. I tried my best to listen to what he had to say, but my mind was a million miles away. *What was I doing here? Did*

229

I really want to get Dailan back that bad that I stooped to this new low?
My ears perked up at the sound of Dailan's name. I stopped him
right away, reminding myself that topic was off limits.

"I'm sorry, but I really would prefer to not talk about Dailan,"
I said.

He looked at me with a wry smile, one that made me feel very
uncomfortable, the same way I always had felt when I was in his
presence. "I'm sorry, I completely understand," he said.

I looked down when I felt his hand on my thigh and quickly
stood up. "I'm sorry, but this was a mistake. I shouldn't have
come here tonight." I threw a ten-dollar bill down on the bar, not
even wanting to accept a drink from him. I walked out to my car
at a faster pace than normal. I got into my car and headed home.
As much as I wanted to hurt Dailan, I just couldn't subject myself
to sitting there with Rick. I didn't know what reasons Dailan had
for hating him, but I had formed my own low opinion of Rick
Kincaide on my own.

* * *

I was actually happy when Monday arrived. Work would be
a welcoming distraction from the loneliness and heartache I had
been feeling all week. Even the thought of dealing with Cameron
Aymes and his mother was better than one more thought of
Dailan. Although seeing Ryan would bring back all those
thoughts that I was so desperately trying to erase. As the kids
piled in, I did my best to put on a happy face, welcoming them
back. I knew that today would be a little bit of an adjustment for
all of them to settle back into a normal routine after having the
week off, so I didn't plan on jumping into anything too intense
with them.

My heart fluttered as I saw Ryan walk through the door. He
gave a huge smile that made my heart sink. I was on the brink of
tears when I realized that I was not only missing Dailan, but I
had missed Ryan as well. I gave him a smile back, trying to make
everything seem as normal as possible for him.

I had made it to lunch without any major complications,
stopping a few times during our spelling lesson to redirect
Cameron. I ate my lunch at my desk while the kids went down to
the cafeteria. I finished up and went outside for the dreaded task

of recess duty. It was a beautiful spring day. I sat on the bench, taking in the warm sunshine while the kids began to pile out and run off all of their excess energy from the morning. I monitored my area closely, making sure that there weren't any problems and I was happy to see that everyone was pretty much getting along nicely.

"Hi." I heard a little voice coming up from behind as Ryan came and took a seat next to me on the bench.

"Hey, Ryan, what's up?" I asked, trying to sound as upbeat as possible.

"Nothing," he said as he swung his legs, which were hanging off the bench, back and forth.

"How was your spring break?" I asked, biting my lip and hoping he wouldn't mention Dailan's name.

"It was fun; me and my uncle went to the aquarium one day and to the zoo on another day. I wish you could have come with us, but he said you were busy."

I bit my lip and nodded, fighting off that all-too-familiar burning in my eyes.

"Well, the next time you got to come, for sure. The monkeys are so funny!"

"Yeah, monkeys are lots of fun to watch," I said, trying to mask my sadness.

I was so happy when Matty, another little boy from my class, came over to ask Ryan if he wanted to join in on a game of soccer. I didn't know how much longer I would have been able to sit there and listen to him without becoming emotional.

I stood up and watched the boys running around and playing soccer. Ryan had come so far from the mischievous little boy that he was in the beginning of the school year. He was so much more grounded and becoming quite sociable with all of his classmates.

The official first day back to school was over. The humming of the overhead clock was the only sound that could be heard in my classroom. I was just finishing up my lesson plans for the week. I looked down at my phone to find a text from Donna:

Friday night, don't make plans – girls' night out!

The last thing I felt like doing was going out. I still didn't feel like facing the world just yet. I was quite content with just going home every night, getting in pajamas and vegging out in front of the TV. I didn't want to put up a happy front for anyone; I was content with being miserable alone.

You're going; no excuses! Another text came through as if Donna was reading my thoughts. I shook my head, forcing a smile. I packed my stuff up and called it a day, hoping that I would feel a little more social by Friday.

* * *

The week progressed along without any major hurdles. I had a knot in my stomach, wondering if Dailan or Lisa would be picking up Ryan from his after-school tutoring. I was pretty sure that it would be Lisa, but I couldn't help but think that maybe he might show up.

Ryan had finished up all of his work and was helping with one of the bulletin boards. I was keeping his mind distracted as much as I could from mentioning Dailan – almost.

"Miss Morgan, don't you like my uncle anymore?" he asked sadly.

I didn't know how to answer. I was totally blindsided. I put the stapler down and tried to gather my thoughts. "Ryan, sometimes adults fight and get mad over things and they need to distance themselves from each other," I said.

"What did he do?" he asked.

"He didn't do anything."

"Then why are you mad at him?"

"I'm not mad at him." I was trying my best to answer the question diplomatically.

"Is he mad at you?"

"I don't know, Ryan. But just remember no matter what happens, you will always be very special to me."

I watched as the tears poured from his eyes as I tried to hold mine back. "I hate my uncle!" he shouted.

"No, Ryan, don't say that. It's not your uncle's fault. It's no one's fault." My heart was aching for him as I finally came face to face with the effects of my and Dailan's failed relationship. I hugged him tightly, trying to comfort him as best as I could. I felt horrible, knowing that I had played a part in breaking this child's heart once again.

I grabbed a tissue from my desk and began to wipe his eyes while he tried to catch his breath. "We're still going to see each other in school every day. I'm still going to be your teacher." I was trying my best to cheer him up, to no avail.

"But I wanted you to be my aunt." He continued to cry even harder. I hugged him again so he wouldn't be able to see the tears that were now flowing down my face as well. At that particular moment, *I* hated Dailan for leaving me to deal with the aftermath of this mess.

I was so happy when I saw Lisa walk through the door. I wiped the tears from my eyes as best as I could, while Ryan's still flowed down his face. She looked at me sympathetically as if she knew exactly why Ryan and I were both so upset. Ryan was silent as he gathered his belongings.

"Are you okay?" Lisa whispered to me.

"Yeah," I said, wiping my eyes. Ever since Dailan had broken the seal, I was no longer afraid to cry in front of anyone.

"Ryan, why don't you go in the bathroom and wash your face," Lisa said.

Ryan walked out with his head hanging low.

"I know it's not my business, but I'm sorry that you had to be the one left dealing with that. Ryan told me that you haven't been coming around lately, so I just figured you guys broke up. Dailan could have at least explained to him what was going on, instead leaving it up to you." Lisa said.

"It's okay. I just feel awful that Ryan is so upset."

"Well, that's Dailan for you. If he knew how to communicate, even a little, then maybe this could have been avoided and -" She quickly stopped herself as Ryan re-entered the room.

"You got everything, Ryan?" Lisa asked.

He nodded, looking down at the ground as he walked out of the room. I was coming to learn that falling in love was the easy part. It was falling out of love that was hard – especially when you were trying to fall out of it with more than one person.

Beth Rinyu

Chapter 43

I still wasn't feeling very sociable by the time Friday rolled around, but I knew there was no way I was going to talk my way out of it. Donna would have come to my apartment and dragged me out, kicking and screaming. So I stood in front of PJ's bar, waiting for Donna, Kara, and a few of Donna's co-workers to arrive. I was relieved when I finally saw Kara pull into the parking lot.

Kara made her way up to the door, smiling widely. We greeted each other with a hug. We stood outside for a little longer, deciding to take our conversation inside and wait for Donna. We ordered our usual drink of choice – margaritas – and found a seat. It was more crowded than usual, due to an up and coming band that was playing tonight. Kara and I were deep in conversation when Donna arrived. She introduced Kara and me to her two co-workers. After a couple of margaritas and lots of laughs, I was glad that I had ventured out of my self-pity cocoon that I had been living in for the past couple of weeks. Even if it was temporary, it felt good to laugh again and not think about Dailan for a while. I drew the line with my happiness when some guy came up and asked me to dance. I declined. Although I might be ready to go out and share some laughs with my girlfriends, I was by no means ready to get involved with anyone, even if it was just one little innocent dance.

They decided to make fools out of themselves on the dance floor, while I took a much-needed bathroom break. I made my way out of the bathroom through the droves of people when I felt someone grab my elbow roughly. I looked up to find myself staring into Dailan's cold, callous eyes. His eyes were glassed over and I could smell the strong scent of alcohol coming off him. Clearly, he had had a little too much to drink.

"So, tell me, Nicole, do you think of me when you're fucking that scumbag Kincaide?"

I couldn't believe how my un-drank drink got back to Dailan and twisted into something else. *Do I even bother telling him that it wasn't true? That I left that night without even having a drink with him?* I looked into his eyes, and through the icy coldness, I saw something else. I saw sadness. I wanted to take him in my arms and tell him it wasn't true. I wanted him to know how much I loved him and wanted to be with him. But then I thought back to that day in his office and how he crushed my heart without even blinking an eye. I wanted him to know exactly how it felt. I didn't even care if it meant that he would think that I slept with a dirtbag like Rick Kincaide. I just wanted to hurt him as much as he had hurt me that day.

"No Dailan, actually I don't think of you at all." The words pained me as they escaped my mouth.

His eyes narrowed and his anger seemed to escalate. He roughly pulled me into him as his lips came crashing down on mine, forcing his tongue into my mouth. I could taste the alcohol on him as I struggled to break free.

"Just a little something to help you remember," he said coldly.

"Get the hell away from me!" I pushed against his chest in an effort to get away. But it was of no use, he just moved in closer getting right near my ear. "What's the matter, Nicole, will *Rick* get upset if he finds out you're kissing me?" I could hear the loathing in his voice at the mention of Rick's name. He began to kiss me again, this time with a sense of urgency as he roughly pulled my body into his and ran his hands up and down my back. I couldn't breathe as I struggled to break free.

"Get off me." I pushed him as hard as I could, barely budging him.

"Oh, don't worry, I won't tell him." I was still wrapped in his arms and even though there was no place on Earth that I would rather be, I still struggled to break free.

"Dailan, please let me go!" I shouted.

Tommy came rushing over and did his best to pull Dailan away. "Dailan, come on; be cool," he said, trying to calm Dailan down.

"She broke my heart, Tommy. I love her and now she's screwing the one person that she knows I hate the most," Dailan shouted in his drunken stupor. I noticed other people who were standing close by looking on.

Tommy just shook his head, placing his hand on Dailan's chest as he came between the two of us. I couldn't believe how screwed up Dailan was. He was the one that broke up with me. He was the one who was having his ex-lovers show up at his job. He was the one that refused to take my calls and he had the nerve to say that *I broke his heart!*

"Nicole, just go. He's drunk. I'm sure he'll feel like a fool when I tell him how he behaved tonight," Tommy said.

I looked at Dailan one last time. I thought about all three times he had said he loved me. The first time, he was under the influence of sleep, the second time was under the influence of sex, and the third time was under the influence of alcohol. I wondered if he had ever really meant it or if it was all just a game to him, much like I felt like our whole relationship was. He was staring at me intently and, unlike him, I felt compassion for the sadness in his eyes. I wanted to wrap my arms around him and comfort him, but I knew it was too late for that. We had both caused one another far too much unnecessary pain.

I worked my way to the dance floor, finally locating Donna and Kara. I didn't want them to know that I was leaving over what had just transpired with Dailan, so I lied.

"You know what, my stomach is bothering me. I'm going to head home."

"Aww," they both said in unison.

I said my goodbyes and headed out the door, happy that they didn't try and badger me into staying. The short walk back to my apartment afforded me time to clear my head. I was more confused than ever by Dailan's behavior. If he truly did care for me the way he had said, then why would he have jumped to conclusions so quickly and break up with me? I knew that it was something deeper. I remembered his reaction to Rick Kincaide at the Christmas party, which was before he and I had even started up any type of relationship. There was some reason that he despised him so much and I knew that it had a lot more to do with just my innocent encounter with him at the coffee shop.

I realized that I had achieved my goal. I had made Dailan feel just as awful as I had that day at his office – only it didn't feel very satisfying after all.

Chapter 44

The weeks were flying by at a rapid pace and fortunately, I had enough on my plate to keep my mind occupied and free of wondering about Dailan. Not that I didn't think about him, but instead of crossing my mind a thousand times a day, it had dwindled down to a mere hundred. We had just celebrated Donna's bridal shower. It was hard to believe that her wedding was only a month away, and so was the last day of school.

My life seemed to be calming down a bit. I still hadn't talked to my parents since the birthday incident, which was fine by me. The less that I heard from them the better I felt. Things had died down with Mrs. Aymes as well. She was now on a new campaign against the art teacher for some foolish reason that I didn't care to listen to. I continued to be there for Ryan as best as I could at school. I became painfully aware that very soon, we too would be parting ways. I was so pleased when his "hero" essay took third place out of the whole school. He wrote it all by himself for the most part, with a little help from me. It was hard for me at first when I saw that his hero was Dailan. But I put my feelings aside and helped him out upon seeing how excited he was to write it. I had wondered if Dailan would be attending the awards assembly – but he didn't. Instead, Lisa was there.

I had a whole hour of free time before the kids would be piling into school for the day. They were all so rambunctious with the warmer weather and wanted to be outside. It made me look forward to this quiet time a lot more than usual.

The air conditioner was on the fritz and it was an unusually hot May morning. I twirled my hair up in the clip that I had hanging on my purse strap in an effort to stay cool. I was glad that I chose to wear my sleeveless summer dress. I was deep in thought, reading over a composition, when I heard a light knock on my door. My heart dropped when I looked up to see Dailan.

"Hi," I said through the butterflies that had erupted in my stomach.

239

"Hey," he replied. He was dressed casually in jeans and a black polo shirt. He was still so devastatingly handsome, but something seemed to have changed about him. He wasn't that same sarcastic man I had met in the beginning of the school year, nor was he the loving man in whose arms I had just been a few months ago. He was flat and expressionless. His eyes seemed to be missing their spark and he looked exhausted.

"I just was in the office picking up some paperwork from Ryan's educational assessment. Sorry I couldn't make the meeting. I was away on business," he said as he moved closer to my desk.

"Oh, no problem," I said, realizing that I was talking to him as if he were just any other parent.

He gazed at me with sadness in his eyes. The silence in the room was becoming blatantly uncomfortable and I knew I had to think of something to say quickly.

"So, when will you be leaving for Dublin?"

"I'm not sure yet, I'm leaving later today to go there and make all the arrangements with my company for the transition, probably in a few months."

"Oh," I said, putting my head down, not wanting to think about Dailan and Ryan being an ocean away.

All of a sudden, I remembered the picture of Ryan from the awards ceremony that I had in my drawer. I fumbled around, finally locating it, and handed it to him.

"I thought you would want this."

It was a picture of Ryan reading his "Hero" composition, the one that I had helped him write. I got up, walked over to the bulletin board, and took Ryan's award-winning composition down. Dailan was still smiling at the picture I had just handed him.

"Here: this goes with it. He was reading from his composition about the greatest hero in his life - you," I said.

He briefly looked it over and smiled. "Wow, who would of thought? He's come a long way because of you."

"Well, I had a lot of help from you too. He's a really great kid. I'm going to miss him." *And I'm going to miss you,* I wanted to say so badly, but I stopped myself in time.

There was sadness in his eyes that just made me want to forget everything that had happened between us and start anew, but I knew it was much too late for that.

"I'm sorry, Nicole, for the way I acted the last time I saw you. I was a little drunk,"

"That's okay; I guess we're even now," I said, thinking back to the first time I had met him when I was a little drunk.

"Yeah, I guess," he said with a sigh.

He moved closer to me. My knees became weak. I breathed in the familiar scent of his cologne and savored the warm touch of his hand on my arm.

"I'm going to be really tied up this next month with work so I don't know if I'll see you before the school year is over. But I wanted to tell you 'thank you - for everything."

I felt the tears building in my eyes and contained them just before they fell. I was pretty sure that he had noticed too. He looked at me sympathetically as if he were trying to comfort me with his eyes.

"Dailan, I know this doesn't matter now, but I need you to know. I never slept with Rick Kincaide. I don't know what he told you, but I swear I didn't. I would never do that to you. Yes, I wanted to hurt you, the same way you had hurt me that day at your office so I agreed to go out for a drink and left before I even had one – I just couldn't."

He was silent for a moment and I wished I knew what he was thinking. He slid his hand down my bare arm, taking my hand in his.

"Goodbye, Nicole." His hand left mine at the same time as a teardrop left my eye. I watched as he walked out of Room 114 for the very last time, leaving a huge hole in my heart and tears flowing down my face. I closed my eyes, wishing things could have been different for us. The one person I was willing to cast aside my fears for had just walked out of my life forever. I wrapped my hand around my wrist and ran my thumb over the silver heart dangling from my bracelet, knowing that the man who had given it to me was the same one that would be in *my heart* forever - Mr. Dailan O'Maley.

Chapter 45

It was the last day of after-school tutoring for Ryan. We switched it up to Tuesday this week because Ryan had plans with his grandfather after school tomorrow. Not that Ryan even needed to be tutored anymore; he was doing perfectly in school now. I knew that he looked forward to spending that extra time with me after school, just as much as I looked forward to spending that time with him. I decided to make it a little more special for him. I had baked brownies and bought them in for us to have after school. His smile was a mile wide when I placed the plate in front of him.

"Did you make these?" he asked.

"Yup."

"They're really good," he said as he took a bite.

There wasn't much schoolwork going on at all, so Ryan and I just talked. He was so excited about his birthday party this upcoming weekend. I listened to him intently as he told me about all the presents on his list. He expressed his sadness over the fact that Dailan was away and wouldn't be there and I did my best to act normal at the mention of his name.

"Miss Morgan, will you come and see me when I come back to visit my Aunt Lisa?"

I felt a lump in my throat, seeing both sadness and hope on his face. Next year, Ryan would be in a different country, and a strange school with new kids and new teachers to which he would have to adjust. He was doing so well here and now he was about to be yanked out of a familiar situation yet again. I knew that he could handle it; he had proven how resilient he was over this past year. I still couldn't help but feel some sadness over the whole circumstance. I swallowed hard to fight back my tears. "Yes, Ryan, I would love to see you when you're here visiting." He smiled, exposing the adorable dimples that I had grown to love and took another bite of his brownie.

By the time Lisa came to pick him up, Ryan was already on his third brownie and second juice box. Ryan was laughing uncontrollably at a joke he had just told me and he was covered in chocolate. "Hey, are you guys having a party without me?" Lisa joked as she pushed a strand of her long brown hair out of her face.

"Miss Morgan made brownies," Ryan said.

I held the plate out to Lisa, offering her one. "Oh, no thanks, I met my chocolate quota for the day," she joked.

Ryan ran to the bathroom to wash the chocolate from his face and hands. "Nicole, I'm having a birthday party for Ryan on Saturday and I wanted to see if you could come. I realize it's Memorial Day weekend and you may already have plans, but if not, it would really mean a lot to Ryan if you were there."

She must have seen the look of hesitation on my face as she continued. "Dailan won't be there; he's in Ireland. He won't be back until next Tuesday."

"Yeah, I know," I said.

"Oh, did Ryan tell you already?"

"No, I talked to Dailan yesterday before he left. He was here picking up paperwork for Ryan. I would love to come," I said, erasing any reluctance from my mind.

"Great!" She grabbed a pen and piece of paper from her purse and wrote down her address and cell number. "We'll see you around two."

"Ryan, Miss Morgan's coming to your party on Saturday," Lisa said as he walked back in the classroom.

"Yes!" Ryan exclaimed. The look on his face was priceless.

Lisa hurried him along as he gathered up his books and loaded them into his backpack with the smile never leaving Ryan's face.

"Bye, Miss Morgan. Thanks for the brownies and thanks for saying you'll come to my party."

"Bye, Ryan." I gave both him and Lisa a smile as they walked out the door.

I sat down at my desk and began to wonder if I would just be making it worse by going to Ryan's party. As much as he wanted me there and as much as I wanted to go, the reality was that soon

I would no longer be in his life. So, was it really good for us to keep building upon this relationship when soon it would be taken away? I quickly dismissed those feelings as I thought of the smile on Ryan's face when he found out that I was going. He deserved happiness and I was happy to provide it to him even if it was fleeting.

I stopped off at the food store on my way home from work. I grabbed a frozen pizza for dinner and couldn't resist the chocolate chip mint ice cream for dessert. I was starving by the time I got home and wasted no time lighting my oven and sticking the pizza in. My apartment was so warm from being closed in all day. I debated about whether to open the windows or turn on the air. I decided to open the windows to let in some fresh air. I changed into my shorts and tank in an effort to cool off. My pizza was just about done when my cell phone began to ring. I was shocked when I saw my sister's name displaying on my caller ID. What the heck did she want? I hadn't heard from her since that day at the ice skating rink. I decided to let it go to voicemail. I was much too hungry to deal with her on an empty stomach. I sat down to eat and pulled out my lesson plans. I quickly glanced at my phone – no voicemail. Guess it couldn't have been too important. As I flipped my calendar to the week ahead, I realized that I was coming up on that dreaded day that I always closed myself off from the rest of the world. I had been so busy these past few weeks that I didn't have time to dwell on it like I had in previous years.

I finished my lesson plans and my pizza and sat down in front of the TV with my ice cream. I had just taken my first spoonful of the cool sweet minty ice cream when my cell phone began to ring from the kitchen counter. "Damn it," I said as I walked into the kitchen, taking my ice cream with me.

Renee, again? What the hell did she want? Her timing was impeccable, just when I wanted to be alone with my ice cream.

"Hello." I finally gave in and answered.

"Nicole," I could hear a sense of urgency in her voice and it almost sounded like she was crying.

"What's up, Renee?"

"Nicole, it's Justin…." The ice cream container fell from my hand to the ground along with my phone. I slid down on the cold ceramic tile of my kitchen floor, hugging my knees and shaking uncontrollably….my little brother was gone forever.

Chapter 46

I was numb. It hurt to breathe and I was quite certain that I wouldn't have made it through the last few days without Donna by my side. My brother's funeral was to be held in the church that we belonged to our whole life, which was five minutes from my house. The burial would take place in the cemetery located up the street from the church. The only detail that I knew about my brother's death was that it was due to an improvised explosive device. I didn't really know what the meant and I didn't want to know.

I had my phone turned off for the last four days, not wanting to talk or hear from anyone. I broke down in tears when I called Valerie to tell her that I would need some time off and I was quite certain that she had informed my co-workers what had happened. I lost it again yesterday when I had received a card made by all of my students. I was sure that it was Valerie's idea and even though I cried upon seeing it, it meant the world to me.

It was a beautiful warm Saturday morning. Memorial Day weekend was always a reminder that summer, my favorite time of year, was just beginning. But now it would always be a reminder of an ending. The ending of a life cut too short. I drove to the church with Donna. I quietly sat in the passenger seat looking out the window when it dawned on me that today was Ryan's birthday party. I felt compelled to text Lisa and let her know that I wouldn't be attending, even though I was quite sure she had figured that out. I knew that Ryan had probably told her what had happened. I finally powered up my phone after its long slumber.

I'm so sorry, Lisa. I won't be able to attend the party today. Please tell Ryan I'm sorry.

I hit the send button and almost instantaneously received a message back from her.

I'm so sorry for your loss, Nicole. If you need anything, please let me know.

I scrolled through all of the text and voicemail messages that were coming in from the last four days, not bothering to open any of them up or listen to them; until I came across a voice mail message from the one name that always made my heart leap out of my chest - Dailan.

Donna looked over at me as I gasped.

"What's the matter?" she asked.

"I have a voice mail message from Dailan."

"What did he say?"

"I don't know. I didn't listen to it. I'm afraid I'll just get myself even more upset if I do."

Donna looked at me sympathetically as we pulled into the gas station. She gave the attendant her credit card and told him how much gas she wanted. "I'm going inside to get some coffee, you want any?" she asked.

"No; I'm good."

I waited until she was inside the mini-mart just outside the gas station before I picked up my phone and dialed the number for my voice mail. I quickly bypassed all of the other messages until I got to Dailan's, which he had left two days ago.

"Nicole, Lisa just told me about your brother. I'm really sorry. I know I'm
probably the last person you want to talk to, but I'm here if you need me."

I played his message over and over again, unable to fight the tears that his voice brought to my eyes. Right now, he wasn't the last person that I wanted to talk to; he was the *only* person. I quickly threw my phone into my purse and wiped the tears from my eyes upon seeing Donna walking closer to the car. She got in the car and handed me the coffee that she decided to buy me anyway.

"You listened to his voicemail message, didn't you?" she asked, obviously seeing the look of despair on my face.

I nodded.

"What did he say?"

I took my phone from my purse and played his message on speaker. Donna looked at me compassionately. "Are you going to call him?"

"I don't know. I just want to get through today first." Donna placed her hand on mine in support as we pulled out of the gas station and headed toward the church.

My stomach was in knots as we entered the church. I hadn't talked to anyone in my family except for the brief phone call from my sister delivering the horrible news the other night. This church held so many memories. It was the place where I had gone every Sunday morning growing up, whether I wanted to or not. I had been baptized, made my first communion and confirmation right inside these walls where I was standing. I never imagined that one day I would be coming here to attend my brother's funeral.

My mother was in the front of the church, standing by the casket. She broke down the moment she saw me, taking me in her arms, and sobbing uncontrollably. I hugged her back, unable to hold back my tears. She held tightly to my hand, making sure I was close by her the entire time. I found it odd that she wasn't hanging all over my sister in this overwhelming time of need, but instead she chose me. My father remained stone faced, showing no emotion at all. He didn't acknowledge me in any way and even though I thought my heart could handle it - it couldn't. It only added to my sorrow. I realized at the moment that he really meant what he said - I was no longer in this family; I was no longer his daughter.

There wasn't a dry eye in the church by the time my brother's best friend Johnny finished delivering the eulogy. It was so heart-felt and true to whom my brother was in life. The military burial that followed was just as heart wrenching, watching them lowering the casket into the ground as the painful melody of Taps filled the air; knowing that I would never see my little brother or feel the excitement of seeing one of his e-mails again was so surreal to me. It was just all too much for me to take. My mother grabbed my hand and pulled me close as I began to sob. I rested my head on her shoulder as she pushed my hair from my face and kissed me on the head. I was spent by the time it was all over. I declined going to the luncheon, even though I knew my mother really wanted me there. I just couldn't bring myself to go. I wanted to go home and be alone, where I could feel however, I wanted without having everyone feel sorry for me. I knew that my sister would be there to help get her through the rest of the day and I actually took comfort in that. My mother hugged me tightly as we were leaving the cemetery.

"I love you so much, Nicole."

"I love you too, Mom."

She finally released her hold on me and kissed me on the cheek. My sister and her husband both gave me a hug and a kiss as well. My dad walked away, striking up a conversation with his cousin, once again achieving his goal of making me feel like an outsider. I bit my lip as Donna took my hand. I knew that she had just witnessed my father's cold reaction and she was feeling sorry for me. She said her goodbyes to my mom and my sister. We walked to her car with her arm wrapped around me.

"Are you okay?" she asked.

"I'm fine." I tried my best to keep together.

I was quiet for the entire car ride, and by the time we pulled in the driveway, I think Donna sensed that I just wanted to be alone.

"Do you want me to come up?" she asked.

"No, I'll be okay." I pulled her close and hugged her tight. "Thank you so much, Donna."

"You're welcome; call me later when you're up to it."

I walked up the stairs to my apartment feeling emotionally and physically drained. I went into my bedroom, turned on the air conditioner, and changed into a pair of shorts and a tank top. I lay down on my bed, falling into a deep catatonic slumber.

Chapter 47

I rolled over in my bed, trying to focus as best as I could at the red numbers on my clock. *Was it really 7 p.m.? Had I really slept for five hours straight in the middle of the day?* I stretched my whole body before getting up, still feeling half out of it. I went into the bathroom, washed my face, and brushed my teeth in an effort to wake up.

I walked out into the kitchen, feeling more alone than ever. I forced half a bowl of cereal down before throwing the rest in the trash. I was feeling so anxious, I was contemplating going for walk, but instead threw on my flip-flops, grabbed my car keys, and jumped in my car.

I pulled into the cemetery, which was now looking so desolate from earlier today, but that's just how I wanted it. I needed to be alone with my brother. I got out of my car and walked up the hill to the freshly dug gravesite. I sat down on the warm ground, gathering my thoughts.

"See what happens when you don't listen to me." I joked the same way that my brother and I always would talk to each other when he was alive. "I miss you so much already, Justin. I don't know what I'm going to do without you." I was suddenly becoming more serious as the tears rolled down my face. I sat in silence, breathing in the sweet smell of wisteria wafting through the warm summer breeze, feeling so at peace. The sky lit up in shades of pink and peach as the sun began to set. Normally, being in a cemetery by myself at night would freak me out, but tonight I didn't feel alone. I knew my brother was there with me; I could feel him. I kissed my hand and placed it on the warm earth beneath me. "I love you, Pooh." I closed my eyes while my hand rested in the dirt, hoping in some small way my brother could feel my touch. The last remnants of daylight had completely faded away, when I finally got up and headed back to my car.

I got into my car and looked at my phone. I held my breath and hit Dailan's name. My stomach began to churn in anticipation of his answer, but not for long. It went straight to his voice mail. I suddenly remembered that it was the middle of the night in Ireland. I contemplated hanging up without leaving a message, but instead took a deep breath, waited for the beep, and began to speak. "Hi, Dailan, thanks for the phone call. I'm so sorry to be calling you in the middle of the night. I totally forgot about the time difference. Anyway, it was really nice hearing from you and I guess…..um, well, goodbye." I hung up, realizing that I sounded like babbling fool.

I turned the key and started my car. I looked up at the freshly dug gravesite one last time. My heart sank when I thought of my brother all alone in the dark cemetery tonight. I turned up the radio to try and erase my thoughts. I pulled into my driveway. It was eerily silent as I got out of my car. Normally, I would hear Elmo barking or Mrs. Tallone's television blaring, but she and Elmo had been away for the past week, visiting her sister. I was once again feeling completely alone. I walked up the stairs and fumbled with my key, trying to find the keyhole in the darkness. I looked up at my unlit porch light, remembering how Dailan would always get so upset when I would leave if off.

"Nicole." I heard a voice in the darkness that made me jump and drop my key. I looked at the bottom of my steps and watched as Rick Kincaide began to walk up them.

What the hell was he doing here? How did he know where I live? I was beginning to feel even more uncomfortable than I normally did in his presence. I tried my best to disguise the state of panic I was beginning to find myself in.

"Rick. What are you doing here?"

A devious grin stretched across his face. I looked down at the ground beneath me, wondering just how badly I would hurt myself if I jumped the ten feet. My body began to tremble as he reached the top and was standing right next to me.

"Did you need something?" I asked.

He reeked of alcohol as he roughly wrapped his arm around my neck. "Open the door," he said through clenched teeth.

"I - I dropped the key." My voice was quivering as I reached down to pick up my keys, while his arm remained tightly wrapped around my neck. My hand was trembling, making me take even longer to open the door, which only seemed to compound his anger.

I finally made the connection with the keyhole, turning the knob and walking in. He kept his arm tightly wrapped around my neck, walking behind me. He moved my hair from my neck and whispered in my ear. The pungent smell of alcohol coming off his hot breath burned my eyes. "I guess we don't have to worry about being interrupted by lover boy tonight, since he's far away." I cringed as I felt his lips graze my neck. I tried to clear my head and think of a way out of this. One hard kick in the groin would allow me time to make it out of the door. I jumped as my cell phone began to ring. He stuck his free hand inside my purse and pulled out my phone. "Ah speak of the devil." He waved the phone in front of my face, teasing me as Dailan's name displayed on my caller ID.

I knew that this might be my only chance; I grabbed the phone from his hand and quickly answered it. "Dailan, please call the police and tell them to come my apartment…"

"You bitch," Rick screamed. He pummeled me across the face. I fell to the ground as my phone went flying across the room. My face was stinging in pain as the warm blood trickled down slowly.

He picked up the phone that was lying on the ground. "See what happens when you leave your pretty little girlfriend all alone? Are you feeling helpless, knowing there's nothing you can do to help her right now? Kind of brings back memories of your brother, doesn't it?" He hung up and threw the phone back to the floor.

I got up quickly and ran into the kitchen. I pulled the biggest knife I could from the drawer and held it up as he slowly approached me. "What are you going to do with that, Nicole?" I was silent, taking a step back for every step he took toward me.

"Well, now we're going to have to make this a little quicker since O'Maley is probably calling the police."

I cringed as he moved closer. I was holding the knife in my shaking hand, unsure if I could bring myself to use it. I just had to injure him enough so I could get past him and run out the front door. He moved closer as I prepared to stick him and before I could, he slapped the knife out of my hand with full force. I ran to grab it off the floor when he pushed me down to the ground. He grasped my leg, pulling me closer to him. "So, you want to play like that?" he asked as he roughly held me down by the arms. I could feel the sweat coming off his skin and was beginning to feel nauseous. "You really are a beauty," he whispered in my ear. I tried pushing him off of me, but I couldn't; he was too strong.

"Why are you doing this?" I pleaded.

"Because of *him*. You can thank O'Maley for this! First, he took away the woman I loved and now a promotion that was supposed to be mine. Now I'm going to take something that's his."

None of this was making sense to me. I hadn't a clue what he was talking about. *What woman? What promotion?* I broke my arm free from his hand and scratched him on the face, which only intensified his anger. I closed my eyes, praying to find some inner strength to get out of this. I couldn't let this happen; I flailed my body about, trying my best to knee him in the groin.

"Now, Nicole, you're not being very nice." His voice was taunting. He was so close to me I could feel his breath on me. I turned my head, unable to look at him. I flinched as he went to kiss my neck, the whole time thinking, this can't be happening to me. But it was useless; he was much too strong for me to fight off. I closed my eyes, feeling defeat. All I could do was cry. Terror overtook me. I was actually coming face to face with my worst fear – I had never felt so helpless in my life.

Chapter 48

All of a sudden, I felt the weight of him lift off me. Everything was happening so quickly as I tried to figure out what was going on. I was frozen as I watched Dailan pummeling Rick in the face. He was relentless as he continued punching him until he fell to the ground.

I finally broke free from my trance and stood up on my trembling legs. "Dailan! It's okay, I'm okay," I shouted, trying to break him from his rage.

He finally looked up as Rick lay knocked out on the floor, just as the police entered the front door. His eyes were full of emotion. He was silent as he rushed toward me and rubbed his hand down my bloodstained face. He hugged me tightly, sending warmth throughout my entire body. I hugged him back and began to sob uncontrollably.

Two police officers made their way into the living room. "Are you okay, miss?" one of them asked.

"I'm fine," I said not letting go of Dailan.

They roughly lifted Rick off the floor and placed him in handcuffs while reading him his rights. I buried my face into Dailan's chest, not able to look at Rick as he walked past me. They were heading out the door when I heard a familiar voice. "Get him the hell out of here." I instantly recognized it as my dad's friend, Don, who was a detective with the local police department. I had just seen him at my brother's funeral earlier in the day.

"Nicole, are you okay?" Don asked as he came rushing over to me, gently placing his hand on my shoulder.

"Yes," I said, finally able to calm down a bit.

"I hate to ask you to do this now, but I'm going to need for you to give me a statement. Are you up for it?"

I nodded as he signaled for me to sit down on the couch. I didn't want to let go of Dailan. I felt so safe in his arms. Dailan must have sensed how I was feeling. "It's okay, I'm just going to get some ice for your face," he said gently.

I sat down and answered all of Don's questions. Dailan brought me over an ice pack for my face and sat back down next to me. I grabbed Dailan's hand when I began to feel myself getting upset once again as I recounted the night's events and came to the realization of what could have actually happened.

"Well, I'm going to get going. If you think of anything else, please call me," Don said as he got up from the couch. "Are you sure you don't want to go to the hospital to be examined?"

"No, I'm fine," I said as I leaned my head against Dailan's shoulder.

"Please, don't say anything to my parents, Don."

He was unresponsive and just looked at me sympathetically. Something told me that he wasn't going to abide by my wishes. "I'll call you as soon as the report is done. I will need for you to come down to the station in the next few days to sign some paperwork."

I nodded.

"You take it easy," he said. He shook Dailan's hand and headed out the door.

Dailan moved closer to examine my face. "I don't know what would have happened if you hadn't called me tonight," I said, shivering at the thought of it.

"I wanted to kill him, Nicole. I have never been that angry in my life." He pulled me closer and hugged me tightly. I closed my eyes, feeling as if nothing could hurt me now. "I don't know what I would have done if something had happened to you," he said.

He pushed my hair out of the way and caressed my face. "I thought you weren't coming back until Tuesday," I said.

"I decided to come back early. I thought maybe you might need someone to talk to; I wanted to be here for you. Besides, no use in being there when I've decided to stay here."

I lifted my head from his shoulder, trying to decipher what he had just said. He saw the look of confusion on my face.

"Nicole, I'm not going back to Dublin. That's part of the reason that he was so angry, because he was up for the position that I decided to take."

"What made you change your mind?"

"I don't know. I thought about how it would affect Ryan and then there's this girl who I'm crazy about."

"Oh, does this girl know how you feel?"

"Don't know; I acted like a real jerk. I really fucked things up with her and I just hope she can forgive me."

I smiled for the first time in days and stretched my neck up to kiss him on the cheek. "She does."

He smiled back and hugged me tightly. I leaned my head back on his shoulder. "This is my fault. I should have never taken him up on his drink offer. I just got so upset that day at your office, when I saw that girl there."

Dailan moved his shoulder forcing me to raise my head and look at him. "What girl?" he looked at me with pure confusion.

"That red-headed girl, you know the one –" I couldn't even finish my sentence. It hurt too much to even say it.

"Nicole, I didn't even see her that day. I have no idea why she showed up. But I told my secretary to tell her I was in a meeting."

"You mean, you didn't –"

He stopped me before I could finish. "No! Nicole, contrary to how I may have behaved toward you, I haven't been able to stop thinking about you. You are the only girl that I've wanted since the day that I met you."

Relief and guilt simultaneously swept over me. I hugged him tightly upon hearing those words.

"This wasn't your fault, Nicole. He did this to you to get at me."

"Dailan, what happened with him? Why did the two of you hate each other so much, even before this happened with your job?"

He sighed deeply. "He and my sister-in-law had an affair."

"Oh," I sat up pushing my hair behind my ear. I suddenly remembered that day at the ice skating rink when Ryan had told me his mom had worked for the company.

"She swore that it only happened once and then she realized how wrong it was, but who knows," he said with disgust.

"Did your brother know?"

He shook his head "no" and for a brief moment, I saw his eyes begin to fill up before catching himself and stopping it.

"How did you find out?" I asked.

"Because that sick bastard told me. I just figured he was lying, but when I confronted Connie, she confirmed it," he said sadly. "I wish she would have just lied. I didn't want to know the truth."

"You never told your brother?"

He closed his eyes and shook his head. "Connie was like my sister. What she did to my brother was pretty shitty, but she was a great mother. She loved Ryan more than anything in this world. She begged me not to say anything. I knew how my brother was and I knew he wouldn't be forgiving. I couldn't do that to Ryan - I couldn't tear apart his family like that. But then maybe if I did, his mom and dad would still be here right now."

"What do you mean?" I asked.

"The night that they got in the -" he had to stop himself to regain his composure. I placed my hand on his arm and rubbed it gently as he continued. "The night that they got into the accident, they were on their way home from a wedding. It was someone that we worked with. I wasn't there; I was back home in Ireland. That asshole Kincaide was there, though. He became obsessed with Connie when she told him it was over. He blamed me for it, said that I had convinced her to end it. He told my brother everything that night, making sure that he knew that I was aware of the affair as well. When my brother confronted Connie, she confessed to everything. It was raining, they were fighting and..."

"How do you know?"

"Right before they crashed, my brother called me. I knew that there was always a chance that he would find out that I knew and I was prepared to deal with it. My brother could be a real nasty son of a bitch, but I always knew how to handle him." He briefly paused, looked straight ahead, and ran his hand through his hair. "That night when he called me, I was in a dead sleep. I thought I was just dreaming when I answered the phone. But even being half asleep, I could hear the hurt in his voice. His last words to me were, 'I can't believe my own brother would have kept this from me.' I tried to explain myself to him, but the phone went dead. There was nothing I could do. I was an ocean away. I tried calling him back..." he took a deep breath as a tear rolled down his face.

"Oh, Dailan, it's okay." I hugged him tightly. "You did what you thought was right for everyone involved." It suddenly became clear to me why Dailan had gotten so upset with me for talking to Rick. He was harboring so much guilt and resentment that he wasn't willing to share. Something I could relate to all too well. I was hoping that he had felt better about himself for finally clearing his mind. I rubbed his back lightly and kissed him on the cheek, wiping away the lone teardrop that was rolling down his face. I got up from the couch and took his hand. He looked at me in confusion.

"Did you forget where my bedroom was?"

"Nicole, are you up for this tonight?" he asked as he stood up and gently rubbed his thumb over my bruised eye.

"I never wanted anything more." Tonight, more than ever, I needed to feel his touch. I needed the security of being in the arms of the man I loved, feeling as if no one could hurt me as long as he was here.

He flashed his crooked little smile at me and my heart dropped. I stood on my tippy toes and whispered in his ear, "I love you, Dailan O'Maley."

His smile became wider upon hearing those words. "I love you too," he said as he effortlessly scooped me up in his arms and carried me to my bedroom.

Chapter 49

The birds were singing outside my bedroom window as the bright sunlight peeked through my half-opened blinds. I looked over at the clock, not even caring that it was almost 10 a.m. and I had slept most of the morning away. I could spend the rest of the day in bed as long as I was wrapped up in the arms of the man lying beside me. I kissed him softly on his chest. His smile was a mile wide when he opened his eyes and looked at me, sending warmth throughout my body.

"Good morning," I said, this time kissing him on the cheek.

"I love waking up with you," he said as he caressed my swollen face. It was feeling much more tender this morning. He pulled me closer and gently grazed the bruise with his lips. He softly ran his fingers up and down my back. I closed my eyes, never feeling as content as I had right now. "Lisa's dropping Ryan off at noon; he's probably wondering what happened to me."

"What do you mean?"

"I was on my way home from the airport to pick him up when I called you last night. I texted Lisa last night and told her that there was an emergency and I wouldn't be able to pick him up."

"Okay, so why don't you get your bag from the car and take a shower, while I make you breakfast before you go."

"You don't have to make me breakfast and you're coming with me. I'm not leaving you here alone."

"Yes I am making you breakfast, and really - I don't need a babysitter."

"Nicole, I'm not leaving you."

I got out of bed and slipped on sweats and a tank top, knowing that I wasn't going to win that battle. Dailan went outside to get his bag while I went into the bathroom and examined my face in the mirror for the very first time since last night. It was bruised and swollen. Shivers went through my spine when I flashed back to the terror I had felt last night. I began to cry, thinking about what could have happened. I knew that the physical marks would heal; it was the emotional ones that wouldn't have if Dailan hadn't gotten there in time to stop it. I quickly grabbed a tissue and wiped my eyes when I heard Dalian coming back inside.

"What's the matter?" he asked as he entered the bathroom.

"I was just thinking about last night. I don't think I would have been able to live with myself if he – "

He tilted my chin and bent down to kiss me, stopping me from saying what I was about to say. He was seemingly just as pained by the thought of it as I was. "You're okay, Nicole. I promise I will never let anything happen to you." I stood on my tippy-toes and kissed him softly on the lips. I reached my hand into the shower, turned on the water, and lifted my shirt over my head. My stomach tingled, seeing the smile that appeared on his face. I smiled back as I lifted his shirt over his head and unbuttoned his pants. We quickly removed the rest of our clothing, stepping into the shower, and let the warm water envelop us.

* * *

I broke down in tears once again over breakfast when I began to tell Dailan about my brother's funeral. He comforted me and listened closely. I knew if anyone could relate to the pain I was feeling it was he.

"Thank you so much for everything," I said as I reached over and ran my hand through his damp wavy hair. "I missed you so much."

"I missed you too."

"Did I ever tell you that I love you?" I asked.

His smile was a mile wide. "I think you did – but you can say it again."

"I love you more than you'll ever know."

"Oh, I think I do know," he said. He got up and stood behind me, wrapping his arms around my waist. He moved my hair away from my ear, bent down, and whispered, "But I think I love you more." I couldn't contain my smile. The wall was finally broken. I was allowing Dailan to enter my heart completely; erasing all the pain and guilt that had been weighing me down for all of these years. My self-imprisonment had ended. I had finally come to the realization that I deserved to be happy.

"We have to get going," he said as he kissed my neck.

I turned around to face him. "Dailan, I just want to throw a load of laundry in and blow-dry my hair, and then I promise I will be over."

"Nicole, I don't want you staying here alone."

"I will be fine. You can call me every five minutes if you'd like. I promise I will be over in one hour."

He looked at me reluctantly. "Nicole-"

"I will be fine."

"Okay, but pack a bag because you're staying over. You're not sleeping here alone."

"Okay." I wasn't putting up a fight. I was actually glad. Daytime I could handle, but nighttime was going to be hard for me for a while.

"Call me as soon as you step foot out of this door and walk to your car," Dailan said as I walked him to the door.

"I will, I promise."

I kissed him softly on the lips, nearly jumping out of my skin at the sound of someone knocking at my door. I looked out my window and cringed at the sight of my dad's car in my driveway.

"Shit, shit, shit."

"What's wrong?" Dailan asked.

"It's my dad. I can't do this, I can't deal with him right now," I said with desperation in my voice.

Dailan took my hand in his and looked directly in my eyes "Nicole, you will be fine; you can do it."

I took a deep breath and slowly opened the door. *So much for his friend Don abiding by my wishes*, I thought. My dad had a look of alarm stretched across his face as he focused in on the bruising on my face.

"Oh my God, Nicole!" He took me off guard when he pulled me toward him and embraced me tightly. I didn't know how to react; it had been so long since my dad had hugged me or showed any type of affection at all. I finally wrapped my arms

263

around him and awkwardly hugged him back. He took my face in his hands. "Are you okay?"

"I'm fine."

He shifted his attention to Dailan. "Dad, you remember Dailan – right?"

"Yes, of course. Thank you, thank you so much," he said as he extended his hand to Dailan.

Dailan nodded. "I'm very sorry for your loss, Mr. Morgan."

My dad looked down at the ground. "Thank you," he said sadly. "Please call me 'Nick.'"

Dailan reached for the doorknob. "Well, I was just leaving. Nicole, I'll see you in a little while. Please just call me when you leave."

"I promise." I gave him a kiss and watched him walk out the door, leaving me all alone to face my biggest critic - my dad.

Chapter 50

"Come in and sit down," I said, leading my dad over to the couch. "Do you want some coffee?"

"No," my dad replied. He stared at my face again as if it pained him to look at it.

"It looks worse than it feels," I said, trying to put his mind at ease.

"Nicole, I'm so sorry for the way I've behaved all these years to you. You didn't deserve it. You're a good girl and I really am proud of the woman you've become."

I felt a lump in my throat as I tried my best to fight the tears. My dad looked broken, almost vulnerable. Not the same strong, impassive man that I was always so used to seeing. I was quite certain that the events that had transpired this past week had a lot to do with it. I didn't know what to say. I sat quietly as he continued talking.

"I was just too worried about myself and what other people would think that I shut out my own daughter. I realize now that life is too short. I want us to have a relationship again. I want to put the past behind us and move on."

"I'm sorry if I disappointed you, Dad, but I can't punish myself over it any longer. I know that I made the right choice."

I watched in disbelief as the tears began to fill my dad's eyes and roll down his face. "I love you, Nicole, and I should have been there for you when you needed me."

"I love you too, Dad." I wrapped my arms around him, unable to contain my own tears now.

We began to talk, something we hadn't done in a long while. We exchanged different stories about Justin over the years, which seemed to provide some healing for both of us. After some time, he looked down at his watch.

"Well, I better go. I know you probably got plans and I don't want to hold you up." He paused for a brief second. "He seems like a really good guy."

A smile stretched across my face. "He's the best."

My dad smiled back as he got up from the couch. "You're mother and I are staying at Ted's and Amelia's until Wednesday. I think she would really like to see you. I didn't tell her what happened yet. I didn't want to get her upset again today."

"Sure, I will definitely come by before you guys head home."

"We're renting a house down here for the summer; your mother wants to be closer to –" he paused for a brief second to regain his composure – "Justin," he finished. I really hope that you come by a lot. You're mother's going to need you and I would really like to get to know this special guy in your life a little better."

"I will." I got up from the couch and walked him to the door. I gave him a hug as we reached the door.

He kissed me on the head and smiled. "I love you, Nicole."

"I love you too, Dad."

I stood in the doorway, watching as he walked down the stairs and got in his car. I closed the door behind me, making sure that I put the deadbolt on. A sense of serenity was overtaking my normally crazy life. I had gotten Dailan back and I had gotten my dad back. I closed my eyes and smiled. The hole in my heart was finally beginning to close.

* * *

I was immediately greeted by Dailan's smiling face at the front door. I had filled him in on what had happened with my dad during the phone call on the way over. He took my hand and walked me back to the great room.

Ryan was sitting on the couch with Jack O'Maley, Lisa, and some other man whom I had never met. Ryan's face lit up when I appeared in the doorway. He jumped up from the couch to give me a hug that melted my heart.

"Miss Morgan, what happened?" he asked sadly, looking at the bruising on my face.

"Oh, it's nothing, Ryan," I said, trying to alleviate his concern.

"Were you playing Rugby with my uncle?" he asked.

I smiled and shook my head.

"Nicole, I'm so very sorry about your brother," Lisa said as she grabbed my hand.

"Thank you, Lisa." I was quite sure that Dailan had filled her in on what had happened last night, since she didn't question why my face was all marked up.

"Oh, Nicole, this is my husband, Warren," she said as a short balding man stood up to shake my hand.

"It's so nice to finally meet you, Nicole. I've heard all about you from Ryan," he said. I gave him a warm smile.

Jack O'Maley had a smile stretched across his face, making it very hard for me to contain mine. He got up from the couch and gave me a hug, whispering in my ear, "I'm glad to see my son made the right choice."

I walked over to the pile of Ryan's birthday presents as he began to show me each one. "This is the second level to the race track that you got me for Christmas," he said excitedly as he picked up one of the boxes. "Uncle Dailan, can we please connect it?"

"Sure," Dailan said.

Ryan jumped up and grabbed my hand "Come on, Miss Morgan – I mean Nicole," he giggled. "Let's go get the other race track so he could put it together!" Ryan led me up the steps to his bedroom. He pulled a chair over to his closet to reach the racetrack that was on the top shelf. I stood by the chair, waiting to grab it from him once he reached it.

"Ahh!" he exclaimed as an array of stuffed animals began to fall down on his head.

I laughed as I bent down to pick them up. My stomach clenched and my hands began to tremble when I looked down and saw the little blue plaid elephant in my hand. The room began to spin and I couldn't breathe. I quickly turned it over to find the initials *JM* written in permanent magic marker on the bottom.

"Do you need some help?" Dailan asked as he stood in the doorway.

I was speechless, unable to breathe. I could feel myself hyperventilating.

"Nicole, what's the matter?" Dailan asked with concern as he rushed over, placing his arm around me to support my trembling legs. I was still holding tightly to the elephant. It was all coming together; yesterday was Ryan's birthday, the day that I always tried to put out of my mind. I was so preoccupied with my brother's funeral that I didn't have time even to think about it. I looked at Ryan and began to burst into tears. I broke free from Dailan and found the strength in my legs to run down the steps, clenching to the elephant as I ran out the front door.

Dailan came chasing after me and I had almost made it to my car before he grabbed my arm and stopped me. "Nicole, what just happened?"

I shook my head, still unable to speak.

"Nicole, please," he begged as he braced his hands on my shoulders.

I swallowed hard, trying to get my voice to work. "Dailan, were Connie and Gerry Ryan's birth parents?"

Dailan looked at me strangely. "No, Ryan was adopted. I thought that you already knew that. Ryan's known ever since he could understand. Connie felt that it was important that he knew he had another mother out there somewhere." The tears began to flow even harder as Dailan tried his best to wipe them away. "Nicole what is wrong?"

"Dailan, Ryan is my son."

"What?" He looked at me with disbelief.

"I got pregnant in high school. I was stupid and careless and I actually believed him when he told me that you couldn't get pregnant the first time. I thought that he really loved me. I found out how much he did, when he left for college that September and I was stuck to face the aftermath alone."

Dailan looked at me sympathetically as he continued to wipe the tears from my eyes. "How do you know that Ryan is your son?"

"This elephant was my brother's. When he was little, he carried it everywhere. He gave it to me when I was eight years old and in the hospital getting my tonsils out. It meant so much to me. I asked my adoption counselor to give this to my child's mother, so he could have a little piece of me." I turned it over to show him the initials on the bottom. "*JM* – Justin Morgan, my brother."

"Wow," Dailan whispered, looking like he was in total shock.

"My dad hated me for it. He was so into appearances that he even went against his religious beliefs and wanted me to have an abortion so no one would know that his teenage daughter was pregnant. I've spent the last eight years of my life punishing myself for what I did."

"What did you do, Nicole?"

"I gave my baby away. A baby that grew inside of me for nine months, that would make me smile with every move that he made. I just gave him away. I didn't even hold him after he was born. I couldn't. I knew I wouldn't be able to let him go if I did. What kind of mother does that?" I broke down once again in his arms.

"Nicole, you didn't give him away. What you did was the most unselfish thing another human being could do. My brother and sister-in-law loved that little boy with all their heart. They were the happiest people in the world the day that Ryan came into their lives." The seriousness in Dailan's voice didn't even sound like him.

I hugged him tightly until I felt myself calming down and able to breathe again. "I don't know what to do, Dailan."

"That's up to you. You can go in there and tell him the truth or you can just tell him you have a phobia of little plaid elephants," he said, sounding more like the Dailan that I knew. I forced a smile as I wiped away a tear. "Whatever you choose to do, I will be here for you, and you will be in his life forever, whether it's as his aunt or his mom."

He took me by surprise. I looked up at him in shock trying to figure out if I had just interpreted his words correctly. "Yes, Nicole, I'm asking you to marry me. This isn't the time or place that I planned to do it, so I'm not quite prepared."

I smiled, this time crying tears of happiness. "Well, that's okay, 'cause I never took you for the down-on-one-knee type of guy anyway," I said.

"So I guess you're going to make me wait for an answer."

"Oh, Mr. O'Maley, whatever happened to your motto of patience paying off?"

"I think I've been patient enough where you're concerned," he smirked.

I took a deep breath, knowing there was nothing more in life that I wanted more. "Yes, Dailan O'Maley, I would be honored to be your wife." I wrapped my arms around him, hugging him as tightly as I could.

He pulled away for a brief moment and extended his hand to me. "What the heck are you doing?" I asked.

"Well, I told you I wasn't prepared for this right now, so let's shake on it until I get you your ring."

"You are crazy, you know that?" I shook my head and smiled as I extended my hand to him. He pulled me toward him and kissed me.

"Dailan, I want to tell him. I don't want any more secrets."

"Okay," he said as he took my hand in his.

We walked into the house. Ryan was in the great room, setting up his racetrack.

Jack O'Maley, Lisa, and her husband immediately stood up. "Is everything okay?" Lisa asked.

I nodded.

"Can you guys please excuse us for just a minute?" Dailan asked. They quickly obliged as they walked out of the room.

I held Dailan's hand as I walked over to where Ryan was sitting down on the floor. "Ryan, I need to tell you something." Ryan looked up at me, smiling widely. I looked into his hazel eyes, finally recognizing them as the same ones that had stared back at me in the mirror my entire life. I took a deep breath and squeezed Dailan's hand tighter, knowing that he would always be there for me, never letting go. *Yes, I could do this....*

Epilogue

The months flew by and before I knew it, Christmas was here again. I had finally put my fear of raw poultry behind me, along with many other fears, and prepared the turkey with ease. Miss Morgan was no longer the teacher in Room 114 - Mrs. O'Maley was. Dailan and I married over the summer with a small intimate ceremony overlooking the beautiful Irish countryside. After a very short engagement, which included a second more formal proposal, the most beautiful ring I had ever seen and, believe or not, Dailan down on one knee - just to prove me wrong , no doubt!

Ryan and I had transitioned from the role of teacher/student to mother/child with ease, thanks in large part to Dailan, who had been there for me every step of the way.

My parents had now become a constant in my life and had opted to extend the lease on their summer rental right into the winter. I had been spending a lot of time with them and they were overjoyed when I revealed Ryan's identity. He seemed to be the best medicine in helping them deal with the loss of my brother.

I thought about my brother often and although the pain was fading, the memories were not. There was nothing in the world I wished for more, than for him to have met his nephew. I felt like he had played an intricate role in reuniting me with my son. If it weren't for that little stuffed animal that he had given me all those years ago, I might have never known who Ryan really was.

I also thought about the woman who had been there for my child when I wasn't able to be. I knew that even though she was no longer here, she played a big part in making the transition so easy for Ryan and me. I was thankful to her every day for being so open with him about his past and allowing a little piece of me into his heart. I, in turn would make sure I returned the favor, never letting Ryan forget that he had another mother in heaven. I only hoped that I would make her proud, taking over where she had left off.

Dailan and I bought a new home together. Well, not exactly new. It was a four-bedroom cape cod, which I instantly fell in love with because it had character, something that I found was lacking in the newer homes. Even though Dailan protested that he wanted something brand new, he finally gave in. I had so much fun lovingly restoring it into something from a magazine. I knew that I was driving Dailan crazy with my indecisiveness when it came to paint colors, flooring, and kitchen cabinets, but he took it all in stride and never once complained. He would just roll his eyes at me in the usual Dailan way.

"Do you need help with that?" Dailan asked as he entered the kitchen.

"Nope, I got it." I smiled.

He wrapped his arms around my waist and whispered in my ear, "Happy Christmas, beautiful."

I gently caressed his face. "Merry Christmas." He pulled me closer and kissed me gently on the lips, still making me melt, like it was the very first time.

I broke free from Dailan's embrace when I saw my mother in the doorway. She was grinning from ear to ear. "Sorry to interrupt, but can I have some scissors before your father hurts himself trying to get the packaging undone from Ryan's toy."

Dailan grabbed the scissors from the drawer. "I'll bring them out to him, Mrs. Morgan," he said as he whisked past my mother.

"Dailan, I'm your mother-in-law. You don't have to call me 'Mrs. Morgan.'"

"Get used to it, Mom. I think he was calling me '*Miss* Morgan' until the day we got married." We both began to laugh as she put her arm around me. I rested my head on her shoulder as we looked out into the living room at Ryan and Dailan battling it out in a video game.

"You lose – again," Dailan teased Ryan.

"That's because you cheated – again," Ryan responded back.

"Sometimes I wonder who the child is," I said to my mother.

I smiled inwardly watching the two of them. I was linked to Ryan by blood. But he and Dailan shared something even more special; they had a history and together we would have his future. Dailan handed the controller to my dad as Ryan began to explain how to use each button.

"Oh, I've got to see this," my mother said as she went out into the living room.

I followed behind her and plopped down on Dailan's lap. I watched the man on the TV screen that was being controlled by my dad run about aimlessly. Ryan instructed him as to which buttons to press. The laughter in the air filled my heart with joy. I rested my head on Dailan's shoulder. "I love you so much," I whispered in his ear.

"I love you too." He placed his hand on my belly, revealing that familiar crooked smile that made me melt.

My eyes fixated to the little plaid elephant sitting on the mantle. I was finally at peace with myself. My relationship with my parents had been restored and I had found my son. A smile stretched across my face as I thought about the new life growing inside of me that would be here in another seven months. It was my little secret for now, one that I shared with only one other person; my hot Irish guy – the love of my life – Mr. Dailan O'Maley.